Dear Reader,

Home, family, community and love. These are the values we cherish most in our lives—the ideals that ground us, comfort us, move us. They certainly provide the perfect inspiration around which to build a romance collection that will touch the heart.

And so we are thrilled to have the opportunity to introduce you to the Harlequin Heartwarming collection. Each of these special stories is a wholesome, heartfelt romance imbued with the traditional values so important to you. They are books you can share proudly with friends and family. And the authors featured in this collection are some of the most talented storytellers writing today, including favorites such as Brenda Novak, Janice Kay Johnson, Jillian Hart and Patricia Davids. We've selected these stories especially for you based on their overriding qualities of emotion and tenderness, and they center around your favorite themes—children, weddings, second chances, the reunion of families, the quest to find a true home and, of course, sweet romance.

So curl up in your favorite chair, relax and prepare for a heartwarming reading experience!

Sincerely,

The Editors

JANICE KAY JOHNSON

The author of more than sixty books for children and adults, Janice Kay Johnson writes Harlequin Superromance novels about love and family—about the way generations connect and the power our earliest experiences have on us throughout life. Her 2007 novel *Snowbound* won a RITA® Award from Romance Writers of America for Best Contemporary Series Romance. A former librarian, Janice raised two daughters in a small rural town north of Seattle, Washington. She loves to read and is an active volunteer and board member for Purrfect Pals, a no-kill cat shelter.

Built to Last

HARLEQUIN HEARTWARMING

Janice Kay Johnson

Built to Last

TORONTO NEW YORK LONDON
AMSTERDAM PARIS SYDNEY HAMBURG
STOCKHOLM ATHENS TOKYO MILAN MADRID
PRAGUE WARSAW BUDAPEST AUCKLAND

Recycling programs
for this product may
not exist in your area.

ISBN-13: 978-0-373-36439-8

BUILT TO LAST

Copyright © 2011 by Janice Kay Johnson

Originally published as TAKING A CHANCE
© 2003 by Janice Kay Johnson

CHAPTER ONE

Jo Dubray was suddenly terrified. Not just nervous, as she'd been at eighteen when she moved into a dorm room with a girl she'd never met. No, she was so scared her hands were actually slick on the steering wheel of her Honda and her heartbeat was drumming in her ears.

What had she been thinking, to commit to living with a group of total strangers?

Pulling up in front of the house, her car piled high with all her worldly goods, she still liked the neighborhood. She made herself notice that much in an attempt to calm herself, to say, *See? The decision can't be* that *bad*.

Not far from the university, this particular street was narrow and edged with sidewalks that twisted and buckled to accommodate the roots of old maples and sycamores. Lovely old homes peeked between leafy branches.

As Jo parked in the one-car driveway, the house itself pleased her as much as it had the only other time she'd seen it, during her fleeting, find-a-place-to-live visit to Seattle. A classic brick beauty, built in the 1920s, the house had the run-down charm of an elderly lady whose proud carriage denies the existence of a sagging hemline or holes in her gloves. Wood trim, once white, peeled. The retaining wall that supported the lawn six feet above the sidewalk had crumbled and the grass was weedy and ragged, shooting up through overgrown junipers someone long ago had planted to avoid having to tend flower beds. But leaded glass windows glinted, the broad porch beckoned and dormers poked from the steeply pitched roof.

Despite an inner tremor, she carried one suitcase up to the house as a sort of symbol: *I'm moving in.* Then, on the doorstep, Jo hesitated. She had a key, but she didn't feel quite right using it yet. In the end, she rang the doorbell.

Kathleen Monroe, her hostess/landlady/housemate, a tall elegant blonde, answered the door with a warm smile. "Jo! You're here at last! What did you do with your car?" She peered past Jo. "Oh, Helen must have found a spot on the street. That's great. You can unload without hauling everything a block.

I'll need you to move before morning so I can get my car out of the garage, though." Her brilliant smile lit her face again. "Come on, I'll take you up to your room, as if you don't know where it is. But on the way you can meet Helen, who makes up our threesome."

Jo crossed the fingers clutching her suitcase. Not having met the third housemate had been one of her reservations about taking the plunge. But Kathleen hadn't *found* another woman when Jo had made the commitment, so it had been a take-it-or-leave-it proposition. Given the fact that she was quitting a full-time job in San Francisco to go back to graduate school at the University of Washington, Jo had taken it. She couldn't afford a condo to herself. Anyway, it might be fun to have roommates again, she had told herself at the time.

"Oh, and you haven't met Emma yet, either, have you?" Kathleen continued, in the same friendly way. "Let's stick our heads in the kitchen—Emma's starting dinner."

The kitchen was shabby like the rest of the house, the linoleum yellowed and peeling, the cupboards painted a peculiar shade of mustard and the counters edged with a metal strip. "I'll be remodeling as I can afford it,"

Kathleen had promised Jo when she'd showed her the house initially. "If you're interested in pitching in with painting and such, I'd welcome you."

Jo had agreed, liking the homey feel to the high-ceilinged rooms, the scuffed oak floors, the pine table in the kitchen laid at the time for breakfast with quilted mats and a bouquet of daisies in a vase. It might be fun to help the house regain her grace.

This time, however, Jo wouldn't have noticed if Kathleen had painted the cupboards purple. She was too nervous about meeting her landlady's fifteen-year-old daughter. What if she had spiked hair, a dog collar and listened at all hours to Eminem at top volume?

No dog collar, but Jo was more shocked than if the girl had worn one. She was painfully thin. Her head looked too large for her pathetically skinny body, and her pale-blond hair was dull and thin. The sight of somebody who had to be recovering from a serious illness—or starving herself to death—stirring spices into a pot of what smelled like spaghetti sauce was beyond weird. She cooked, but did she eat? Why hadn't her mother said anything about her problem to Jo when she'd mentioned having a teenage daughter?

Kathleen gave no sign now that anything was wrong, either. "Emma, meet Jo Dubray. Jo, my daughter, Emma." Her voice was proud, her smile allowing no option but for Jo to respond in kind.

"Emma, how nice to meet you. I hope you don't mind having a stranger down the hall."

"Well, you won't be strangers for long, will you?" Kathleen said brightly, not allowing her daughter to respond. "Now, let's say hello to Helen and then I'll let you move in."

Jo gave a weak smile over her shoulder at the teenager, who was rolling her eyes. Then she let herself be led toward the stairs.

"Oh," Kathleen tossed out, as if the tidbit were trivial, "did I mention that Helen has a daughter?"

She hadn't.

Anxiety cramped anew in Jo's chest. How much more had Kathleen not thought to mention?

"No," Jo said. "How old?"

"Ginny is six. She's just started first grade."

Oh, no, Jo thought in acute dismay. A teenager had sounded okay; she'd be hanging out with friends most of the time anyway, wouldn't she? Jo didn't remember being home much herself when she was fifteen and sixteen. But a six-year-old was another story. She'd be watching Disney movies on the TV and bringing friends home after school so that they could shriek and chase each other around. She'd interrupt at the dinner table, ask nosy questions and pop into Jo's bedroom, her private sanctum, without the courtesy of a knock.

Jo didn't want to have children herself, which made the idea of living with one unsettling.

Struggling to remember the details of their agreement that would let her move out if she hated living here, Jo almost bumped into Kathleen, who had stopped in the doorway of the small, back room she'd called the den.

Jo peered around her.

A woman who looked about thirty sat at the desk, staring at an open phone book in front of her. A gray sweatshirt hung on her, and the one vibrant note in the room, her auburn hair, was bundled in a careless knot, as if it were an inconvenience instead of a vanity. A thin, pale child leaned against her. When she saw Jo and Kathleen in the doorway, she ducked behind her mother in apparent panic before peeking around her shoulder to stare with wide eyes. The woman didn't even look up.

"Helen," Kathleen said, in a voice that had become notably gentler, "I'd like you to meet our new housemate. Jo Dubray, this is Helen Schaefer and her daughter, Ginny."

Helen lifted her head, but slowly, as if it ached. Her gaze took a minute to focus on Jo. The smile looked genuine but wan. "Oh, hi. I'm glad you're here."

Ginny hid behind her mother.

"Nice to meet you," Jo said insincerely.

On the way up the stairs, she whispered, "Why's the girl so scared of people?"

Kathleen touched a finger to her lips. "Ssh. I'll tell you about it in a minute."

Jo felt sick to her stomach. What had possessed her to think this was a good idea? For the same monthly rent, surely she could have found a room somewhere that, however tiny, would have been hers alone.

Companionship, she had told herself. Instant friends, even, in this new city.

Instead she was going to be living with a perky Princess Diana look-alike who was in serious denial, an anorexic teenager, a sad woman and a first-grader whose huge, vivid eyes showed secret terrors.

In the large bedroom that looked down on the overgrown backyard, Jo set her suitcase on the floor and said firmly, "Tell me."

Kathleen hesitated, then sat in the overstuffed, flowered armchair beside the dormer window. "Helen is really very nice, and Ginny won't be any trouble. Poor thing, she's as quiet as a mouse."

"What," Jo asked, with a grimness she failed to hide, "is wrong with her?"

"Ginny?"

"Both of them."

"Helen was widowed recently. About three months ago." Kathleen made a face. "I felt sorry for her. But I should have consulted you."

"It's your house." A fact that Jo had thought wouldn't matter. All for one, one for all. That's what she'd imagined.

Echoing the absurd, visionary sentiment, Kathleen said plaintively, "But I want us to live together as equals. All of us." She sighed and looked down at her hands, fine-boned and as elegant as the rest of her. "I didn't really want us to take on a child. For one thing, we don't have another bedroom, unless we make over the den for her. For the time being, she's sharing with her mother. The thing is…" Troubled lines creased her forehead, and at last she said with a faint, twisted smile, "I suppose I…identified with her. In a way we don't have anything in common, because as far as I can tell, Helen loved her husband, and he died instead of deciding…" She stopped, apparently choosing not to say what her ex-husband had decided. "But we're alike in that we both suddenly find ourselves on our own, with the horrifying knowledge that we have no real job skills and are rather lacking in everyday competence. Do you know, the last job I held was in college, when I waited tables?"

Shocked, Jo asked, "What *have* you been doing?"

"Being a wife." Kathleen met Jo's eyes, her expression stark. "Putting on charity luncheons. Entertaining. Being a wealthy businessman's prop." Her laugh was brittle. "Sad, isn't it? I'm half a century out of date."

Jo could think of a million things to say, starting with: How did you let yourself be used like that? But they didn't know each other well enough for her to be so tactless.

"Helen," she said instead. "Is she always so…withdrawn?"

"No. Oh, no. She was nerving herself to call her attorney, who hasn't been doing what he should be. He was their attorney—Ben's, really, and now she's thinking she shouldn't have left so much in his hands, but she's having a hard time being assertive enough to insist on more control, or to fire him."

Being assertive had never been hard for Jo, who had difficulty imagining turmoil or timidity over something as simple as firing an incompetent lawyer.

"Is her little girl always like that?" she asked.

Kathleen hesitated. "She's very quiet," she said at last. "I don't think she'll bother you."

The expression in those big, sad eyes would bother Jo, but she only nodded.

"Emma..." Her question—questions—died unspoken in the face of Kathleen's blandly inquiring expression.

"She's trying to take Ginny under her wing, but that poor child is very shy." Kathleen's brow crinkled. "I worry about how she's doing in school. At home, she doesn't want to be away from her mother even for a second. She stands out in the hall when Helen goes in the bathroom."

An image of the little girl just waiting,

a small insubstantial presence with that haunted gaze fixed on the closed door, flickered through Jo's mind. She almost shivered. Ginny reminded her of a kid in a horror film, she couldn't remember which. The kid had probably turned out to *be* a ghost. No, what Ginny reminded Jo of was herself, in the year after *her* mother had died.

Kathleen shook her head and then smiled with the brilliance of a hundred-watt bulb. "Well. Can I help you carry stuff in?"

Tempted to snatch up her suitcase and flee, Jo ran through her options and came up with no viable one. It might not be so bad. She could stay for a few days, a week, see how it went. Maybe Helen *wasn't* as lost in grief as she seemed. Maybe the little girl was just painfully shy. Maybe Emma…

Here, Jo stuttered to a stop. Maybe Emma would sit down at the table and tuck into the spaghetti tonight? Maybe she was recovering from a debilitating illness and not anorexic at all? Feeling a surprising sting of sadness for the girl with the sweet smile and fragile body, Jo couldn't believe any optimistic possibility.

But maybe living here would work. At least long enough to find something else.

"Thanks," she said. "I have a bunch of boxes."

Kathleen stood. "Then let's go get them."

EMMA DIDN'T EAT dinner. She'd nibbled so much while she was cooking, she felt stuffed, she said. Her mother didn't argue, although Jo thought she saw strain briefly on Kathleen's face. Why didn't she *make* her eat? Jo wondered.

The teenager puttered in the kitchen, cleaning up, while everyone else sat around the table twirling spaghetti on forks and making conversation. Jo felt as if Emma were the ghost at the feast. Two ghosts now, she thought morbidly, both children. Every time she looked at Ginny, who ate with tiny, careful motions, taking sips of milk only after shooting wary glances around, Jo was sorry. Happy children were bad enough, but unhappy ones were worse, she was discovering. She longed for the pathetic girl to bound out of the chair and interrupt the adults with a noisy announcement that she was going to go play video games. Loudly. In the next room.

"What good spaghetti!" her mother said. "Thank you, Emma."

Everyone murmured agreement. Emma

smiled with apparent pleasure and offered seconds.

Kathleen tapped her glass of milk with her spoon. "I propose that we have a round-table discussion after dinner. We can talk about rules, expectations, pet peeves...whatever anyone wants."

Jo shrugged. "Sounds good to me."

"Why don't we clean up first?" Helen said, in the first minor burst of initiative Jo had seen from her. "Emma cooked. She shouldn't have to wash dishes, too."

Wash dishes? Aghast, Jo took a more comprehensive look at the kitchen. No dishwasher? Was it possible?

It was.

She dried while Helen washed and Kathleen put food away. Emma, shooed from the center of activity, sat with Ginny and murmured to her, her head bent and her ash-blond hair forming a curtain that hid both their faces. Twice, though, Jo caught sight of Ginny peeking around the teenager to fix anxious eyes on her mother. To make sure she was still there, Jo supposed, and hadn't slipped away.

As her father had.

Helen didn't say much as they washed, but

she seemed…normal. Present. She gave Jo a couple of shy smiles, apologized when she bumped into her and asked once, "Are you all moved in?"

Jo thought of the pile of boxes in the corner of the upstairs bedroom and the larger pile of boxes and furniture she'd left in storage in San Francisco and shook her head. "I meant to get here earlier in the afternoon, but traffic into Seattle was awful."

They had one of those innocuous conversations where they discussed the rush hour and the respective traffic jams in the Bay area and Seattle. If she didn't look toward the starving teenager and terrified first grader, Jo could almost feel reassured.

The women were just pouring cups of coffee and herb tea—soda for Ginny—when a knock on the front door made Jo jump. Seeming unsurprised, Kathleen said, "I'll get it," and left the room. She came back a moment later, followed by a man.

And what a man, Jo thought with a burst of pure, disinterested admiration. Well, okay. Maybe not disinterested.

Broad shoulders, smiling eyes, thick, dark-blond hair streaked by the sun, and a craggy, intelligent face interested her very much.

"Jo, my brother, Ryan Grant," Kathleen said, rolling her eyes. "He gets lonely and can't stay away."

"Don't make fun of me," the man said mildly. Gray eyes met Jo's for a strangely electric moment before he turned to hug Emma. "How are you, kiddo?" he asked in a low, gruff voice in which Jo recognized gentleness.

"Uncle Ryan!" Emma's pixie face brightened. "Cool! *Are* you lonely?"

"Nah. I just like all of you." He touched Ginny's shoulder. "Hi, Hummingbird."

Hummingbird? The tiny bird's quivering energy seemed the furthest thing from Ginny's repressed, frightened self.

But the name provoked a small smile, quickly hidden but startling.

The man—Kathleen's brother—smiled in return, seemingly content, and said, "Do I get a cup of coffee?"

"There's spaghetti left," Emma told him eagerly. "I can warm some up for you if you want."

"Thanks, but I've eaten."

"We," his sister said sternly, "were just going to have an official round-table meeting to discuss rules."

"I can make up rules," he said obligingly.

"*You* don't live here. Contrary to appearances."

"I'll referee."

With a tartness Jo appreciated, Kathleen said, "Unlike men when they get together to play, women rarely need a mediator."

Jo could see the resemblance between sister and brother, both what she thought of as beautiful people. Kathleen, though, had the carriage and confidence of someone who had grown up with money—the easy poise, the natural ability to command, the chic French braid—while her brother had shaggy hair and wore faded jeans, work boots and a sweat-stained white T-shirt under a torn chambray shirt, hanging open. His hands were brown, calloused and bleeding on one knuckle. He looked like a working man. Intrigued, Jo continued to watch their byplay as Kathleen told him with mock firmness that he could stay and eavesdrop, but not contribute—unless he wanted his name on their chore list.

Ryan chose to pull up a chair just outside the circle when the women sat back down at the table. He hovered behind Ginny and Emma, elbows resting on the backs of their chairs, his quiet murmurs eliciting giggles that Emma let peal and Ginny buried behind a hand.

Kathleen had grabbed a pen and spiral notebook, now open in front of her. "Well, let me say first that I'm really glad you're both here." She smiled warmly first at Helen and then Jo. "I think this is going to be fun."

Jo had thought so, too, until she'd nearly chickened out before knocking on the front door. Despite her apprehension, she let herself believe that it really would be. Both girls still knew how to laugh. Whatever troubled them, they weren't beyond hope. Sure, she hadn't wanted to live with kids, but they weren't hers. She'd probably see them only at meals—and apparently Emma wouldn't be sitting down with them for hers, if she ate any at all.

"Now," Kathleen continued, "I genuinely don't want to be in charge. I hope we can agree on how we want to run the house, the levels of cleanliness and noise and privacy we all find acceptable. It's one reason I chose both of you, women close to my own age. I thought we'd be likelier to enjoy the same music, have the same…well, standards, I guess." She looked around. "I'll start. I figured we should divvy up chores."

They decided each would cook dinner two nights a week, with Sunday either a joint effort or an everyone-on-their-own day. Other meals, they'd take care of individually. The two who hadn't cooked would clean the kitchen together after dinner.

"Unless Ryan invites himself," his sister said dryly, "in which case *he* can clean up. By himself."

"Hey!" he protested. "I've been known to bring pizza. Or Chinese takeout."

"You should see his refrigerator at home," Kathleen told the others. "Soda, cheese, mustard... Classic male on his own."

The question, Jo decided, was why such a gorgeous man was on his own at all. He had to be in his early thirties. Guys with smiles and charm like his had been snapped up long before his age. So...what was the catch?

Oblivious, thank goodness, to Jo's speculation, Kathleen added, "And I hope everyone will clean up after themselves in the morning and after lunch?" The question was more of a tactfully phrased order.

Jo and Helen murmured assent.

Otherwise, they agreed that everyone would pitch in on Saturday mornings to clean house. Bedrooms would be sacred to their owners—knocks were mandatory, and a closed door should be interpreted as a desire for privacy.

Very conscious of Ryan Grant's interested gaze, Jo said, "We should discuss our schedules as we know them, so we're not all trying to use the bathroom at the same time. Fortunately, my first class isn't until 9:00 a.m. this semester, but that may change."

She'd made the decision to go back for a graduate degree in library and information science. She'd been lucky enough to have risen from page—her job while in high school—to clerk and finally branch manager in a San Mateo County public library. She loved books and libraries. What she hated was knowing that, although she had the same responsibilities as branch managers with master's degrees, she didn't get equal pay. And she wasn't going to be offered any more promotions, or ever have the chance to rise to director. In fact, if she were to move, she would never be offered even a comparable job. Jo was too ambitious to settle for what she had.

Two years of penny-pinching, with full-time graduate school and part-time work, and *she* would be a degreed librarian. No more subtle condescension. Jo had every intention of ending up director of a major library system. The only drawback to moving away from the Bay Area was that she was farther from the only family she cared about: her brother, Boyce, who lived in San Francisco, and her aunt Julia in L.A. But once she had her master's degree, she could go back to California.

She'd worked until the last possible day. Today was Saturday; Monday she started classes.

In response to Jo's suggestion, Helen said, "I start work at 9:00 a.m., too. Ginny's bus picks her up at 8:25 a.m. I usually leave right after. I guess the three of us will be the ones fighting for the bathroom."

Emma's bus left at what seemed the crack of dawn. Apparently high school started obscenely early and let the kids out before two o'clock. Kathleen, too, left the house by 7:30 a.m.

"I'm looking for another job." She wrinkled her nose. "I can't seem to convince anyone that I have the skills when I haven't held paying jobs. The fact that I've nearly run several charities doesn't seem to impress anyone. Anyway, I'm going to check books out of the library so I can learn to use some other software packages."

"I can't do much but write a letter or send email on a computer," Helen admitted timidly.

Why wasn't she surprised? Jo thought uncharitably, then was ashamed of herself. She had no idea what Helen Schaefer had been like before her husband died. Perhaps grief had changed her personality.

To make amends, Jo asked, "Where do you work, Helen?"

"At Nordstrom. Do you have Nordstrom stores in California? It's an upscale department store. I'm in the children's department."

"So you work on commission?"

"Partly." Her smile showed a shy prettiness Jo hadn't suspected. "I'm actually pretty good at it."

Ryan cleared his throat. "Aren't you going to ask me what I do?"

Jo couldn't help smiling. "Okay. What do you do?"

The smile that touched his eyes seemed to be for her alone. "I'm a contractor. We do remodeling. Mainly residential." With a sidelong glance at Kathleen, he added, "I would love to work on this place, but my sister won't let me."

"I can't afford you."

A frown tightened his face, and Jo knew she was forgotten. An old argument was apparently resuming. "I'm not asking to be paid."

"I know you're not," his sister said gently. "But I can manage. I'll let you pitch in on a Saturday afternoon. I won't let you send in your team and swallow the expenses."

"Stubborn," he grumbled.

Yes, but Jo had to admire her roommate for not accepting charity, even if it was from her brother.

"We're all going to help," she chimed in.

"Uh-huh." He spared her a glance. "My sister can't drive a nail. What about you?"

Jo knew that frustration at having his desire to help thwarted was behind his scoffing, but she hated it nonetheless.

Her chin rose a fraction and her eyes met his. "As a matter of fact, I can. I can use a table saw and change the oil in my car, too."

A glint of something in those gray eyes briefly softened her irritation, but then he said in a hard voice, "Can you update the wiring?

Tear up the roof and replace the shingles? Fix cracks in the foundation?"

No. She'd never done any of those things and was pretty sure she couldn't—for one thing, she was scared of heights—but Jo was fired up enough to lie. She had her mouth open when Kathleen saved her.

"Don't pick on Jo. I'm the one who said no. If the roof leaks this winter, I'll save my pennies to replace it next summer. The bank okayed the mortgage, which must mean the appraiser didn't see dangerous wiring. And of course the foundation is cracking! The house is ninety-plus years old. I don't think it's going to fall down any time soon."

Emma's head swiveled as she watched first her mom and then her uncle. Eyes already too big for her face were wide, and Jo wondered what she was thinking. Did an argument, however mild, frighten her? She seemed to like her uncle Ryan better than she did her mother, so perhaps she was hoping Mom would be bested. Or, in a teenager's self-centered way, maybe she just resented living in a shabby house when she could have a gorgeous, remodeled showplace to bring her friends home to.

If she had any friends. People didn't just

become anorexic without other problems, did they? Assuming that's what was wrong with her.

Ryan abruptly shoved back his chair, lines carved deep in his forehead. "Well, since I'm not any use here, I think I'll get home and let you women decide which room you're going to paint first."

Kathleen started to stand, too. "Ryan…"

"It's okay." His grin was resigned. "I wish you'd get it through your head that I can afford to take a hit for you and Emma, and I'd feel happier if you'd let me. But I guess stubbornness runs in this family." He ruffled his niece's hair. "See? It's not your fault, kiddo. You inherited it."

She smiled uncertainly up at him. Ryan kissed Emma's forehead, gave his sister a passing hug and let his gaze linger on Jo with a certain deliberation as he said, "Good night, all. Kathleen's right. I'm always here, butting my nose in. Call me on it if I'm a nuisance." With a last nod, he left. A moment later, they heard the sound of the front door opening and closing.

Kathleen laughed, the sound wry. "That's my brother."

And wouldn't he make life here more interesting, Jo thought, more conscious in his absence than she'd been in his presence of the way he'd seemed to charge the room with energy. Oh, be honest, she told herself: with the way *she* had responded to him.

What's more—miracle of miracles—she had a feeling he'd been attracted to her, too.

Maybe she wouldn't regret moving in here after all.

She cleared her throat. "I have a proposal. What do you say we show that brother of yours what we're made of? Let's tackle a job next weekend. Maybe the upstairs bathroom? Isn't that one of the projects you had in mind, Kathleen?"

"But…plumbing…" Helen protested, in her soft, uncertain voice.

"We're smart women." Jo looked from one to the other. "I'll find a how-to book. How hard can it be?"

Kathleen's smile was the most genuine Jo had seen from her. "Those sound like famous last words. But you're right. We can learn. I'm game. Helen, what do you say?"

"It might be fun," Helen agreed tentatively.

"Emma?" Jo asked, when her mother didn't.

The teenager shrugged with a hint of sullenness. "I don't know how to do anything."

"You can learn," Jo said.

Her mother gave a decisive nod. "Then let's go shopping tomorrow night. We can pick out a new vanity and sink and what-have-you together. Home Depot, here we come!"

CHAPTER TWO

"UH-OH," JO WAS the first to say.

She knelt with one strip of the ancient, cracked linoleum in her gloved hands. Beside her, Kathleen gaped in horror at the rotting floorboards beneath where the toilet had been pulled up.

"What's 'uh-oh'?" Helen asked from the hall behind them. Ginny peered around her.

Hovering outside the bathroom door, Emma asked eagerly, "Did you do something bad?"

"Great. Wonderful," Kathleen muttered.

"It's okay." Jo was already envisioning the work to be done. Way more than she'd signed up for, considering this wasn't her house, but she wasn't the quitting type. Besides, she wanted to take a shower again someday. With false confidence, she said, "We'll tear the boards up and lay down plywood."

"What if the beams underneath are rotting?"

Brutality was sometimes necessary. "We call your brother."

Kathleen's jaw hardened. "Then let's pray," she said, and began yanking up the linoleum again.

Jo couldn't quite figure out why Kathleen was so determined not to accept Ryan's help. Pride—sure. She'd been a dependent wife, now she wanted to show the world she could manage very nicely on her own, thank you. But her determination also struck Jo as a sort of competition—*I can do it better than you can.* A childish game. When you got right down to it, wasn't it a little silly that three women who knew nothing about construction were refusing to let a willing contractor help gut the bathroom, just so they could prove… what? That they could do it, too? Could do it better?

Yeah, right, Jo thought with humorous derision. Do it? Maybe. Make a dozen mistakes? That, too.

"Well," she decided, while Helen was carrying the tattered roll of linoleum out, "we'll definitely need the circular saw. But let's pry a few boards up and see how bad it is."

The first board splintered—well, *disintegrated* was probably closer to the truth.

Squished into pieces. But under it, the thick, rough-hewn beam looked solid. Jo pulled out nails and moved on to the next board. Somehow, as the only one with any know-how whatsoever, she was ending up doing most of the work. But she'd always enjoyed doing simple projects like building a floor-to-ceiling bookcase in her last condo. She'd been proud of the results. This was more than she'd bargained for when she had shrugged and said, "Sure, I don't mind helping," during that interview/visit this summer. But it wasn't as if she had any friends with whom to spend a sunny Saturday, and she liked a challenge.

"It looks okay," she announced, after the second board shattered with a soggy sound. "These boards weren't rotted quite through."

Kathleen sank back on her heels and sighed. "Thank goodness for small favors. Okay. Tell me what to buy, and I'll go back to the lumberyard while you and Helen pull up the floor."

Jo measured the dimensions of the bathroom floor. "Ask somebody what kind of plywood you should buy. Tell them we're tiling on top of it. Oh, and what kind of nails. Get a circular saw..."

"But we already bought a saw," Helen protested.

"That was a jigsaw. We can't cut big pieces of plywood with it, not and make straight lines."

"Oh."

Kathleen was busy writing notes. "We'll probably need the tools when we work on other projects anyway. We should have bought one in the first place."

"The thing is," Jo paused, the hammer suspended in her hand, "we really need to get a plumber."

Kathleen looked dismayed. "A plumber? Why?"

Jo put it in simple language. "Something was leaking. I don't know what."

"But you know we'll never get anyone out here on Saturday or Sunday. And that'll leave us without a bathtub or shower, never mind a toilet upstairs, until next weekend at least, when we have time to tile."

"Uncle Ryan could fix it," Emma said. "If you'd let him."

"He'll promise to come and then not show up until tomorrow evening." Kathleen sounded waspish.

Jo raised a brow, but didn't comment on

this assessment of Ryan Grant. Instead she pointed out, "Tomorrow evening would be better than Monday, when one of us would have to be home to let a plumber in."

"That's not true anyway!" Emma's face flushed red. "He always comes when he says he will!"

"You haven't known him as long as I have," her mother said crisply. "If he were more ambitious, he wouldn't still be working with his own hands. He'd be running the business instead of driving nails."

"He *likes* working on houses!" the teenager cried.

"If he wanted to be successful..."

Apparently he didn't, at least to his sister's standards. Maybe he didn't like wearing a white shirt and tie and spending his day sending emails and talking on a cell phone.

On the other hand, Jo amended, maybe he was one of those irresponsible men who'd rather go fishing on a nice day than show up to do the work he'd promised to. Just this summer, when she put her condo up for sale and needed to lay a new vinyl floor in the kitchen, the first two days she'd stayed home from work to let workmen in, they had neither come nor called.

Her interest in Kathleen's brother waned. Not much for lazing around herself, she liked workaholics, not playboys.

Still...

"You'd better call him," she advised.

Kathleen made a face. "Oh, all right." As she backed into the hall, she explained, "Emma, it's not that I don't like Ryan..."

"You don't!" the teenager cried. The venom in her voice startled Jo into swiveling in time to see bitterness transform the fifteen-year-old's expression as she finished, "Maybe he has dirt under his fingernails sometimes, or he smells sweaty, or he doesn't know what to wear to one of your parties, but he's *nice!*"

Kathleen seemed frozen in shock. "I've never said..."

"You have!" her daughter flung at her. "I heard you and Dad! You were embarrassed by Uncle Ryan! Just like you're embarrassed by me!"

With that, she turned and ran. Jo heard the uneven thud of her feet on the stairs, and then the slam of the front door.

None of the women moved for what seemed an eternity. Ginny had her face pressed into her mother's side.

Kathleen finally gave an unconvincing laugh. "Teenagers!"

Helen smoothed her daughter's hair. "I was awful when I was thirteen."

"Me, too," Jo admitted. "And when I was fourteen, and fifteen, and sixteen…" Actually, she hadn't quit rebelling until at eighteen she'd realized that her father didn't even notice her snotty comebacks or sulky moods. She wasn't upsetting him, she wasn't even making a blip on his radar screen. That's when she left home and never went back.

Looking unhappy, Kathleen left the room. A minute later, her voice floated up the stairs. "I left a message on Ryan's voice mail."

"Okay," Jo called back.

Helen and Ginny made repeated trips up and down the stairs, carrying boards from which Jo was careful to remove all the nails. In her quiet way, the six-year-old seemed to be enjoying herself. She'd hold out her arms and wait for Jo to pile on a child-size load, then carefully turn and make her way out of the gutted bathroom. Sometimes she even went ahead of her mother, or reappeared before her.

Kathleen had been right, Jo had discovered: Ginny wasn't any bother. Living with her was more like having a mouse in the house than a child. Tiny rustles marked her presence.

Once, when Ginny reappeared ahead of her mother and stood waiting patiently while Jo pried at a stubborn board, she felt compelled to make conversation.

"Your mom says you're in first grade. How do you like it?"

"I like to read."

"Really? Better than recess?" The hammer slipped and banged her knee. "Ow!"

"Did you hurt yourself?"

"Yes!" Jo moderated her voice. "Not permanently. I just…whacked myself."

"Oh." Ginny cocked her head at the sound of her mother's footsteps on the stairs.

"So, what do you do at recess?"

The solemn gaze returned to her. "I stay in if Teacher lets me."

Jo sank back on her heels. "You stay in?" she asked incredulously. She could remember how much she'd longed to be outside, pumping herself so high on the swing that she momentarily became weightless, or skipping rope with friends to nonsensical songs that still had to be sung perfectly.

Ginny's face showed no expression. "Kids make fun of me."

Jo frowned. "Have you told the teacher? Or your mom?"

She shook her head.

"Why not?"

"Why not what?" Helen asked from the doorway, her voice dull, as if she had to force herself to ask. She often sounded that way. Jo wanted to shake her sometimes and say, Wake up! But what did she know about grief?

Knowing Helen wouldn't care enough to be suspicious, Jo improvised quickly. "I asked why she isn't wearing overalls and leather gloves and a tool belt, since she's a carpenter now."

A tiny smile flickered on the pale face, whether at Jo's attempt at humor or because she'd kept Ginny's confession confidential, Jo didn't know.

"Well, maybe we should get her one." Helen gave a rare smile, too, her hand resting lightly on her daughter's head. "She'll grow up an expert on how to do all this stuff." Her voice became heavier. "I don't want Ginny ever to feel helpless, about anything."

"Well, she'll learn right along with us," Jo said heartily. "Right, kid?"

Very still under her mother's hand, Ginny said nothing.

Jo took a deep breath and pried again at the board. It groaned and squealed in protest. She braced her feet and used her full weight to wrench upward. It snapped free and she landed on her behind just as the doorbell rang.

"Jo! Are you all right?"

"I'm fine." She picked herself up. "You'd better go get that. It might be Kathleen with her hands full."

She flipped the board over and hammered. The nail popped out, and she started on the next.

Should she tell Helen what Ginny had said about recess and the other kids taunting her? Or was that betraying a confidence?

Why had the little mouse confided in *her?*

"You look like you're pounding meat," an amused male voice commented. "I think it's already tender."

Ryan. Of course.

Jo focused on the board, where a deep indentation showed that the hammer had more than pushed the nail out. "I was brooding," she said, before oh-so-casually glancing up.

He was gorgeous, even if he was a slacker.

A smile deepened creases in his cheeks and crinkled the skin beside his eyes. Today he wore jeans again and a gray T-shirt that bared nicely developed muscles in his upper arms.

He *must* have a girlfriend.

"About what?"

"Oh…" She thought fast. "Just about school. Nothing earth-shattering."

"Speaking of which…" Ryan crouched beside her. "You must have a real problem for Kathleen to relent and call me."

"I insisted." Jo gestured with the hammer. "Behold the rot."

He did, and grunted. "Why am I not surprised?"

"I can cut up sheets of plywood and replace the subfloor, but real plumbing is beyond me."

He smelled good, she was disconcerted to realize. Or maybe she was disconcerted to have noticed. She caught a hint of sweat, aftershave and something else warm and male.

Jo scowled, but he didn't notice. He was frowning, too, as he studied the exposed pipes.

"Can you tell what's wrong?" she asked.

He grunted again. "What isn't? I've been telling Kathleen the pipes all need replacing. Look at the corrosion."

Every pipe she could see was rusty and wet. "Can you replace them?"

The frown still furrowing his brows, he looked at her. "I can, but it's going to be a big job."

Her hand felt slick where it gripped the hammer. She had to tear her gaze from him.

Jo took a deep breath. "We don't have a shower until we get this bathroom done."

Oh, no. Did *she* smell?

If so, he didn't seem to mind. Forehead still creased, his expression no longer looked like a frown. He was studying her with disconcerting intentness, his eyes smoky, darkening...

A bumping sound gave away the presence of someone else. Ryan jerked and swung around. "Hummingbird!" he said, voice gentle and friendly, his smile so easy, Jo was sure she'd imagined the moment of peculiar tension. "You're helping?"

"Yes, I am," the little girl said solemnly, her big eyes taking in the two adults, her thoughts inscrutable.

Ryan rose with an athletic ease that Jo envied. She was beginning to feel as if her knees would creak and crack when she stood.

"Oh, dear." She wrinkled her nose. "I've been sitting here like a slug, not getting anything done. I don't have another load for you yet."

Helen stuck her head in. "Has Ryan figured out our problem yet?"

"Ryan figured it out before his sister made an offer on this house," he said dryly. "She just didn't want to hear it."

"You didn't think she should buy it?" Jo asked in surprise. "It's a great house."

"Yeah, it is," he agreed. "Given real estate prices in Seattle, what she paid was fair, too. She just didn't want to recognize that the place was a bargain because it needed so much work. She figured she could get by with cosmetic fix-ups. A little paint, maybe eventually a new roof..." He shrugged. "It was built in 1922. The wiring hasn't been updated since about 1950, and the plumbing needs to be completely replaced."

He looked and sounded exasperated.

"If she can't afford it..." Jo said tentatively.

Through gritted teeth, he answered, "She should let me do it."

It was hard to engage in any kind of meaningful debate when you were squatting at a man's feet, but Jo didn't let that stop her. "Don't you admire her independence?"

"Sure I do." His mouth twisted. "But I'm

not Ian. Her ex," he added as an aside. "Why can't her pride handle a little help from her brother?"

Helen's face showed the same struggle Jo felt—sympathy for both points of view.

"How would *you* feel if Kathleen was trying to help you out financially?" Jo asked.

"I'd take the check, if my kids depended on it," he said brusquely. Then he gave a faint laugh. "Sorry. It's not your fault that Kathleen and I butt heads. I'm just glad that you apparently *do* have some construction skills."

She felt an absurd glow of pleasure at the compliment. Some women wanted to be told that they were beautiful. She apparently reveled in being praised for competence.

Perhaps, she thought ruefully, because she wasn't beautiful. Not like he was, or his sister. Pretty, maybe, if the beholder was generous. But she had not spent her life fighting off suitors.

At the sound of a car engine, she smiled as if he hadn't both pleased her and stung her feminine vanity all at the same time.

"I do believe Kathleen's home," Jo said. "The two of you can go at it to your heart's content."

ALTHOUGH HE'D HAVE RATHER stayed and worked beside Jo Dubray, who was far too petite to be wielding a hammer so ably, Ryan went outside, argued briefly with his sister and headed home to get the supplies he needed to work on the bathroom.

He hated doing plumbing. Wood was his passion. He liked building and restoring equally. Rebuilding a curving banister in an old house, recreating the molding that would have framed tall windows in the 1890s, baring and polishing and laying hardwood floors, those he enjoyed.

But for his sister and Emma, he'd do anything. And why not? Now that his kids had moved a couple thousand miles away with their mother and her new husband, his weekends and evenings would be empty if it weren't for Kathleen and Emma. What they hadn't realized was that he needed them more than they needed him.

By the time he got back Jo had managed to remove the entire subfloor and replace parts of it with thick plywood. She'd left the plumbing and glimpses of the downstairs ceilings exposed. As he dropped his first load, he heard the distant sound of a saw, but didn't see her.

Heading back downstairs for another load of PVC pipes, he grimaced. He'd had better things in mind for this weekend. Indian summer, the end of September, the day glowed with golden warmth that had chased away the night's chill. He'd intended to start with a run around Green Lake, then pick up the apples rotting on his lawn and finally mow it, he hoped for the last time this fall.

Well, maybe plumbing didn't sound so bad after all. Especially not with an interesting woman popping into the bathroom to check on him. Maybe bringing him a can of soda, commiserating if he scraped a knuckle, admiring his muscles—he thought he'd caught her doing that already.

He'd wondered about his sister's taste in roommates after meeting Helen Schaefer and her sad little girl. Pity and kindness had a place, but he figured Kathleen had enough to handle with Emma. Did she have to take on a befuddled, grieving woman and her painfully insecure child, too?

"Wait until you meet Jo," Kathleen kept saying. "You'll like her."

Jo. The name sounded masculine enough that he'd pictured a man/woman, like the high school vice-principal who'd scared every kid who'd ever considered pulling a prank, if not worse. Jo, he now realized, must be short for something feminine and French, like Josephine.

Five foot four or so, she wasn't unusually short, but her bone structure was delicate. Yet she crackled with energy and intelligence, making him wonder if she ever completely relaxed. Her big brown eyes, assessing and judging, were the furthest thing from pansy soft. Her hair, a deep, mahogany brown, was thick and straight and shiny, cut in a bob below her jawline. She had a habit he guessed was unconscious of shoving it back with impatience that seemed characteristic.

He didn't mind that about her. In fact, Ryan preferred smart, strong women. Funny, considering how his sister irritated him. Nonetheless, when married he'd have rather his wife had yelled at him than wept.

So how had he ended up married to a woman who seeped tears more easily than he adjusted the angle of a saw cut?

Old news. Old failure. Mouth set, he dumped a load of pipes and fittings and started back for more. Why thinking about Jo Dubray and the sharp, interested way she looked at him had evolved into self-recrimination about an ended marriage, Ryan didn't know. Couldn't he imagine kissing a woman without relating it to his marriage?

He worked all day, taking a brief break for a sandwich. He had to cut a hole in the wall in the downstairs bathroom, which had Kathleen shrugging.

"We have to wallboard anyway."

"This floor is probably rotting, too," he said.

She stared at the toilet with the expression of someone who'd just seen a tarantula scuttling out of sight. Or someone who'd imagined herself sitting on a toilet when it plummeted through the rotten floor.

"I guess we could go ahead with this room, too," she decided, deep reluctance in her voice. "Next weekend. If, um…" The words stuck in her throat. "If you can help."

He grinned and slapped her on the back. "Didn't think you could spit it out."

"Ryan!" she warned.

Laughing, he said, "Yeah. I'll be here Saturday morning."

He didn't see Jo again until he was ready for the new toilet upstairs. She'd already cut out the piece of plywood it would sit on, and he helped cut the hole around the flange. Together, they nailed it down, the rhythmic beat of their hammers somehow companionable.

"Are you planning to lay vinyl yourself?" he asked.

"Tile," she told him. "It's downstairs."

"So I can't install the toilet."

"I guess not."

"You know this job is going to take you days," he said, frowning.

Jo nodded. "But we can take a bath—carefully—if you get the plumbing done."

He grimaced. "Yeah. Okay."

Crazy women, thinking they could gut a bathroom on Saturday and be washing and primping in it by Monday morning. Had any of them ever tiled before? Did they understand the necessity of letting the grout dry and then sealing it?

Jo did reappear a time or two during the afternoon, although her visits were strictly practical. Maybe he'd imagined any spark of interest.

Maybe he should ask her to dinner and find out.

He'd have to think about that some, he decided. He'd dated a few times since his divorce, and hadn't enjoyed any of the experiences.

When he was ready, they laid more plywood and then nailed up wallboard. Miraculously, by early evening he pronounced the bathroom ready for tiling and fixtures.

Admiring his work, Kathleen asked with unusual meekness, "Could you possibly help carry the tub upstairs before you go?"

He stared incredulously. "What, the three of you were planning to do it if I hadn't happened to be around?"

She stiffened. "I thought we could bribe the teenage boy next door to help."

"Is it cast iron? Do you know what the thing must weigh?"

She flushed. "We're stronger than we look."

"Are you?" He scowled at her. "And where is Emma? I haven't seen her all day."

His sister looked behind her and saw that they were alone. With a sigh, she admitted, "We had a fight. No, not a fight. She got mad. I can't seem to do anything right."

As irked as he was with her, Ryan wasn't going to judge her parenting. He took the chance of laying an arm over her shoulders and giving his too-proud sister a quick hug. "You did one thing right. You left Ian."

A stunning expression of sadness crossed her face. "Was it right?" she asked quietly.

"Or am I kidding myself that he was the problem? It would appear that Emma doesn't think so."

"You and Emma have things to work out," he said, feeling awkward. "But you have a chance now."

"I don't know where she is," she said starkly. "It's seven o'clock, and she's been gone all day."

"Have you called her friends?"

"Does she have any anymore?"

He didn't know. He tried to be here, but knew it wasn't enough. Emma chattered to him as if to fill Hummingbird's silence, but what did she really say? Nothing of any substance. She never said, *I understand why I'm starving myself to death.*

He settled for, "She'll be home."

"Yes." Kathleen gave a tiny, twisted smile. "Mostly she's…civil. And almost a homebody. But this terrible anger flares sometimes, most of it directed at me."

"You know," he reminded her, "don't forget that she's a teenager. Sure she has an eating disorder, but that isn't *her.* Seems to me fifteen-year-olds are famous for yelling at their parents."

She half laughed. "That's true, I'm afraid.

And stalking out. It's what she said…." She stopped abruptly.

Ryan stowed his hammer in his toolbox. "What was that?"

"Oh…nothing." She shook her head and backed toward the door. "Just implying the usual. That I never think she's good enough. Pretty funny, isn't it, when she never thinks anything *I* do is adequate, either."

He sensed that she was being evasive, but he never had gotten anywhere either cajoling his sister or battering down her defenses. Born two years after her, he was at a disadvantage. She'd forever be his tough, know-it-all big sister.

"All right, let's get the tub," he said instead.

Maneuvering the thing, still in its box, up those steep stairs and around the sharp corner at the top was a lousy finish to the day. The only payoff, as far as Ryan was concerned, was catching glimpses of Jo.

Everyone's patience was eroding by the time they made it through the bathroom door and eased the tub to the raw plywood floor.

"I'm glad you were here." Jo rubbed her shoulder. "We'd never have made it."

"Tubs are heavy. I assumed you were having it delivered and carried up."

"No, we're the original do-it-yourselfers," she said lightly.

His sister had fetched a knife to slice open the cardboard and cut off the wrappings. With some maneuvering, they heaved the white porcelain tub into place.

"Fixtures?" Ryan asked.

Kathleen produced the faucet, shower head and drain. "You could come back tomorrow," she said tentatively.

"Nah, I'd rather finish."

"Do you mind if I watch?" Jo asked.

"Not at all." He gestured to the floor. "Have a seat."

She grinned at him and settled herself comfortably.

Downstairs, Ryan heard the front door open and close. He cocked his head, but caught no more than the murmur of voices.

"I hope that's Emma."

"She scares me," Jo said unexpectedly. "I keep waiting for her to…"

He glanced at her. "Collapse?"

"Something like that. She's so…frail."

"Starving yourself can damage your heart and other internal organs. Her head knows that, but then she tries to eat, and that's what scares her."

A job as easy as installing a faucet required no thought. Wrench in hand, he automatically juggled tiny seals and baskets and sleeves.

Jo was watching him, but who knew how much she was taking in. Her forehead was creased. "It scares her more than the idea of dying?"

"Apparently." He applied a bead of sealant.

"Does it have to do with the divorce?" Jo still sounded unusually hesitant.

He guessed she was used to forging ahead and found it unnatural to tiptoe. But she had the sense to know an issue like this was a minefield, waiting to blow up around her.

"The divorce had to do with Emma's problems," he corrected, looking for a wrench that he'd set down. It was just out of his reach, but Jo picked it up and laid it in his hand. Ryan continued, "Ian didn't think she looked that bad. He didn't want to be bothered with counseling. All she had to do was eat, he declared. He lost his temper one night and started shoving food down her throat. She was screaming and sobbing and almost choked to death. I guess Kathleen was beating at him, trying to get him off Emma." He clenched his jaw. "Bad scene."

"Poor Emma," Jo said somberly.

"Kathleen said counseling or else. He chose 'or else.'"

Her big brown eyes were pretty. They were a deep, near-black color, like espresso, surrounded by long, thick lashes.

"Thank you for telling me all this," she said carefully. "I didn't like to ask."

"I figured." He would have felt the same.

"She loves you."

"She likes me." He rotated his shoulders as he worked. "There's nothing emotionally loaded about our relationship. I pretend she doesn't have any problems. She thinks I'm fun."

A smile flickered at the corners of Jo's mouth. "Are you?"

Was he imagining things, or was she flirting with him? "You bet." He grinned at her. "That's me. A laugh a minute."

Her smile went solemn again. "Your hummingbird seems to think so."

"I like kids." And missed his own with an ache that went bone-deep. Calls were no substitute for hugs and laughs and the chance to toss a football or lounge on the living room floor watching the expressions on his kids' faces as much as the movies playing. Before he and Wendy had had children, he'd never imagined loving someone so much that he could do nothing for hours but drink in the sight of her face—his face, when Tyler came along after Melissa.

Jo shoved back her hair and said, "I've never been around them much."

"Yeah? Well, here's your big chance. Although Hummingbird is not standard issue."

"I assumed that."

Ryan groaned and got to his feet. "What say we turn on the water and see if it flows?"

"But what about…" She gestured at the pipes protruding from the wall where the vanity and sink would go.

"I've installed shutoffs for the toilet and sink."

"Oh." Her expression was longing. "You mean, I could take a bath tonight?"

"I don't see why not."

"You're a miracle worker!"

He basked in the radiance of her smile. Who wouldn't enjoy a moment of pretending he was a hero?

Outside the bathroom, he discovered that Emma was indeed home, although closeted in her bedroom. He knocked and invited her to the ceremonial turning-on-of-the-water.

She climbed from the bed with the care of

a brittle seventy-year-old. "Cool!" Her tone turned scathing. "And Mom said…" She stopped, bit her lip.

"Mom said what?"

Her face turned mulish. "Nothing."

Mom had insulted him, he diagnosed, and Emma had realized belatedly that she might hurt him if she echoed Kathleen's remarks. Appreciating his niece's sensitivity, he didn't push.

Water ran into the tub on command, a cascade that began dirty but turned clear quickly. He flipped the lever to test the shower, but ran it for only an instant so as not to get the wallboard wet.

"Ladies," he pronounced to a full house, with even Ginny looking with apparent awe around her mother's hip, "you have the power to get clean."

"Dinner's ready," Kathleen announced.

Ryan took a minute to organize the rest of his tools and sweep bits of piping up. He liked a neat work site.

Jo found the bar of soap and they took turns washing their hands in the tub. Presumably by chance, he and she were the last, Emma having headed down the stairs as he was drying his hands.

"You were great today," she said, her glance unexpectedly shy.

"You were, too." He barely hesitated. "Kathleen implied that you were single. Is there any chance I could take you out to dinner sometime?"

She looked surprised. "Me?" Then she flushed. "I mean, I didn't realize..." Finally she took a deep breath. "I thought maybe... But I'm not that..."

"Yeah, you are." He let her see his appreciation as he admired the effect of pink staining her cheeks. "And I am."

"Oh." She gnawed on her lip, without any apparent awareness of how tempting that was. "Then, um... Yes." She squared her shoulders and gave a little nod. "Yes, I'd like to have dinner with you."

His triumph was disproportionate to the occasion, but his tone was easy. "Good. How about Monday night?"

"I can't be out late," she warned, "but... sure."

He handed her the towel. "Then, what say we go have dinner now, in the romantic setting of my sister's kitchen?"

CHAPTER THREE

Jo STRETCHED and flipped shut her textbook, then the binder she'd had open beside it on the long, folding table she used to work. Her laptop was unopened, her printer silent. She didn't need them for her cataloging class.

She had never been interested in cataloging, already knew her Dewey decimal numbers well enough to walk to almost any subject on the shelf in a public library and had no interest in working in an academic library, which meant she'd forget the Library of Congress classifications as soon as the semester ended and she passed the final. But the course was required, so she was taking it.

She didn't mind that it was time to change for her date with Ryan. Casual, he'd said, maybe pizza, but she had been grouting tile earlier, so she was dressed in a frayed sweatshirt and jeans.

Jo had worked a good ten hours Sunday, surprised that her best helper had turned out to be Helen. Helen was the one who'd told her what she knew about Ryan's divorce.

At ten last night Jo'd said, "Gosh, you look tired. I'd like to finish around the tub, but if you want to go to bed…"

Weariness showing in dark circles under her eyes, Helen looked up and said simply, "Why? I can't sleep anyway."

"Oh. I didn't know. You never said…"

Helen concentrated on splitting a tile in half and handed one piece to Jo. "The doctor thinks I should take sleeping pills, but they make me groggy. Besides, I don't want to get addicted."

No wonder she seemed dazed half the time! Jo realized in shock. Lack of sleep would do that to you.

Tentatively, she asked, "Do you miss your husband—Ben—the most in the evening?"

Head bent, Helen shrugged. "No, it isn't that. We hadn't slept together in a long time. He had cancer, you know. It was…slow." She gave a sound that might have been a laugh, as if the one small word was so utterly inadequate she could almost find humor in it. "It's just that, when I go to bed, my mind starts to race. Don't you find that?"

Jo nodded. "If I'm worried about something, or trying to make a decision, I can't sleep, either."

"I think about Ben, or how scarred Ginny is by all this, or how I'll manage financially—" She broke off with a small, choked sound.

Jo sneaked a look at her averted face. She never quite knew what to say in situations like this. Other women seemed to have a knack she didn't. Her inclination was to fix problems, to offer practical advice, to charge ahead. In some ways, she had become aware, she had more in common with men than other women.

"Sometimes," Helen continued drearily, "I'm not thinking at all. I just lie there, so tired. I think I've forgotten how to sleep."

"But you must sleep!" Jo exclaimed. "Some, at least."

"Oh, eventually. A few hours a night." She scored a tile. "I'm sorry. I didn't mean to go on about it. It's just that I'd rather have something useful to do anyway."

Jo was actually a little irked at Kathleen, who after all did own the house and would be the only one of them to truly profit from their remodeling. She'd worked, of course, but off and on, with a distracted air. She and Emma had had another fight Sunday morn-

ing, one that had left Kathleen looking...
older. She had to be thirty-five or thirty-six,
but was such a beautiful woman Jo had never
noticed lines on her face before. Sunday they
had been there.

Even so, she didn't have to be so eager to
let Jo be in charge.

"I'm so glad you know what you're doing!"
she'd exclaimed several times, always right
before vanishing for an hour or more.

It was especially irritating given that Jo
didn't know what she was doing, not in the
sense of actually having done it before. She'd
picked out a do-it-yourself book at Home
Depot and was following the directions. Any
competent person could have done the same.
Helen had quietly taken over cutting tiles to
fit, and she'd never done it before, either.

Kathleen, Jo was beginning to think, was
a little bit of a princess.

Now Jo changed to a pair of chinos and
a scarlet tank top with a matching three-
quarter-sleeve sweater over it. She brushed
her hair—what else could she do to it?—and
added a pair of gold hoop earrings and a thin
gold chain with tiny garnet beads. Inspect-
ing herself in the mirror, she decided the
result was...fine. She was the same old Jo,

just cleaned up. What you saw was what you got. Her makeup was basic, eyeliner, a touch of mascara, lipstick.

Besides she refused to get very excited about this date, after learning that Ryan had two kids. She didn't know any more about them except that they lived with his ex-wife. She hadn't wanted to sound too curious, so Jo hadn't asked about them. But if the kids were at his place half the time and he was constantly juggling dates because he had them, she wasn't interested.

At a knock on her door, she said, "Come in."

Emma opened it and slipped in. Closing the door behind her, she inspected Jo critically. "You look really nice."

"Thanks."

"Your stomach is so-o flat." She came to stand beside Jo and look into the mirror, too. "Oh, yuck. I'm so fat."

With shock, Jo said, "What?"

Their side-by-side images horrified her. The contrast was painful even though she had always been wiry. Emma was pale, her cheeks sunken, her hair dull, her limbs like sticks, while Jo felt almost obscenely healthy in comparison, with high color, shiny thick hair and noticeable muscles and curves despite her narrow hips.

"Look." The teenager splayed her hands on her abdomen, covering the bony jut of her pelvis. "My stomach pooches." She turned from side to side, making faces. "I'm eating too much. I know I am! I shouldn't have had that Jell-O last night..."

Was she *serious?* "But you're so thin! Too thin. Anyway, wasn't the Jell-O sugarless?"

"But it was sweet." Emma sat on the edge of the bed. "I shouldn't eat dessert," she said with finality.

Feeling as if she were arguing with the Queen of Hearts in Wonderland, Jo tried anyway. "Emma, you're so skinny, I'm afraid you'll break! Why do you think you're fat?"

"Oh, I guess I'm not really." She shrugged. "Not now. But I was. You should have seen me two years ago. I was, like, pudge city. So now I'm just really careful, so I don't gain any weight."

If she weighed ninety pounds, Jo would have been astonished. "Boys don't usually like skinny that much."

"The other girls are so jealous!" the teenager said with pleasure, as if she hadn't heard Jo or didn't care what boys thought. "They're, like, pigs. They can't make themselves not eat pizza and ice cream and junk like that. They want to think *everybody* eats it, but then I don't, so they know they're lying to themselves."

"Jealousy isn't the best basis for friendship," Jo said carefully.

Emma looked at her as if she were crazy. "I'm not going to be *fat* just to make them feel better."

"You don't have to be fat. Just don't..." Jo had the sense not to say, Rub their noses in it.

Emma wasn't listening anyway. "Uncle Ryan is here. Did I tell you?"

No. She hadn't.

Jo grabbed her small purse and stuffed her wallet, a brush and lip balm in it. "You don't mind that I'm going out with him?"

"No. You're cool."

Jo smiled over her shoulder as she reached for the knob. "Thank you. I'm touched."

"Mom's showing him the bathroom. She's bragging, like *she* did all the work," Emma added spitefully.

Jo hurried down the hall.

Ryan's voice floated from the bathroom.

"This tile looks great. I can't believe how much you've gotten done."

"We worked hard," his sister said.

We? Jo's temper sparked.

But Kathleen, seeing her, smiled graciously. "Jo is our expert. And Helen has become a whiz at cutting tile. She's hardly broken any."

The bathroom did look good, if Jo said so herself. Ryan did, too, but she tried to concentrate on the room, not his big, broad-shouldered presence or the slow smile he gave her.

They'd gone with a basic, glossy, four-inch-square tile in a warm rust. The grout was a shade lighter. The floor was still raw plywood; Jo was concentrating on getting the bathtub surround and the countertop done so the sink could be reinstalled. Wallpaper would be last, an old-fashioned flower print in rust and rose and pale green.

"I just did the grout this afternoon," she said. "I guess I have to wait a couple of days to seal it."

Ryan nodded absently. "I can put the sink in tomorrow evening if you'd like."

"We'd like!" Kathleen exclaimed. "Now, if only we had a toilet upstairs…"

Feeling as if she'd just been criticized, Jo

reddened. "I'm sorry. Maybe I should have done that part of the floor…"

Kathleen laid a hand on her arm. "Don't be silly. You're a miracle worker. I'm just whining. I got up in the middle of the night last night and fell down the last three stairs. Ms. Graceful."

Behind Jo, Emma laughed, the tone jeering and unkind.

Kathleen flinched.

"That's not very nice," Ryan said. "Laughing at your mother having hurt herself."

"She was a cheerleader. And homecoming queen. You don't think it's funny that she fell down the stairs?"

"No. Any more than I'd think it was funny if you had."

"But *I* do things like that all the time," Emma said resentfully. "*She* never does."

Rather than angry, Jo saw with interest, Kathleen looked stricken.

"I don't cut myself with a table saw, either." Ryan kept his voice calm. "Would it be funny if I did?"

His niece stared at him. Her voice rose. "That's different! You know it is!"

He didn't let her off the hook. "Why?"

Color staining her cheeks, Emma cried,

"Because…because *you* don't think you're perfect!" With that, she whirled and ran down the hall. Her bedroom door slammed.

The adults stood in silence for a painfully long moment. Jo wanted to be anywhere else.

Ryan and Kathleen looked at each other. He had a troubled line between his brows, while her face looked pinched.

"She's been impossible lately." Hysteria threaded Kathleen's voice.

"Like I said before, she's a teenager."

Trying to be unobtrusive, Jo edged back into the hall.

"You know it's more than that." Tears glittered in the other woman's blue eyes.

Her brother squeezed her shoulder. "The therapist told you there weren't any easy answers."

"Yes, but I thought…" She pressed her lips together. "I hoped…"

"I know," he said, in a low, quiet rumble.

Kathleen turned almost blindly to Jo. "I'm sorry we keep throwing these scenes. You must wonder about us."

They were both looking at her now. She couldn't go hide in her bedroom. "No," she lied. "I…"

"She has an eating disorder." Tears wet Kathleen's cheeks. "I suppose you noticed."

Jo nodded dumbly.

"I thought my husband was the problem." For a moment her face contorted before she regained control. "It would seem I was wrong."

"Emma's the one with the problem," Ryan reminded her, in that same deep, soothing way.

"Is she?" Kathleen wiped her cheeks with the back of her hand. Her eyes had a blind look again. "Excuse me." She brushed past Jo and a moment later her bedroom door shut with another note of finality.

This silence was uncomfortable, too. Both spoke at the same time.

Jo began, "If you'd rather not..."

"Makes you glad you live here, doesn't it?" Ryan said at the same time.

They both laughed, in the embarrassed way of people who don't really know each other.

"Yeah, I'd still like to go out." He raised his brows. "If that's what you were going to say?"

Jo nodded.

"I don't think we can expect dinner here," he said wryly.

Jo gave another, less self-conscious laugh. "Actually, it's Helen's night. Lucky for her and Ginny."

His deep chuckle felt pleasantly like a brush of a calloused finger on the skin of her cheek. Jo loved his voice.

"Let's make our getaway," he said, grasping her elbow and steering her toward the stairs. "Unless *you've* changed your mind."

"No."

Masterful men usually irritated her. This one gave a wry smile and she crumpled. Ah, well. She hadn't been charmed in too long.

She had to scramble to get up in the cab of his long-bed pickup truck. She'd noticed that weekend how spotlessly clean and shiny it was. The interior was as immaculate. Either he'd just bought it, or he loved his truck.

He'd be appalled if he saw the interior of her Honda, with fast-food wrappers spilling out of the garbage sack, books piled on the seats and dust on the dashboard. To her, a car was a convenience, no more, no less. You made sure it had oil changes so it would keep running, not because lavishing care on a heap of metal had any emotional return.

"What are you thinking?" he asked, starting the powerful engine.

She looked around pointedly. "That you're a very tidy man."

He shrugged. "I like everything in its place."

Jo liked to be able to find things when she wanted them. Not the same.

"You and your sister."

"She's gotten better." He sounded apologetic.

"I put away groceries. She rearranges them behind me. Alphabetically." That had freaked Jo out. Who had time to care whether tomato soup sat to the right or left of cream of mushroom?

"She's always been…compulsive." The crease between his brows deepened again. "She and Ian had this showplace. Housecleaning staff. Kathleen made gourmet meals, entertained brilliantly, ran half a dozen charities with one hand tied behind her back. When she does something, it's perfectly."

His echo of Emma's cry had to be deliberate.

"Was she always like that?"

He handled the huge pickup effortlessly on the narrow city streets, lined on each side with parked cars. Porch lights were coming on, although kids still rode skateboards on the sidewalks.

"Yes and no. Kathleen was a hard act to follow." He glanced at Jo. "She's two years older. Always straight A's. The teachers beamed at the mention of her, probably groaned once they knew me. She was… ambitious. Dad's a welder at the shipyards, laid-off half the time, Mom was a waitress. Kathleen wanted better."

Jo had begun to feel uncomfortable again. Did he think she was criticizing his sister, that he had to explain her?

"I like Kathleen," she said, not sure if it was true, but feeling obligated.

They were heading south on Roosevelt, a busy one-way street, almost to the University district, which she had yet to explore at any length.

Ryan didn't seem to read anything into her slightly prickly comment. "I like her, too. Most of the time. I admire her. Sometimes she bugs me."

He turned right a couple of blocks and into a parking lot across the street from a restaurant called Pagliacci's. A big multiplex movie theater was next door.

"Eaten here?" he asked.

Jo shook her head. "I've grabbed lunch a couple of times at places farther down University. Thai or Mongolian."

"Pagliacci's has good pizza. For pasta, my favorite is Stella's over by the Metro or Trattoria Mitchelli's, down near Pioneer Square. Owned by the same people, I hear."

"I love pizza," she confessed. "I haven't tried to find a good place yet in Seattle."

As they waited on the sidewalk for a cluster of college students to exit, Ryan asked, "Why Seattle?"

"The UW has a great graduate program in librarianship. It's supposed to be one of the best. That's what I wanted."

He gave her a teasing grin. "You sound like Kathleen."

"I'm ambitious, too," Jo admitted. "Just not..."

When she hesitated, he finished for her, "Compulsive?"

"Neat." Jo laughed up at him as he held open the door for her. "Does that scare you?"

"Would I have to wade across your room?"

She let him steer her to the counter, his hand at her waist.

"Maybe," she confessed, before slanting a

sidelong look at him. "Assuming you had any reason to be walking across my room."

"Touché," he murmured, head bent, his breath warm on her ear. "What do you want?"

A kiss... Oh, no, how close she came to saying that out loud! She was especially embarrassed when she realized he'd effortlessly shifted gears from flirtation and was asking what kind of pizza she wanted to order.

"I like plain cheese, veggie or everything. You decide."

"Veggie is good." He bought a pitcher of beer and they found a table up a step toward the back, where the space was quieter, more intimate.

Talking to him was easy, listening easier yet. With that voice, he should have been a DJ.

He talked about his business, the personalities among his crews, the irritations of dealing with homeowners who changed their minds every five minutes and couldn't seem to remember to pay bills.

"But, hey," he said finally, with a grin, "they let me play with their houses, so who am I to complain?"

Jo could just imagine how Kathleen would

react to that attitude. "A man who has bills of his own to pay?" she suggested.

"There is that." He was silent for a moment, hand cradling a pint of beer. "Why are you aiming to be a librarian?"

"Because I already am one." She let out a huff of breath. "But without the graduate degree, I wasn't paid like one, and couldn't keep advancing." She told him about starting as a page shelving books, about working nights as a clerk while getting her college degree, about stepping in as acting branch librarian. "Library budgets are always tight. Somehow they just let me stay. I did the job, they saved money. After a while, I resented that. And openings would come up that might have interested me—in outreach, or reference at headquarters, or the step above me, the librarian who oversaw branches—and I, of course, wasn't eligible. I decided I could stew, or do something about it."

"How long is the program?"

He listened in turn and encouraged her to talk about her classes, her need for a part-time job and her decision to rent a room at his sister's rather than look for an apartment on her own.

"Are you glad? Sorry?" he asked.

"Undecided," Jo admitted. "They're both nice women, but I hadn't bargained for the kids, and I'm used to more privacy than I have now."

His attention never wavered. "You didn't have a roommate? Or a significant other?"

She shook her head. "I owned my own condo. I'm afraid the equity is financing my tuition."

"Boyfriend?"

"Nobody serious." She didn't tell him "serious" wasn't in her game plan. "You?"

Ryan shook his head in turn. "I've been divorced less than two years. Most of my spare time until a few months ago was spent with my kids." A ripple of emotion passed through his eyes. "My ex remarried and this summer they moved to Denver."

"Can she do that?"

"Regrettably, yeah." He abruptly stood. "That's us."

Us? Jarred, she realized their pizza was ready.

Once they started dishing up and eating, Jo didn't ask any more about his kids. Obviously, he missed them. But because they lived half a country away, she wouldn't have to have anything to do with them. Good thing—she couldn't see herself pretending to have great fun taking someone else's children to the zoo or the water slides. Maybe this relationship had more promise than she'd feared.

As though tacitly agreeing to avoid subjects too personal, Ryan started in on local politics and the resultant taxes on a small business like his, grumbling about years ago having to help pay for SafeCo Field for the Mariners. "Blowing up the King Dome." He shook his head. "Can you believe it? Perfectly good stadium."

"Aren't you a baseball fan?"

"Yeah, sure I am." He grinned. "I even like SafeCo Field. It's cool that they can roll back the roof on a sunny day. But they just keep piling on the taxes, and I can't afford it. I sure don't make any more money when the Mariners are successful."

Corralling a long strand of cheese, she said, "No, I suppose not."

"Hey." He set down his mug. "Want to go to a Mariners game someday?"

Jo couldn't help laughing. "I'd love to. Although, the Mariners… I don't know. Maybe they're an acquired taste. Now, me, I'm an Oakland A's fan."

He pretended shock, and they bandied mild insults along with a few stats.

Enjoying herself, Jo was also aware of feeling more self-conscious than she normally would on a casual date like this. It was Ryan, of course, who was responsible for her nervousness. He was the most handsome man she'd seen in a long time—okay, forever. Excitement ran through her, just a tingle that occasionally made her shiver. But she was disquieted by her powerful reaction to him.

Women did dumb things when they fell too hard for a man.

The pizza they hadn't eaten grew cold on the table while they continued to talk. He was a reader, too, she discovered, and had even written poetry when he was in high school.

"Romantic, tragic garbage," he said with a laugh. His tone became smug. "Girls loved it, though."

"I'll bet they did," Jo said with feeling. "*My* boyfriend in high school sometimes got really romantic and told me that making it with me would be as good as hitting a homer. A real high, he said."

Ryan threw his head back and gave a hearty laugh. "Did you punch him?"

"Yeah, actually, I think I did." Jo chuckled,

too. "I still remember the look of complete bewilderment on his face. He didn't understand why I wasn't clasping my hand to my heart to bestill its pitty-pats."

Eyes still laughing, Ryan said, "Yeah, well, he's probably long-married and his wife is lucky if once in a while he tells her she's put on weight but she still has a pretty smile."

Jo made a face. "If there's any justice, she grabs his big belly and tells him it doesn't ripple like it used to, but she doesn't mind love handles."

"You think he has one?"

"Yeah. He was kind of beefy. A jock, you know. Sure," she nodded, "he'd have gone to seed. How about your high school girlfriend?"

A certain wryness entered his voice. "Want to know the truth?"

Jo cocked her head to one side. "Yeah."

"I married her. She still looks good."

"You *married* right out of high school?"

Ryan dipped his head in acknowledgment. "Big mistake, but, yeah. I did."

"Did Kathleen like your wife?"

"Hated her. The feeling was mutual," he added. "Kathleen said Wendy was self-centered and shallow." His mouth twisted.

"She was right. Isn't it awful, when your big sister is always right?"

"Is she?" Jo asked quietly.

He made a sound low in his throat. "I used to think she was. I think *she* thought her life was pretty close to a state of perfection." There was that word again. "But you know the saying."

"Pride goeth before the fall?"

"That's it. Her pride is taking a real battering."

Jo asked about their parents, and learned that their mother was dead of cancer and their father was still on-again, off-again employed, living in a run-down little place in West Seattle. "Likes to go to the bars. He was plenty mad when Emerald Downs closed." Seeing her confusion, Ryan added, "The horse racing track."

"Ah."

"Dad's your classic blue-collar, uneducated guy. He's happy with what he is. Which," Ryan's grin was wicked, "irritates Kathleen no end. She's spent a lifetime trying to improve him."

"She hasn't started trying to improve me yet," Jo said thoughtfully.

"Oh, I'm making her sound worse than she

is." The skin beside his eyes crinkled when he smiled. "But here's a piece of advice. Don't leave dirty dishes on the counter."

Jo didn't admit that she already had one morning, when she hit the snooze button and overslept. They'd been washed, dried and put away when she got home. At dinner, she'd thanked whoever picked up after her. Kathleen had smiled and said, "We all have those mornings occasionally."

Oh, no, she wouldn't feel guilty! She was working off any sins of commission or omission. Jo hadn't expected the remodeling job to be as all-consuming as it had turned out to be.

"Did you really think the tile looked okay?" she asked.

"Better than okay. Hey!" He pushed away the half-full pitcher of beer. "Want to work for me sometimes?"

"Are you serious?" Both flattered and startled, she felt an annoying frisson of excitement. He liked her. Well, he liked the way she used bullnose tiles.

How easily she was pleased.

"Yeah." He seemed surprised. "Yeah, I am. We have a guy we call for tiling, but he's been unreliable. I've considered looking for someone else."

"I'm a complete amateur!"

"Job you did in there didn't look amateur."

Her cheeks were turning pink. "Thank you. It wasn't just me, though."

"Wasn't it?" Ryan asked shrewdly.

"Helen did most of the cutting."

"Could you learn?"

"Well, sure." Jo frowned. "Are you saying your sister is lazy?"

"Lazy?" She'd earned raised brows. "No. Just…used to the peons doing the work. It's actually why I've been skeptical about her determination to be independent. Make sure she does her share."

Jo nodded. "I will. Um…how often do you need someone to tile?"

After he gave her an idea what kind of hours and pay she could expect, she promised to think about whether she'd want to work for him, and they left it at that.

On the way out, they briefly discussed seeing a movie, but decided they had to get up too early in the morning. "Maybe Friday night?" Ryan asked.

"Sure." Jo enjoyed the feeling of his hand

on her lower back as he opened the outside door.

On the short drive home, Ryan asked out of the blue, "Here's my profound question for the night. What do you want out of life?"

An audible hint of defensiveness crept into her voice. "A satisfying job, a nice home and good friends."

In the darkness between street lights, she felt as much as saw his head turn. "Marriage? Kids?"

She wouldn't lie. "Neither are for me."

He was quiet for a moment, until he had to brake at a stop sign. "Why?"

"How many happy marriages have you ever seen?" she asked bluntly. "You and your sister are zero for two. My parents should never have married. My friends are in and out of relationships and marriages. If by some wild chance you are happy, then you face grief like Helen's feeling now. What's the upside?"

Pulling to the curb in front of his sister's brick house, he set the hand brake. "Having it all."

"Can't you do that without getting married?"

"No desire for children?"

Jo shook her head firmly. "I'm not maternal."

"Until you have them…"

"You don't know? Uh-uh. Haven't you noticed how many people stink at being parents? I wouldn't wish that on anyone, and I sure don't want to be a failure at something I never intended to do in the first place."

"You're a hard woman."

Did he mean it?

"No. Just…cynical."

"But you haven't sworn off dating altogether?"

"No, I like companionship. Just so the man understands I'm not interested in forever."

"Aren't I the one who should be saying that?"

"That is traditional, I believe."

"I don't mind breaking tradition." He bent toward her. "If you don't."

"It seems to come naturally to me," she whispered, just before he kissed her.

Oh, so softly, his lips brushed hers. She sighed. He took his sweet time and let her take hers. She was boneless by the time he lifted his head.

"You are a very beautiful woman, Jo Dubray," he murmured, nuzzled her ear.

"Me?"

"Oh, yeah." He seemed to be enjoying the texture of her hair as he ran his fingers through it. "Definitely you."

"You're, um, not so bad yourself."

She loved the rumble in his chest when he laughed. "Am I something like a good book?"

Jo tried to sound dignified. "Isn't that better than a home run?"

"I don't know." He shook his head doubtfully, the grooves in his cheeks betraying his amusement. "I think we need to work on how to give compliments."

It never had been her strong suit. Her mother, she didn't remember that well. Her father had never said anything more than, "Looks good," or "That's fine." Never once had he beamed with pride in a small accomplishment of hers, or lavished her with praise. How did you learn to say, You're wonderful, if you'd never heard it?

"Okay, how's this? You're hot."

"I already knew that." Now he was openly grinning. "Emma tells me I am. She likes it when I drive her places, because the other girls say I'm hot."

"Well, they're right. And I do believe someone is peeking out the front window."

"So they are." He sounded regretful. "So much for another kiss."

"Another time?" Did she have to make it a question when she'd intended to be oh, so cool?

"Count on it."

A moment later, she let herself into the house and watched his pickup pull away.

Companionship. Could she enjoy such tepid pleasures with Ryan, and not make the fatal mistake of falling in love?

CHAPTER FOUR

ONE WEEK AND a couple of dates with Ryan later, Jo was contemplating the less than absorbing problem of whether a given title should be classified in the Dewey Decimal 500s, as a scientific work, or in the 200s, as a metaphysical piece of crackpot science, when the knock came on her bedroom door.

"Come in," she said, turning in her chair, pleased with the interruption and hoping it would be lengthy.

Emma came in, Ginny behind her.

"We're going for a walk," the teenager said. "We thought you might like to come."

Jo hesitated. A stroll down city sidewalks with a first-grader and a high school girl was not her idea of a thrill a minute. On the other hand, it was a beautiful fall day, and besides... Her gaze slipped back to her open textbook.

"Sure! Thanks for asking." She rose, a little embarrassed at her alacrity. "Just let me grab a sweater."

Neither girl's mother was home from work yet. Jo knew the two often went for walks in the afternoon, sometimes to Cowen Park, or to the grocery store to buy a Popsicle for Ginny, or just to wander, she supposed.

Today they set out the eight blocks to Whole Foods, a treasure Kathleen and Helen had pointed her to shortly after her arrival. The huge grocery store on Roosevelt specialized in organic and earth-friendly foods and toiletries. Cosmetics weren't tested on animals, and the produce department had the most incredible mountains of glorious fruits and vegetables she'd ever seen. The bars where shoppers could construct their own wraps and salads were to drool for.

Head tilted back to look up at the leafy canopy, touched with the pale yellow of autumn, Jo decided aloud, "Maybe I'll buy a scone. Have you tried them?"

She immediately felt guilty. If Emma had ever eaten anything like that, she didn't now. But it was really hard never to talk about food. Maybe if people did, she'd be tempted, Jo thought, trying to justify raising a subject that was seldom mentioned around their house.

Ginny walked just ahead beside Emma,

holding her hand. Her brown hair was French-braided, probably courtesy of Emma. She looked over her shoulder. "What's a scone?"

"Um…sort of a sweet biscuit. Really dense." A blank look told Jo she needed to elaborate. "Not fluffy and light like bread, but heavy like…"

"Mom's bread when it doesn't rise right," Emma finished.

"Oh." Ginny nodded, satisfied.

"And you can get them with blueberries or cranberries or bits of orange. They're scrumptious."

"Scrumptious," Ginny repeated, in her solemn way.

Jo bent to pick up a whirlybird seed pod, fallen from a maple. Tossed in the air, it spun gently to the sidewalk.

"Oh!" Ginny said again, with more animation. Letting go of Emma, she picked one up, too, and threw it. She almost smiled, watching its spinning progression.

They stood there for five minutes, playing. Jo felt a little silly when she saw laughing faces in a passing car, but, after all, she'd started this. And Ginny looked absorbed and happy, in her quiet, withdrawn way.

In the next few blocks, Jo and the two

girls talked about hairdos, books and why
an Indian woman who lived in the neighborhood had a dark spot on her forehead. Jo had
to admit Ginny and Emma were easy to talk
to—easier than she'd expected, but maybe
that was because they weren't normal children, either of them. Death shadowed both,
in different ways, subduing them. Making
them more thoughtful, Jo would have liked
to think, but the truth was, Emma seemed
to think and talk about little except food and
how fat she was. Except, Jo amended, when
Emma was with Ginny—then she seemed
more child than teenager.

In the fourth block, Ginny stopped. "Oh!"

Her favorite word, Jo thought dryly, before
she saw the sign, too, easily read even by a
first grader. In block print painted on cardboard, it read, Free Kittens.

"Can we look at them?" Ginny whispered.

Sensing dangerous territory, Jo hesitated.
"Uh…"

"Sure," Emma said, hurrying forward with
the smaller girl towed behind. "We can ask
anyway."

"I'm not sure that's a good idea…." Jo
called after them, lengthening her steps to
catch up.

But they had already turned up the narrow driveway, where they'd spotted a boy shooting baskets into a hoop that hung crookedly above the garage door.

Bang! The garage door rattled when he missed, and Ginny jerked and tried to stop. Determined Emma hauled her onward.

"Hi!" she said.

The lanky boy, who had to be close to her age, turned at the sound of her voice. Dribbling the ball, he said, "Hi." His gaze went to Jo, behind the girls. Warily, he asked, "Um… you looking for somebody?"

"You have a sign for free kittens. Can we see them?"

His face cleared. "We only have one left, but you can look at him, if you want. We really need to find him a home. Dad said any of the kittens that didn't get homes by this weekend have to go to Animal Control."

"We're not really looking for one," Jo felt compelled to say.

"Maybe Mom would let us," Emma said, making Ginny's tipped-up face hopeful.

Jo couldn't imagine. Kathleen didn't strike her as a woman who'd like having a kitten clawing the furniture and hanging from the blinds and shedding on her pillow.

"Does your mother *like* cats?" she asked doubtfully.

"Sure. We used to have a Persian. He died of cancer. The vet said they do a lot."

A Persian. Well, they did shed, she supposed, but she wondered if they ever dangled from window blinds. In every photo she'd ever seen, the Persian was neatly composed on a velvet pillow, apparently content to gaze vacuously at the world.

The boy let the basketball fall. "He's under a bush in the backyard, I think. Come on." He started around the corner of the house, beneath a huge bush with shiny green leaves that seemed to be blocking one of the windows in the house.

"Are you spaying the mother cat?" Jo asked. She had never been an animal person, but in her opinion, you shouldn't have a pet you couldn't adequately care for. And keeping a female cat from having endless, unwanted litters of kittens seemed like basic care.

"Dad said we could keep her if I can earn the money to pay for her spaying. I mow lawns. Hey!" He looked eagerly over his shoulder. "Do you need yours mowed?"

The gate hung crookedly on bent hinges.

He had to scrape it across the concrete walk to open it. Jo winced.

"No, but we're remodeling the house. We might be able to pay you to haul debris out to the Dumpster, that kind of thing." She'd pay him out of her own pocket until that cat was spayed.

The backyard could have used mowing, but Dad apparently didn't care. Dandelions were displacing the original sod. The handle of a mower stuck out of a rusting metal shed that seemed to be otherwise full of junk. Jo was beginning to think the boy had way more initiative than his father.

"Kitty, kitty, kitty!" the boy called.

At a tiny meow, Jo turned. A creamsicle orange-and-white ball of fluff walked out from under an overgrown rhododendron.

"Oh," Ginny breathed happily.

The kitten picked its way through grass that reached over its back, the tail a flag, waving high. Even Jo felt a dangerous melting sensation.

But when it was about ten feet away, they all saw that one of his eyes was… Oh, my, Jo thought. It was actually dangling out of the socket.

Even as they gaped in horror, they heard the happy whir of a kitten purr.

Ginny shrank back against Jo, and even Emma recoiled. On gathering anger, Jo asked, "Did you know?"

The boy turned a shocked face to her. "He wasn't like that." His voice shook. "Something happened. I bet the neighbor's dog got him."

"Will your parents take him to the vet?" The hard tone was unlike her.

His mouth worked, and finally he shook his head. "I think Dad'll take him to Animal Control."

Jo bent and gently scooped up the kitten, whose purr intensified. He weighed hardly anything. "We'll take him to the vet," she said. "Maybe his eye can be saved."

She was hurrying out of the yard before she grasped what she'd done. The girls behind her were starting to babble.

"*Can* it be fixed?"

"Will we keep him?"

"I don't know," Jo said to both questions. In the driveway she stopped and turned to the boy. "Can you remember our address?" She made him repeat it twice. "I'll pay for the mother cat to be spayed, if you'll promise to work to pay me back."

He nodded jerkily, his eyes full of tears.

"I'll see you Saturday morning, then. At nine o'clock."

"I promise." He swiped the tears on his shirtsleeve.

The kitten was trembling in Jo's arms. As she hurried toward home, she kept stealing glances at his eyeball and the caked blood around it. This hadn't just happened, maybe not even today. He felt hot. Hotter than a cat should, she thought.

"Is he okay?" Emma asked for the third time, as they turned the corner onto their block.

"He needs to go to the vet," Jo told her. "Now. Will you two come?"

They both nodded, eyes wide and scared.

"Emma, I need my car keys and license. My purse is on my bedside table. Will you run up and get it?"

The teenager nodded and raced into the house.

"Ginny, will you go get a towel out of the linen closet? An old one, preferably?"

The six-year-old obeyed without a word. Waiting, Jo wondered anxiously if she was doing the right thing. Both girls had such problems. Was she traumatizing them further by letting them think they might save this poor creature? But what else could she have done? If she'd hustled them away, they'd have all had nightmares. At least this way they could tell themselves they'd done their best.

She murmured softly to the kitten, who began again to purr. He hadn't struggled once. He was such a soft, sweet thing, his one good eye trusting.

"We'll fix you," she whispered, scratching his back gently with one finger. "You shouldn't have been out where that scary dog could find you."

Behind her, Jo heard the deep rumble of a truck. Startled when it turned into the driveway, she turned.

"Ryan!"

In his work garb of heavy boots, faded denim jeans and torn flannel shirt, he climbed out of his pickup, his smile a caress. "Jo, I came by to see…"

Ginny tugged at Jo's sleeve. Wordless, she held up a towel.

At almost the same moment, Emma tore down the stairs. "Here's your purse!"

"What's the emergency?" Ryan asked.

As Jo shifted the small, furry bundle in her arms so she could wrap it in the towel, his gaze shifted.

"What the…?"

"Long story," she told him. "We're on our way to the vet. Um…do you know of a vet?"

"There's a clinic just off Roosevelt. I pass it all the time." He nodded to his truck. "Hop in."

The moment he opened the door, they all saw the huge tool chest on the back seat. "But you said we could go!" Emma protested. "Uncle Ryan doesn't have room."

Taking a deep breath, Jo faced the girls. "Are you sure you *want* to come? You know, there's a chance that, um…"

Emma lifted her chin. "He'll die?"

Jo nodded.

"We still want to come. Don't we?"

They all looked at Ginny, who knew too much about death snatching a loved one. Small and pale, she tucked her hand in Emma's. "Yes," she said softly but very clearly. "We want to come."

"Well, then," Jo turned back to Ryan, "we have to take my car. But thank you."

"I'll drive." He held out his hand.

Masterful man, once again. Also once again, Jo was chagrined to realize she didn't mind. After all, he knew where he was going, she told herself. Besides, she didn't want to jar the kitten by handing him over to someone else.

"Emma, can you dig out the keys?"

The teenager found them and passed them to Ryan, who waited only until everyone was buckled in before rocketing away from the curb.

Righting herself, Jo said, "I don't think another minute or two is going to matter."

He glanced at the kitten. "Why is it purring?"

Tiny paws kneaded Jo's arm. "I think he's happy. Or maybe he's purring to comfort himself. I'm not sure."

Ryan made an inarticulate sound and tore around a corner. Jo clutched at the armrest and saved her breath.

Within minutes they screeched to a stop in the small parking lot beside a veterinary clinic. Everyone trailed Jo in.

"May I help you?" asked the heavyset woman behind the counter.

"We…found this kitten." Jo held it up for her to see. "He really needs help."

The pleasant smile vanished. "Oh, my! Just a moment." She disappeared through a doorway, returning almost immediately. "Let me take you back to a room."

She carried a clipboard with them into the small examining room, where all four crowded with her. "Dr. Mills will be right with us. Let me get some information first."

With a twinge of what did I get myself into, Jo gave her name as the owner, along with her address and phone number.

"Does the kitten have a name yet?"

Had the boy called him by anything? She couldn't remember hearing anything but "kitty, kitty."

"I don't think so," she admitted. "This has all happened so fast."

Ginny piped up unexpectedly. "He should be Pirate. In case he has to have an eye patch."

Jo looked down at the orange-and-white face, made grotesque by the damaged eye. "Pirate," she whispered.

Silent since she'd carried him in, he started to purr again.

Jo smiled at Ginny. "Pirate it is."

After the receptionist had left, Emma said, "Mom's going to wonder where we are, if she gets home first. Maybe I should leave a message."

Jo nodded. "Good idea. We don't want to scare her."

Emma disappeared to use Jo's cell phone, left in the car. A moment later, the door opened and a young woman in a white lab coat with a stethoscope around her neck came in.

After introducing herself and shaking hands, she said, "Let's take a look."

Emma slipped back in to join the anxious circle watching while the vet took the kitten's temperature, listened to his heart and studied the inside of his mouth for reasons mysterious to Jo.

"He's certainly in shock," she said with a frown. "And he has a fever. You don't know when this happened?"

Their heads shook in unison.

"We'll give him some fluids and start him on antibiotics right away."

"Is Pirate a he?" Emma asked.

She grinned. "It's a boy."

It was Jo who asked nervously, "What about his eye?"

The veterinarian made a humming sound in her throat as she gazed at Pirate for a long moment. "Well," she said with a sigh, "the obvious course would be to remove the damaged eye." She held up a hand when they all began abortive questions. "Cats do very well with only one eye. He'd never know the difference. Of course his vision wouldn't be quite as good, and he'd have to be indoor-only—"

"Can his eye be saved?" Jo interrupted. She'd been watching Ginny's distress.

"I can't save it. However, I can refer you to a specialist who might be able to. I do think it's possible. The eye looks to be in good shape and the socket isn't damaged badly. However," she warned, "you'd be looking at a pretty big bill."

In the end, Jo decided to let her buckle an Elizabethan collar around the kitten's neck so he wouldn't scratch the eye, put ointment on it and gently cover it with a bandaged cup. With antibiotics and instructions in hand as well as the address for the eye specialist, they left with Pirate.

Dr. Sullivan had agreed to look at him right away. They stopped at home first, where Helen decided to come as well.

"I'll leave a note for Kathleen," she said,

hurrying back into the house and reappearing in remarkably short order.

Dr. Sullivan looked with some amusement at the crowd, but let them all in while he examined Pirate.

"I think we can save his eye," he concluded, "although it's difficult to tell how much of his vision will be intact."

"We'll never know, will we?" Jo laughed shakily. "He can't read an eye chart for you, can he?"

He laughed, too. "We do have ways to check. His eyes will follow movement, for example, just like ours. But no, I won't be able to tell if his vision is twenty-twenty."

The cost, as he outlined it, made Jo's heart sink. They shouldn't have come at all. She couldn't afford a bill like that. And she didn't even want a cat!

But Emma and Ginny both looked at her with anxious eyes. "Is that too much?" Emma whispered.

"Can we have a minute to talk about it?" Jo asked the veterinarian.

"You bet. There's no one else in the waiting room. You have it to yourselves."

They huddled, conscious of the receptionist

within hearing distance. Jo cradled Pirate in one arm.

"I can't afford anywhere near that much," she said bluntly, feeling horribly guilty with the tiny bundle looking up at her with his one good eye. He looked so pathetic in the wide plastic collar that was almost bigger than he was.

Ginny shrank at Jo's words.

Helen wrapped her arms around her daughter. Biting her lip, she said quietly, "I can't, either, but maybe we could pool our money. I could come up with…oh, two hundred dollars. I know that's not much, but…"

"I'll bet Mom would, too!" Emma declared, eyes filled with hope. "I'll call her!"

Hating to think what Kathleen would say about today's adventure and seriously doubting that she would pony up money for a cat she wouldn't want, Jo nonetheless offered her cell phone.

While she dialed, Ryan said gruffly, "I'll contribute."

"But…you don't even live with us," Jo said, then realized how it sounded.

His gaze rested on Ginny, and his voice was brusque. "I care."

Emma handed the phone to Jo. "Mom wants to talk to you."

Jo explained the situation. Kathleen was silent for a long moment. "Just what we need," she muttered.

"No kidding," Jo admitted. "I'm sorry. This is my fault."

"What else could you do?" She sighed. "It really seems to matter to Emma. Lately, not much does."

Jo was silent.

Another sigh. "I can afford, say, three hundred dollars. Is that enough to help? We can put off doing the downstairs bathroom. Maybe I'll get a different job soon. One that pays better."

"Okay. Thanks. I'll let you know," Jo said, breaking the connection.

They added up their contributions and realized they needed a few hundred more. Jo, wishing she'd lined up a part-time job, mentally tallied her bank account and her bills, trying to decide if she'd have enough for tuition if she made up the difference.

"I'll pay the rest, too," Ryan said. "Despite what Kathleen seems to believe, I have more money than I have any use for. She just doesn't like to take it from me. But this isn't for her."

Emma started to cry. Jo was shocked to feel a sting in her eyes as well. "Thank you," she whispered.

Ginny asked, "Can I hold him until they take him?"

Jo nodded and knelt to gently transfer the bundle of kitten and towel into the little girl's arms. Then they returned to the reception desk.

"We've decided to go ahead and try to save his eye," she said.

"Oh, good!" The receptionist smiled at Ginny. "He's such a handsome boy. He's going to be a beautiful cat!"

"He is, isn't he?" Jo took one last look at the small face with the huge ears and the cute orange splotch on the otherwise white face. She felt like crying again. What if he didn't survive the surgery? The other vet had said he was in shock. And he was so small! Maybe he wasn't strong enough…

"We'll take good care of him," the receptionist said gently, taking Pirate from Ginny. "I promise. Dr. Sullivan will do the surgery this afternoon. We'll call as soon as he's finished."

"Okay." Jo swallowed. "Thank you."

They trooped back out into the late-afternoon sunlight. "Well," Jo said, "that wasn't quite the walk we had in mind, was it, girls?"

Emma laughed even as she sniffed and wiped her wet cheeks. "I'm being dumb. It's not like we've had him forever."

Ginny tugged at her mother's sleeve and looked up at her rather than Jo. "We can keep him, can't we?"

Helen's eyes met Jo's for a brief instant. "Honey, it's not going to be my decision. The house is Kathleen's."

"But Mom's going to help with the vet bill!" Emma exclaimed. "That must mean—" She stopped.

Jo admitted, "I didn't ask her. I guess I assumed, too..."

Ryan came to the rescue once again. "I'll take Pirate to my house if Kathleen won't let you keep him. You can visit all you want." He smiled wryly. "But you know what? I think you've got a cat."

In the car, Jo moaned, "Oh, no! It's my turn to cook! I should have put the casserole together. I'm sorry. Dinner's going to be really late."

"Let's just have leftovers," Helen said practically. "We have a whole bunch of dibs and dabs in the refrigerator. Ginny is happy with macaroni and cheese, and I wouldn't mind a salad and some of those scalloped potatoes from yesterday."

Flooded with gratitude, Jo asked, "Really? I'll make my casserole tomorrow night."

They had to park half a block away, an inconvenience that was going to become an annoyance when winter rains and chill came. Every morning, Jo had to think where she'd left her car the afternoon before. Once, she'd had to park two blocks away. She'd liked having her very own reserved spot with her condo.

Ryan came in with them as if it were a matter of course. The way he chose to walk beside Jo gave her a warm tingle, too, as if he liked being with her, or maybe was giving physical form to his support of her if his sister was mad.

Kathleen must have been hovering, because she appeared from the living room the moment the front door opened. "Well?" she demanded. "What happened?" She saw that their arms were empty. "You didn't…?"

"He's going to have surgery," Jo said. "With

your contribution, we came up with enough money."

"Oh!" She pressed a hand to her chest. "You scared me for a minute."

"He's really cute, Mom." Emma's face was alight. "He's orange and white and fluffy, with the sweetest face. And he purrs even though he must hurt."

"I'm glad you rescued him," Kathleen said with a smile for her daughter and a swift, meaningful one for Jo. "You would have felt terrible if you hadn't."

On the spot, Jo decided that maybe she liked Kathleen after all. So she was a princess; any divorced woman had to adjust. But she'd had the guts to leave her husband for Emma's sake, and she had enough pride to refuse to live on her brother's charity. So what if she had a little bit to learn about not assuming other people were willing to work for her just for the sheer pleasure of it? Obviously, her heart was in the right place.

Emma gazed beseechingly at her mother. "We can keep him, can't we?"

Kathleen's brows rose. "Are you kidding? After we spend a fortune on him? You think we'd just give him away?"

"You mean…we *can?*" the teenager said in wonder.

"Of course we can." Kathleen gave her a quick hug, as if hoping she wouldn't have time to reject the embrace.

Emma squealed, and she and Ginny danced around. The adults smiled and watched. Under her breath, Kathleen said, "When the cat claws the couch, remind me how happy he made Emma."

"I will," Jo promised.

Ryan just grinned. "Trim his claws," he advised.

"Well." Kathleen drew herself up with her customary briskness. "I don't know about you, but I'm hungry."

"We have lots of leftovers we can heat in just a few minutes," Helen said again.

"Works for me," Ryan said easily.

For once, his sister didn't ask who'd invited him. Her gaze did flick speculatively from him to Jo, however.

But all she said was, "Then let's go inspect the refrigerator."

Jo was very careful not to look up at the tall man who stood so close, his powerful upper arm brushing her shoulder. He might have seen her interest stamped on her face.

But then, she thought, it was beginning to look as if she might get what she wanted. That is, *who* she wanted. Why not? She'd set the ground rules, and he hadn't even tried to negotiate them. Probably he was no more interested in marriage at this point in his life than she was, never mind having children. After all, he already had two.

In fact, he was perfect for her. Unattached, distanced enough from his marriage to be fun but not so far from it that he was cruising for wife number two. Jo and he could be friends. With neither of them wanting more.

Jo had begun to be very glad she had decided to rent a room in this house.

CHAPTER FIVE

PIRATE CAME HOME two days later, his eye stitched shut and covered, to Ginny's delight, with a patch. He was still stuck in the Elizabethan collar, which he shook with ferocity and frequently managed to wedge in narrow openings, where he would scream until someone came to rescue him.

A couple of times, Jo heard Kathleen mutter, "I can't believe we wasted that kind of money," but never in either of the kids' hearing. Jo also caught her crooning to Pirate as she rescued him or cradling the sleeping kitten almost absentmindedly while she paid bills or dusted. Work on the bathroom continued and Jo saw Ryan a couple of times, but life centered on Pirate.

The girls came rushing in the door from school every day, dying to see the kitten. Ginny had never looked so much like an ordinary little girl.

At dinner one night, she asked if she could take him to show-and-tell in her class. "I asked Teacher specially, because they don't usually let you bring your pets, and she said yes if you come, too, Mom, so you can take him home after." She fixed hopeful eyes on her mother.

Helen, who had been especially quiet until now and had dark circles beneath her eyes, said, "Oh, dear. When is show-and-tell?"

"Friday."

"But I work." She sighed. "What time?"

"Two o'clock, Teacher says."

"Oh, honey." Helen's voice ached with regret. "I don't see how I can. If we could take him in the morning…"

"It has to be for show-and-tell." Ginny's shoulders slumped, and she whispered, "That's okay."

Jo could not believe she was doing this, but she offered, "I could take him." When Ginny's head shot up, Jo said, "I know you'd rather have your mother, but I don't have a Friday afternoon class. I'll bet Emma would come with me, too."

"Yeah!" Emma was hovering in the kitchen doorway, unwilling to sit down at the table heaped with food but also reluctant to miss any conversation that might have to do with her. "That would be cool! We could hang around afterward until school lets out."

Oh, joy, Jo thought. But it wouldn't kill her. She didn't have to like kids to want to see Ginny's face brighten the way it did now.

"Really? You could bring Pirate?"

"Sure. If that's okay with you, Helen."

"Bless you," the girl's mother said fervently.

When the phone rang, Emma pounced.

"It's for you, Jo," she said a moment later, looking pouty.

Done eating anyway, Jo took the phone to the living room.

"Jo? It's Aunt Julia." Her aunt, an attorney, explained that she was flying tomorrow to Fairbanks to depose a witness and had arranged a night stopover in Seattle on the assumption that she'd be able to see Jo. "I could rent a car if you can't make it to the airport...."

"Don't be silly!" Jo exclaimed.

Aunt Julia had been the next-best thing to a mother she'd had. There had been tension between Aunt Julia and Jo's father when she was a child. Her father had to have known that his wife's sister didn't particularly like him. But he hadn't stopped her visits to Jo and Boyce.

Jo and her aunt had visited more often when Jo had been in the Bay Area; business seemed to bring Aunt Julia up from L.A. every few months. But now it had been... oh, as much as five months since Jo had seen her.

Thus she found herself at the airport the next evening, waiting for disembarking passengers at the Alaskan Airline gate. Businessmen in dark suits carrying laptop cases strode briskly out without a glance, while a young, weary-looking mother with two toddlers came through the gate, scanned the crowd, then burst into tears when she saw the face she sought.

"Daddy! Daddy!" The older of the two children broke away from her mother to run to the man who swept first her, then the woman into his arms.

"They cried and cried..." Jo heard, as the family moved away.

Jo shuddered. Imagine traveling with two kids that age! Better yet, imagine how everyone sitting in their vicinity had suffered.

"Josie!"

She jerked her head back, to see her petite,

stylish aunt parting a family cluster as if she were Moses and they, the Red Sea. Aunt Julia was rather like that, her gaze fixed on her own goals so firmly that others generally did give way.

Jo hated being called Josie by anybody but Aunt Julia. From her, it had always felt like an endearment. The closest thing to an endearment that anybody ever called her, at any rate.

"Aunt Julia!" she said with genuine pleasure.

The two women embraced. Her aunt pulled back to eye her critically.

"You look well. I'm so glad you've chosen to go to graduate school. You were wasting yourself at that backwater library. You're far too intelligent to settle when you can have more."

Her aunt's mantra, one Jo had adopted. Why should she settle?

"Thank you. You look wonderful," she said warmly, meaning it.

Her aunt was approaching fifty, but seemed to defy age to touch her smooth olive skin or frost her dark hair. She wore her thick hair in a short, sleek style that emphasized elegant cheekbones and commanding brown eyes.

Today's beautifully cut suit was fire-engine red, as were her fingernails and lipstick.

"My dear!" she said with raised brows. "I make a point of looking wonderful."

Jo laughed. "I wish I had half your presence."

"You do. You just don't know it." Her aunt gave a man who dared to jostle her a withering stare. "Well? Why are we wasting time? I do have baggage—it's important I look good for my meeting in Fairbanks. Fairbanks in October! Why couldn't it be Honolulu?"

Jo, assuming the question to be rhetorical, hurried to catch up with her aunt, who was briskly walking away. "I wish we had a guest bedroom. Did you make a reservation?"

"Nearby at the Radisson," her aunt told her. "My flight is quite early in the morning. I won't expect you for breakfast."

"I have a nine o'clock class," Jo said. Which she would undoubtedly have skipped, had Aunt Julia commanded it.

"Ah." Her aunt tapped one red pump irritably as they waited for the 'people mover,' SeaTac's subway from one concourse to another. "I assume you haven't seen your father?" she asked.

A knot of hurt inside Jo seemed to gain a

new tangle. "No. We rarely talk. You know that."

"Idiot man," her aunt pronounced.

Actually, he seemed content enough to Jo, now that he didn't have to shape his life around the children he'd had to parent alone since their mother died when Jo was seven. Jo had always believed that she and her brother, Boyce, were unsatisfactory as children went. As an adult, she now understood intellectually that the fault hadn't been theirs. Their father hadn't signed on to be a single parent. He'd expected to be the breadwinner while his wife handled school lunches, the PTA and skinned knees. He did his duty when he got stuck with all of the above, but he hadn't enjoyed it and was visibly relieved when first Jo and then Boyce had left home. If he had regrets, they were well hidden.

Jo said nothing. He was what he was. He'd raised her in a way that had shaped who she was. She wouldn't repeat his mistakes. Heredity did not suggest she would be much of a mother.

Aunt Julia let the subject of Jo's father drop, talking about the deposition she'd be taking in Fairbanks and the triumph of winning a recent, high-profile murder case.

"With no body, juries are hard to persuade," she said with satisfaction. "But we all knew the man did it, and he allowed his smugness to slip out a few times. Juries may be made up of people who never read a newspaper, but that doesn't mean they're dumb."

Jo hid her smile. When the defense won, Aunt Julia was just as inclined to rant about the idiocy of people allowed to sit on juries.

Aunt Julia's luggage was the first to appear, naturally. As children, Jo and Boyce had been awed by her incredible luck. Parking places always opened before her, traffic lights turned green, coveted items went on fifty-percent-off sales, tables in front of the window became available when she stepped foot in exclusive restaurants. She simply sailed through life assuming she would get her way.

Jo grew up wanting to be Aunt Julia.

Her memories of her mother were mere snapshots, a child's impressions. Mom had been petite and dark-haired, too, with a face that in photographs could have been Jo's own. Lately she'd realized that she was nearly the age her mother had been when she died. The idea bothered her. In one way it made her feel closer to the woman her mother had been, but that wasn't totally comfortable. She didn't like to suspect that her mother had felt any of her own uncertainty and doubt and childish anger.

Pulling Aunt Julia's suitcase, Jo led the way to her car. The Radisson Hotel wasn't five minutes drive from the airport. Settled in the restaurant, they continued to talk.

"Do you know, it's been almost two years since Boyce and I had Christmas with you in L.A.?" Jo said, after mentally counting on her fingers. "I'm so glad you had an excuse to pass through Seattle. I think that's the last time we were all together."

Her aunt sipped her coffee. "You know you're welcome to visit me anytime."

Jo smiled fondly. "Some Friday night I'll shock you by showing up on your doorstep. You'll just be changing into a glamorous little black dress for a night out with your latest boyfriend, who happens to own some dot. com, or is lighting in L.A. between wars that he covers for the *New York Times*. You'll be appalled to see me."

The tiniest of lines deepened beside Aunt Julia's mouth, adding years. "Oh, come, Jo. My life is hardly that exciting."

It had to be a trick of the candlelight, Jo told herself. Aunt Julia would never age. Or perhaps she would, but beautifully, so that even white-haired she'd be strikingly beautiful, a woman who stopped conversations when she passed. By then her boyfriends would be far younger than she, still brilliant or powerful or wealthy. Why else would they interest her?

"I always imagined it that way," Jo said, her smile becoming reminiscent. "I remember watching you dress up one night for a date with that senator you were seeing. I think he was a senator. I couldn't have been more than seven or eight. I thought you looked like a princess. I would have loved to be able to peek from a stair landing at the ball."

The lines vanished as Aunt Julia laughed. "I suspect the ball was some tedious political gala, and he needed somebody decorative on his arm. I don't even remember it."

"Or him?"

"Oh, I remember him." She waved a hand dismissively. "He was lovely to look at, but I learned he was a puppet with several other people pulling the strings. Not nearly as interesting as I thought he'd be."

"What about now?" Jo asked, leaning forward. "Are you still seeing that federal judge?"

"George?" Her aunt sounded uncaring, but some emotion pinched her face, bringing back the wrinkles. "No! He fell for a thirty-year-old law clerk and married her. I understand she's pregnant with twins."

Jo frowned. Men didn't leave Aunt Julia for other women. At least, Jo had never imagined that they did. Perhaps her aunt had already lost interest in him, and he was seeking consolation.

"You two seemed so…cozy, that Christmas Boyce and I spent with you. Almost settled."

"Settling isn't in me," Aunt Julia snapped. "You know that."

Startled by the edge in her voice, Jo bit her lip. "I didn't mean…"

"He was good company." She set down her coffee cup with a sharp click. "That's all."

"Are you seeing anyone now?" Jo asked tentatively.

"It seems as if everywhere I go, the men are married." Her aunt snorted. "Men my age are pushing strollers. Ridiculous."

"Do you ever wish…?" Jo hardly knew how to frame her thought.

"Don't be absurd!" Aunt Julia's laugh was hard. "Can you see me, of all people, in a

Lamaze class? Changing diapers, instead of writing briefs? I'm hardly the hausfrau type."

"Women do seem to juggle work and family more successfully these days." Why was she arguing, when she felt the same? Yet the words kept coming. "Maybe because employers are more sympathetic. Women don't have to give up so much anymore to have children."

"Nonsense!" Aunt Julia signaled the waiter with a flick of her hand. He bustled forward, deferentially taking her order for a sorbet. When he was gone, she continued, "I don't know a single serious practicing attorney with children. It's simply impossible to put in those kinds of hours and be any kind of parent or keep a husband content. Oh, there are ones on the lower echelons who put their careers on the back burners for years while they raised children, but they'll never regain what they lost. And at least law is something you can take up again! Your poor mother had to sacrifice any chance at all of making it as a singer. Not that she didn't love you, of course." This was said offhandedly, in a way familiar to Jo, who had heard it a hundred times. *Not that she didn't love you, but...*

Jo dared voice a question she'd always

been afraid to ask. "Was Mom really sorry? I mean, did she say that she was?"

Her aunt chose to answer indirectly, if it could be called an answer. "Do you know, she never sang after you were born? Do you even remember lullabies?"

Jo had to shake her head, although she felt a shimmer of memory, a soft voice crooning in the darkness as they rocked, rocked, rocked. She sensed the warm bundle of her baby brother on her mother's other shoulder. So the song hadn't been for her. If there had been a song at all.

"There you go then." Aunt Julia picked up the spoon in her sorbet as though this subject, too, was closed.

On a flicker of exasperation, Jo asked, "Why did you ask about Father?"

Her elegantly dressed aunt looked up from her dessert with surprise. "I always do."

"No." Jo felt oddly combative tonight. "You didn't say, How is your father? You said, I assume you haven't seen him, as though… I don't know." But she did. Aunt Julia had said it as though she were seeking confirmation of something that pleased her.

For the first time, Jo wondered if Aunt Julia wanted to be more important to her niece and nephew than their father was. If, in her mind, there wasn't a competition. Almost as if *she* were their mother, long divorced from him.

"I can't imagine what you mean," she said coolly. "If I phrased my question poorly, I apologize. I merely sought to discover whether your relationship with him had improved."

It would never do that, Jo knew. Once she would have cared, but no longer. Instead she followed the intriguing idea that Aunt Julia, of all people, actually possessed maternal feelings.

If that were true, it meant she could have been a mother. Or even wished she had been. Was that possible? Would she ever admit it, if it were so?

"You've been very much like a mother to us," Jo said. "You know how grateful we both are."

Her aunt hid an expression of pleasure, but not quickly enough. "Whatever brought that out?"

"I've just…done more thinking lately about Mom, and children and parents in general. Both of the women I live with have daughters—I think I told you that."

"I can't believe you moved into a house full of kids. How do you get any studying done?"

"They're both quiet. Too quiet. I actually," she cleared her throat, "I, um, like them better than I expected to. Even Ginny, the six-year-old."

Aunt Julia threw back her head and gave a derisive laugh. "Please don't tell me your biological clock is ticking, and you too are starting to imagine the joys of warming a bottle for a screaming infant at 4:00 a.m."

"Of course not!" Jo snapped. "Ginny and Emma are hardly the kids to make me think parenting would be a breeze anyway, since they both have problems. It's just that their mothers love them. I never have the feeling they wish they weren't burdened with children."

There, she thought with relief. That's what she'd begun to notice. Helen, grieving though she was, never seemed resentful of her daughter, any more than Kathleen, who had chosen her child over her husband.

No, neither woman had had to balance a career with motherhood. Perhaps one of them had made sacrifices when she found she was pregnant. Jo didn't know. But they *were* struggling financially, both of them. If they ever wished that they didn't have to put another person first, they hid it well.

It was too bad Emma in particular didn't realize how lucky she was. Maybe Jo should tell her.

"Then you must be seeing a man," her aunt decided, scrutinizing her. "Is it serious?"

Annoyed, Jo said, "No! I mean, yes, I'm seeing someone, but I've just met him. Neither of us is interested in marriage or anything like that. He already has kids, but they live with his ex. I'm happy with my life, Aunt Julia. I don't see why expressing appreciation—"

"You're right," her aunt interrupted. "I'm sorry. I just don't want to see you making the same mistake your mother did."

But I wouldn't be here if Mom hadn't chosen marriage and motherhood, Jo thought in automatic protest.

"You knew that Boyce broke off with that… Jennifer person," Aunt Julia said. "I'm glad. I couldn't listen to a word she said when I visited him last time. All I could do was stare at that dreadful row of hoops through her eyebrow."

"I didn't know." Jo was disturbed that her brother hadn't called her. They weren't so close that they spoke weekly, but usually they updated each other on major life changes. "I'll have to call him."

Her aunt's smooth brow furrowed. "He seemed upset. I didn't care for her, but I'm afraid he did."

On an impulse almost immediately regretted, Jo asked, "Do you miss your judge? Wasn't it...nice, having somebody you knew so well? Who knew *you* so well?"

The answer was predictable, an arrogant, "I don't need anyone to know me."

Jo just wasn't sure she altogether believed it anymore.

MOODILY, RYAN SLUMPED in his worn leather club chair, propped his feet on the ottoman and used the remote to flick on the television. He'd missed the Mariners playing the Cleveland Indians when he went to Kathleen's earlier. Now he flipped through channels without finding anything that interested him. Frowning, he killed the television.

Why hadn't Jo said that she wouldn't be home this evening? When he asked Kathleen, she'd dredged up a vague memory that Jo was meeting somebody for dinner, and later he hadn't liked to ask the others. A man had some pride. Maybe she had a study group getting together at a coffee house.

Even if she was on a date, it wasn't his business. He and she had barely started seeing each other. Neither had even hinted that they should be exclusive.

Which didn't keep him from brooding over the mental image of her with another man. Laughing with quick pleasure, a sparkle in those rich brown eyes, or pursing her lips before expressing an opinion. He wondered if she knew how provocative she was when she did that.

The house had felt empty without her there tonight! He'd always liked hanging out with Emma and even little Hummingbird. Irritating his sister was a lifelong hobby that still gave him childish pleasure. Since Kathleen had ditched Ian and bought the Ravenna district house, it had been a home away from home for Ryan.

Tonight, he'd hung around for a while, but without enjoying any of the conversation. Emma had asked for help with some complicated form of graphing that might as well have been Greek to him, and he'd felt stupid. Ginny was more interested in the kitten than in him, Kathleen was paying bills with a Grand Canyon-size frown furrowing her forehead and Helen disappeared right after dinner. When Ryan offered to mow the small back lawn, Kathleen told him the boy who'd been Pirate's previous owner had already done it. In fact, he'd done several chores Ryan usually handled.

Out of sorts, Ryan went home.

Not that his mood had improved here. He supposed he ought to run some laundry or sweep or scrub the shower or some useful thing, but he didn't get up from his easy chair. He was bugged by the knowledge that he was dependent for his state of mind on a woman.

How had that happened so fast? They hadn't gone out half a dozen times: dinner, a movie, a drive up to Mt. Rainier. She had been as blunt as a woman could be about her lack of interest in permanency, marriage, children. He was supposed to be having *fun* with her. He wasn't supposed to be ready to kick the first small child that crossed his path merely because an evening had gone by without his having talked to her or seen her.

"Not now," he said aloud, then jumped a good six inches when the telephone rang. Despising himself for his eagerness, he snatched up the cordless, which sat on the end table beside him, then made himself wait through three rings before answering. "Yeah?"

"Ryan." The voice belonged to his ex-wife. "Um…hi."

His mouth tightened. She wanted something. Wendy was as cold as a penguin's morning swim when she didn't. He was pretty sure she didn't know how obvious she was, or she'd employ a subtler touch.

He tried not to antagonize her, however. For the kids' sake, they had to get along. Trying for a reasonably genial tone, Ryan asked, "What's up? Tyler and Melissa okay?"

"Of course they're fine. They're both in bed. I wanted to talk to you when they couldn't hear."

He wondered how stupid she thought they were. Whatever she was going to ask of him, their kids would find out eventually. Unless it was money, but that was rare. Her new husband made plenty.

"Didn't you get my check?"

"Oh." She sounded flustered. "Yes. Of course I did! Thank you."

"Then?" He was sorry right away for his brusqueness, which she tended to bring out in him. If only she'd just once in her life come right out and say what she wanted.

"Melissa did really well on a big math test today." She offered it like a sprig of olive in a bird's beak: a tentative peace.

Ryan shifted the phone so that he cradled it between his shoulder and ear, freeing him to take a swig of pop. He needed it. "Good."

"Tyler is loving soccer. Ronald videotaped the last game. We'll send you the tape."

As if wobbly, grainy images on the television screen could make up for never being able to see his own kid on the field. For not being able to pace the sidelines, yell encouragement, give quick hugs, see the triumphant grin dawn on the eight-year-old's face when he made a gigantic save.

By moving, she'd cheated him of all that. He tried hard to be adult about this. He couldn't expect her not to remarry, not to move when her husband got a better job. Ryan did his best not to resent her too much for what she'd stolen from him.

Most of the time, he failed.

"Yeah." Voice gritty, he forced himself to add a curt, "Thank you."

She started chattering about Ronald's family and their holiday traditions, as if Ryan cared. "So you can see why we want a break," she concluded.

Frowning, he reran what he remembered of her narrative and couldn't find a connection. A break from what? From whom?

"Yeah. Sure."

"So you won't mind having them? You don't have other plans?"

He sat up, gripping the phone. Okay. He'd missed something, big time. Who was he supposed to be having? Ronald's family?

He gave his head a shake. No. She wanted to ship the kids to him.

"For Thanksgiving," he said tentatively.

"Actually, I thought it wouldn't hurt if they missed a couple of days of school." She gave a high nervous laugh. "Well, three days, technically, but you know the Wednesday before Thanksgiving they have only a half day, and that's a joke, what with class parties and all the excitement about having a break and—"

He interrupted ruthlessly. "When do you want to send them?"

"Friday night? Before Thanksgiving?"

"For a week stay."

"Weren't you listening?" she asked in exasperation.

Ryan drew a breath. "I was supposed to get Christmas this year, and you Thanksgiving. Are you suggesting we switch?" He loved

Christmas! The kids had two weeks off. He'd been really looking forward to that.

"No," Wendy said. "I know that's not fair, especially not when I'm asking you for a favor. You can have both, if you're okay with that."

Okay? He was jubilant. On his feet and pacing, Ryan suppressed the exultation in his voice. "Yeah, you know I always like to have them. Have you told them…"

"No, I wanted to clear it with you first. They'll be excited."

"You're sure?"

"Ronald really wants us to do something with just the two of us. We've had so little time alone," she said apologetically. "Ronald has been terribly nice about taking on two school-age children. He's really good to them. But we haven't been married very long, and sometimes we want to do something romantic."

Ryan said nothing. It had been a long time since he'd wanted to do anything romantic with Wendy. Listening to her light, quick voice, to the breathy apology and the clutter of details that obscured the point of her call, he couldn't remember ever having loved her. He knew he had—or knew he'd *thought* he was in love—but his primary emotion now was gratitude that Ronald wanted Thanksgiving without Melissa and Tyler, thus forcing Wendy to be uncommonly generous.

"Just let me know what flight they'll be on," he said. "I'll give them a call tomorrow night after you've had a chance to tell them about the change in plans."

"Wonderful!"

The rush of relief in her voice seemed excessive, giving him pause. It had seemed to him the kids had been conspicuous lately in how careful they'd been *not* to mention their stepfather.

Was her marriage in trouble? What kind of pressure had "terribly nice" Ronald put on her to ditch the kids? Ryan was suddenly very glad he'd have a chance to talk to Melissa and Tyler about their mom and stepdad. Over the phone, it was too awkward to ask, "How do you feel about Ronald?" Let alone ask if he ever laid a hand on them, or if he scared them in any other way. Ryan could never be sure that Wendy wasn't listening in on another phone, or to the kids' end of the conversation. And in the time since he'd seen them, the talks on the phone had become stilted. It scared him to think that he might already be becoming a stranger to them, a man they didn't really know but were obliged to maintain a relationship with. Having them for a week now, for two at Christmas, then for two months next summer... That would help.

Yeah. It would help a lot.

A knot of unhappiness in his chest loosened, and he said quietly, "I'll look forward to seeing them, Wendy. Don't worry during your getaway. We'll be having a good time, too."

And Jo could meet his kids, too, Ryan thought a moment later, after he'd hung up the phone. Maybe she didn't want any of her own, but there was no reason to think she wouldn't like his. Look how good she was with Ginny and Emma!

Yeah. Smiling, he drained the can of soda, resumed his seat and reached for the remote control again. They'd have a great week.

CHAPTER SIX

PIRATE'S VISIT to school was a huge success. Jo watched with pride and delight as Ginny, lovingly cradling the kitten, carried him around the circle of first-graders seated on the floor so each could pet him. Pirate purred indiscriminately. The clumsy plastic collar appealed to the little boys, and the softness of his fluffy orange-and-white coat evoked oohs and aahs from the girls.

For once the object of envy and admiration, Ginny glowed. "We rescued him," she told one student in response to a question. "He probably would have died if we hadn't taken him home."

Emma, in the circle with the little kids, said, "He gets his patch off next week."

One little girl waved her arm in the air. Signaled by the teacher, she asked, "Can he come back so we can see him again?"

The teacher smiled. "We'll see. Now, does anybody else have something to share?"

Fortunately, nobody did, as the entire class was still entranced with the kitten.

The teacher strolled around the circle to Emma and Jo. "I understand you two plan to stay until the end of the day to wait for Ginny?"

"That's right," Jo agreed with a smile.

"Any chance I could talk you both into listening to some of the kids read while you wait? We never have enough volunteers, and so many of the students don't have anyone at home who encourages their reading."

Jo felt a moment of panic, quickly quelled. She had done plenty of preschool story-times in the library, and competently, too, she'd always felt. She could do this.

"I've done it lots of times," Emma said, jumping up from where she'd sat cross-legged. "My sixth-grade class used to go once a week to help first-graders."

"I'd be happy to," Jo lied.

Thus they found themselves stationed at two back tables. An eager boy carrying a book came to Jo first. Whipping it open, he said, "I know how to read! Want to hear?"

"You bet," she said.

He opened it, planted a finger under the first word, and began. "The...bbb...aa...ttt."

His face drew into a scowl as he listened in his head to the sounds, then cleared as he declared triumphantly, "Bat! The bat!"

Jo grinned. "Right!"

Okay, this was kind of fun, really.

"The bat and...the...ccc..."

It could also get old, she decided after half an hour of listening to six-year-olds torturously sound out words, but it was still satisfying and even exciting in those magical moments when they managed the feat of putting all the letters together.

She felt some relief when the teacher clapped her hands and called, "Five minutes, everyone! Time to put your work away."

The little girl beside Jo whispered, "Thank you," closed her book and slid off the chair. "I wish you'd come back," she confided, before scooting back to her desk.

Jo felt a peculiar squeezing in her chest.

Emma plopped down on the first-grader-size chair, her knees poking up almost as high as her shoulders. "I don't remember it being that hard to read."

"Me, either," Jo admitted. "But it must have been."

Emma watched the kids bustle around gathering their backpacks and coats, setting their chairs on their desks and lining up at the door. "I kind of like doing that. Maybe I could come regularly."

"Ginny would love that."

Just then, her miniature housemate approached, her daypack slung over her shoulder and Pirate back in his cardboard carrier. "Teacher said I could leave before the bell, since I'm with you," she said importantly.

"Cool," Emma said. "I always liked having an excuse to beat the crowd."

Obviously pleased by the moment, Ginny held her head high as they passed the line of students, thanked the teacher and exited into the still empty hall. They had almost reached the outside door when the bell rang and hordes stampeded toward them.

"Wow. Let's get out of here," Jo said, shoving the door open.

They made it outside in the nick of time. Within minutes, the playground and parking lot were a scene of chaos familiar from her own school days. A long line of yellow school buses waited, as did parents on foot and in cars. Walkers dawdled on the playground, sixth-grade girls murmured in trios and tried to look fifteen while the boys wrestled and whooped and the teachers and playground aides wielded whistles to induce order.

Jo shook her head, smiling reluctantly. "I should make Aunt Julia come and listen to first-graders read."

The girls' heads turned. "What?"

"Never mind. Let's go home."

Pirate rode on Ginny's lap. Despite being the object of a group rescue, he seemed bent on becoming her cat. Tiny and puzzled by the irritating collar, he must have felt safest in her quiet presence.

Jo hadn't been home long when Ryan called. "Hey," he said. "Long time no see."

She'd wondered why he hadn't called or stopped by the evening before. It had irked her even to be aware of his absence. Couldn't she get by for a couple of days without seeing him? Aunt Julia would be ashamed of her!

"Have you been busy?" she asked.

"Me? I came by Wednesday night. You weren't home." It wasn't quite a question, as if he knew he didn't have the right to ask this one.

She wouldn't have minded if he had asked, Jo realized.

"I had dinner with my aunt Julia. She

stopped over at SeaTac on her way to Fairbanks. We haven't seen each other in months."

"Ah." He was quiet for a moment. "I got stuck having dinner with some clients last night."

Relieved for reasons she preferred not to examine, Jo teased, "It was that bad? What did they serve, liver and onions?"

A smile in his voice, he protested, "Hey, I like liver and onions!"

"No!" She wrinkled her nose. "Really?"

"Afraid so."

Jo sat sideways in an easy chair and hung her legs over the arm. "I always knew there was something strange about you."

"I'll bet you haven't tried 'em. Why don't I make them for dinner tonight…"

"You do that," she said. "Just be sure to air out your house before you invite anyone over."

He laughed. "Okay. I can take a hint. How does Thai sound to you?"

They agreed he'd pick her up at six, and they would consider a movie later. Tonight was Helen's turn to cook, and Jo wandered down to the kitchen.

"Hi," she said. "I wanted to let you know I won't be here for dinner."

Helen turned from the sink. "Ryan?"

"Mm."

"Thank you for doing that for Ginny today." Carrying a can of cola, Helen joined Jo at the table. Popping the top, she said, "I need a caffeine boost before I put dinner on. Thankfully today's Friday."

"You look tired." Jo studied her. "Are you *sure* you shouldn't be taking sleeping pills?"

"Then I'd really be dragging. No. What if Ginny needed me during the night? Or I got addicted to them?" She shook her head firmly. "I just have to…wait it out. Normal sleep will come eventually." Under her breath, she added, "I hope."

Jo got herself a can of pop. "I had fun taking Pirate today. I really didn't mind."

"Moving here was the best decision I've made yet on my own," Helen said unexpectedly. "You and Kathleen and Emma have been lifesavers."

Jo felt a pang of guilt for her unhappiness when she'd discovered she would be living with a six-year-old. Thoughts didn't count, she told herself, only actions, and she'd been nice to Ginny. Hadn't she?

"I had qualms about moving in with a bunch of strangers," she admitted, "but I'm glad I did, too. It makes me realize how lonely living by myself was."

Helen nodded eagerly. "That's it exactly! Friends call and ask how you're doing or want to have lunch once in a while, but they aren't *there* when you're running late in the morning and can't find something, or are too tired to cook dinner, or whatever. Emma has been so good to Ginny, and now you, too."

More guilt warred with Jo's pleasure. "It wasn't that big a deal, just a couple of hours."

"But I couldn't do it." Helen's face twisted. "I don't see how I'm ever going to be able to do things like that. And Ginny needs me to." She stood up quickly and turned her back. Voice muffled, she said, "I should start dinner."

"Helen…"

Facing the refrigerator and not turning around, Helen shook her head hard. "I know I'm not the only single parent. Kids are adaptable, and we'll be fine. I just wanted you to know that I'm grateful."

"Any time." Jo bit her lip. "Can I help now? Ryan isn't picking me up until six."

Wiping her cheeks, Helen turned at last. Her eyes were still damp, but her expression defied Jo to comment. "Really? Would you mind starting the hamburger frying while I run up and change? I'm making stroganoff."

"No problem."

She'd cut up and added the onions and garlic before Helen came back in jeans and a sweatshirt, her face scrubbed clean and her auburn hair pulled back in that severe—and unflattering—ponytail.

"Thank you!" she said, reaching for the spatula. "I should take your next turn cooking…."

"Don't be silly." Jo caught sight of the clock. "I'd better go change."

"Yes." Helen's grin made her look about sixteen. "You had."

"That bad?"

Upstairs, Jo discovered it *was* that bad. Her jeans had acquired a mysterious gray spot on the rump that she decided, on examination, might be rubber cement. Possibly a permanent fixture. She'd spattered hamburger grease on her T-shirt, her hair stuck out every which way and her mascara had run. Making a face at her image in the mirror, she decided she should be grateful Ryan hadn't been loitering here this afternoon.

They ate at a small Thai place on University Avenue, where Ryan asked about her family. "This Aunt Julia. Are you close?"

Jo found herself talking more openly about her childhood than she ever remembered doing with anyone but Boyce.

Propping her elbows on the table, she said, "I was seven when Mom died. I wish I remembered her better than I do. I should. I was old enough. It's weird. Even Boyce, who's three years younger than I am, will pop up with things sometimes that I just don't remember."

Ryan listened, his eyes intent. "Maybe forgetting was your way of dealing with the trauma of losing her."

"Maybe. But Aunt Julia—who's Mom's sister—makes it sound as if my mother regretted marrying and having children. So maybe there's more that I'm blocking out."

"Regretted?" Ryan frowned. "I don't know anything about your father, so maybe their marriage stank. But I can't imagine how she could regret having you."

Jo gave him a brief, wistful smile. "Thank you. But you see, she was a singer. A hybrid between folk and country, according to Aunt Julia. Sort of like Mary Chapin Carpenter. Really talented. Then she fell in love—" Jo made a face "—had kids and quit. I actually don't remember her singing at all, even around the house."

But then, she thought for the first time, she'd blocked out a great deal. Maybe this was one of the things her childhood self had chosen to forget for reasons she couldn't conceive.

"This Aunt Julia." Ryan was still frowning. "Do you believe her? Are you sure she doesn't *want* to think her sister was unhappy?"

Because he had so exactly echoed her own disloyal reflection, Jo had to scowl back at him. "Why would she lie to me? She *loves* me!"

"Maybe she disapproved of your dad. Maybe she was jealous." He shrugged. "She might not be lying. She might just have skewed the way she remembers things."

"No!" The idea upset Jo, making her tone pugnacious. "That's ridiculous! Aunt Julia says Mom loved us. She just regretted sacrificing her career. Who wouldn't?"

He stared her down. "A woman who'd made the choice knowingly."

"People are famous for making foolish choices when they first fall in love," she said defiantly. "Thus the American divorce rate."

"What's your dad say about all this?"

Jo looked away. "He doesn't say. We're not close."

"You've never asked him?"

"No." Jo toyed with her food, still unable to meet those penetrating gray eyes. "I guess I didn't want to hear the answer. Assuming he would have told me." She jerked her shoulders. "Assuming he even *knows* whether my mother was happy or miserable. I think he was the kind of husband who came home from work, expected dinner to be on the table, then planted himself in front of the TV. Your All-American husband."

"I could resent that," Ryan said mildly.

"You could," Jo admitted.

He chose not to make an issue out of it. "What kind of father was he?"

"Joyless, stern." Her moue was designed to hide the pain that still stabbed, however dully. "He put food on the table, came to parent-teacher meetings, gave us warnings if we made too much noise. Sometimes he'd be watching TV or reading the paper, and when one of us interrupted he'd look up with this irritated, disconnected expression, as if he didn't know who we were." Jo moved her shoulders to indicate indifference that she couldn't quite feel. "He didn't enjoy having children."

The compassion in Ryan's eyes was a balm. "Do you still see him?"

"Oh, I'm a dutiful daughter." She gave a sharp laugh. "I send birthday and Christmas cards, call every so often. I haven't actually seen him in three or four years." Three years, three months and…oh, ten days, give or take a few. She'd felt compelled to drive by the house, saw his car in front and stopped on a little-understood impulse. He'd come to the door, looking as if he barely recognized her. After he'd apparently reminded himself that she was someone he should know, he'd been…pleasant. The familiar hurt and resentment had kept her from going back again, although she knew Boyce, less determined to hold grudges, had seen their father at least once a year.

"You know," she said, relieved to have an excuse and wishing now that she hadn't started talking about her family, "we'd better get going or we'll miss the movie."

Ryan glanced at his watch, then reached for his wallet. "You're right."

The French film was a romance. Jo was always conscious of Ryan, but not usually *self*-conscious. Sitting in the dark theater, upper arm bumping his, she was. Painfully so.

The movie had been her idea, although she hadn't realized quite what it was about. She'd thought it was a drama with the usual quirky French flair. Now Ryan must be thinking she'd suggested it as a hint.

The movie ended at last with Jo shell-shocked. Ryan kept a hand on her back as they made their way up the aisle and out through the lobby into the damp, cold night. His touch burned through her sweater.

"Well," he said, and she heard the amusement underlying his matter-of-factness, "that was interesting."

She gave a laugh that sounded false, even to her own ears. "I know how to pick 'em, don't I?"

His grin was wicked. "You sure do."

She punched his arm. "I thought the couple in front of us would never stop kissing."

Under the street lamp, she couldn't be sure, but it seemed to her that his eyes darkened when he said, "I was tempted to imitate them."

She had to clear her throat. "Were you really?"

A group of students almost enveloped them in their laughing circle.

Ryan's gaze didn't waver from her face. "Yeah." He took her hand. "Let's go to the car."

Unfortunately, they were parked five or six blocks away, a curse of city living. After a couple of blocks of silence, they reached his pickup truck, parked on a dark side street.

He faced her and said, "I want to kiss you."

"Oh."

Brilliant, she chided herself, feeling the flush of embarrassment in her cheeks. Way to flirt.

Cheeks now flaming hot, which thankfully he couldn't see, Jo said in a small voice, "I was beginning to think you didn't, um, want me as a girlfriend."

She felt him jerk.

"What?"

"If you'd like to be just friends…" she began.

His head bent so fast she didn't see it coming, his mouth capturing hers.

He lifted his head, and she said, "I guess that answers that question."

CHAPTER SEVEN

OVER THE NEXT COUPLE OF WEEKS, Jo was blissfully, absurdly happy. As much fun as tiling the bathroom had been, she'd turned down Ryan's offer of a job. Instead, she was working part-time in the university undergraduate library. When she wasn't there or in class, it seemed she was with Ryan. Evenings, he either hung out at the old Ravenna neighborhood house or she was at his. More often the latter. She was embarrassed at how often she'd switched her night for cooking or opted out of dinners Kathleen or Helen had made.

She had only one cloud on her horizon. Well, two, both connected to Thanksgiving.

The day after the awful French film, Ryan had mentioned casually, but with delight, that his kids would be with him for Thanksgiving. He and Jo were on their way to his place, groceries in the back. They intended to make a southwestern-style bean and rice wrap.

"They'll be here for the whole week." Behind the wheel of his pickup, he reached out for her hand and squeezed. "I expected to have them for Christmas, but not for Thanksgiving, too. Wendy's new husband apparently planned a romantic getaway for them."

Obviously, any romantic activities she and Ryan might have indulged in that week would be on hold.

"You've really missed them, haven't you?" she said diplomatically. What was one week?

"Yeah, I can't believe they're coming. I talked to them a couple of nights ago. It was almost like old times."

He fell silent, his expression suddenly brooding. His hand left hers and gripped the steering wheel.

Jo had an attack of guilt, because she never encouraged him to talk about his children. She knew why, of course; she was pretending they didn't exist, even though she knew how much he loved them.

"What do you mean?" she asked.

"Talking to them has gotten hard. I don't know what to say, what to ask about. I mean, I know Tyler plays soccer, but except for some videos I've never seen a game. I don't know how good he is, I don't know the boys on the team, who they play. So I say, 'How was the game?' and he says, 'Fine.' Maybe, if I'm lucky, he tells me he scored a goal."

"Didn't you say they moved just this past June?"

"Five months is a long time in their lives." Stopped at a red light, he grimaced. "Oh, it's not as bad as I'm making out. It just scares me, when things get stilted. I imagine the years going by with us having less and less to say to each other, and me calling less often. Maybe them coming to visit me only because it's court-ordered and their mom marches them onto the plane."

"Oh, Ryan." Seeing the unhappiness on his face, she had to swallow a lump in her throat. She reached out and laid a hand on his arm. "You're too good a father for that. I'll bet they can hardly wait to come."

He pulled into his driveway, set the emergency brake and turned off the engine before he looked at her. "How do you know I'm a good father?"

"Because I've seen you with Emma and Ginny," Jo said with conviction. "They adore you."

In a way, it bothered her to see how good he was with the girls. Sometimes she felt inadequate with them in comparison. Worse yet, it reminded her that at heart he was a family man. He'd have fun with her for a while, but he wouldn't be content with a girlfriend. One of these days, he'd want a wife again, and maybe even another child.

He shrugged. "They've both latched on to me in place of their fathers. Who else is available?"

"Well, you're gloomy tonight!" Jo said with exasperation. "Who would be better to have available?"

"In Emma's case, it would be Ian." For a moment, his expression was dangerous. "Doesn't he know how rejected she feels?"

"Do you think she *wants* to see him, after what he did to her?" Jo asked dubiously.

"Yes!" Ryan raised a brow. "Did you ever give up on your father?"

Her first reaction was fiery and instinctive. "Of course I did! Eventually," she added less strongly, before making a face. "I think I have. Okay. Point taken. Every kid really, really wants her parents to love her. Which—" she went on the attack "—makes me wonder why you'd expect your kids to be any different."

"My kids?"

"Yeah. Why do you think they're going

to lose interest in you? You're their father! They're going to be desperate to know that you still love them."

For an unnervingly long moment he stared at her, but she was far from certain he was really seeing her. "Yeah," he finally conceded. "Maybe."

"It's just going to be up to you to make sure they don't forget you," she said firmly. "Is there any reason you couldn't fly to…wherever they live for a visit? Think how cool it would be for them to spend a weekend with you at a hotel with a swimming pool. If you plan right, you can take Tyler to a soccer game or Melissa to…whatever she does."

Once again she was embarrassed. He had undoubtedly told her where his ex-wife had moved, and what his daughter loved to do. She just hadn't listened.

But he didn't seem to notice. "Yeah," he said again, his tone odd, wry. "You're right. I've been so busy sulking, I haven't been very creative about staying in touch. I could have flown out there this fall. We could email, too."

"Buy them a digital camera for Christmas, and that way they could send you pictures all the time. Silly ones of when they have friends over or are just goofing off. They'd think it was fun."

He gave her a crooked smile. "You know, you have the instincts of a mother."

She was shaking her head even before he finished. "I don't think so. Making suggestions is one thing. It doesn't mean I want to apply my own advice."

"No?" He didn't push the issue, for which she was grateful, but his amused, confident expression made her both wary and irritated. Surely he wasn't already getting ideas.

The conversation was dropped once they carried the groceries in and started work on dinner. But she couldn't forget it. She found herself in the next week watching when he was with Emma or Ginny, seeing even more clearly the gentleness and humor he employed with them, the easy way he teased without ever hurting feelings, the pleasure in his own laugh when they teased back. She had flattered herself that he was hanging around so often because of her, but she began to wonder. The two girls assuaged a loneliness she couldn't touch.

Seeing him with the two girls awakened other, unsettling emotions and memories. He made such a painful contrast with her father, she'd find anger welling in her chest, leaving her breathless. Why couldn't Dad have listened to her like that? Smiled at her with such affection and approval? *Ever?*

She'd stop at the public library and have a flashback: herself as an eager young girl, excited about a book she'd found, a discovery she'd made, racing to her father. "Daddy! Daddy!" He'd angrily shush her, even punish her for being too loud by not letting her check out the book. Or she'd remember dinnertimes, their father silent and withdrawn, the kids expected not to bother him. What a cold man! she marveled now. How had he won her mother's love, convinced her to give up music for him?

Perhaps it was fitting, in the midst of a week where she was brooding so much about family, that her brother chose to call. It was one of the rare nights when Ryan was busy. Conversation at the table had been sparse, with Helen so tired her eyes looked unfocused and Kathleen nursing a migraine. Ginny picked at her food and said nothing, while Emma, as usual, absented herself. Dinner was barely over when Emma answered the ringing telephone in the living room and came into the kitchen with it a moment later.

"For you," she told Jo.

"Hey!" Boyce said without preamble. "How's it feel to be a kid again?"

"A kid?" Jo left the others cleaning off the table. She'd cooked, so she was entitled, although she'd intended to offer to do it so that Helen and Kathleen could both go lie down.

"Back in school?" her brother nudged. "Do you feel middle-aged compared to the other students?"

"Sometimes, when I'm walking around the campus," Jo admitted. She curled up on one end of the sofa in the living room. "But not in the library school. Half or more of the students haven't come directly from their undergraduate years. Most have been working for at least a few years. I have a classmate who is fifty-five."

"Cool!" Boyce said cheerfully. "At least there's one guy for you to date."

"Brat," she said without malice. After a moment's peaceful pause, she continued, "Aunt Julia tells me you and Jennifer have parted ways."

"Yeah." He was quiet. "I really liked her, even if she was weird. You know?"

The piercings and tattoos, Jo presumed. "Uh-huh," she said meaninglessly.

"Thing is, I liked her too much. I made her nervous."

Jo knew something about that. "You were thinking 'til death do us part, and she just wanted to party."

"Pretty much," Boyce admitted.

"I'm sorry," Jo said, and meant it.

"Yeah, well, I'll get over her." He sounded, suddenly, very young. Her little brother. "Thing is, I was wondering if you could come down for Thanksgiving."

She blinked. They didn't do these family occasions, having no center, no *home*. They'd gone to Aunt Julia's a few times, when she wasn't escaping winter in the Bahamas, but most often holidays didn't mean family to either Dubray.

"Do you have room to put me up?" she asked cautiously.

"Now that Jennifer isn't here, sure. Um, did you already have plans?"

"No-o," she said. Actually, this might be a good thing. She could meet Ryan's children, make nice with them, then escape. He'd have a few days with just them, feeling no obligation to include her. "No," she repeated more firmly, "I was just going to hang around with my roommates. And, to tell the truth, I don't know what *they* have planned. They may both be intending to get together with family."

Boyce cleared his throat. "Uh, there's just one thing."

At his tone, her eyes narrowed. "What?"

"I invited Dad."

She sat up. "You did *what?*"

"You know I see him more often than you do." There was defensiveness in Boyce tone.

"Yeah." She snorted. "Although why you bother…"

"I don't resent him as much as you do."

"So, is he staying with you, too?" Their father still lived in Pasadena, near L.A., where Boyce and Jo had grown up.

"Nah," her brother said. "You know what my place is like."

Slobby. A typical bachelor pad. Jennifer hadn't possessed any housewifely skills or interests, which should have been a clue to Boyce.

Jo stared darkly at the wallpaper, yellowed and peeling at the seam. "I'd just have to see him at Thanksgiving dinner."

"Pretty much."

Why did she feel as if she was being set up? "You're not doing this because you think he and I will magically fall into each other's arms and beg forgiveness, are you?"

Her brother hooted, answer enough.

"Okay," she conceded. "You're not stupid. I knew that."

"You don't have to come." He was silent for a moment. "I just, uh, I guess I was feeling lonely. Sometimes even a tense family get-together seems better than eating turkey by yourself, or as a guest at someone else's family functions."

She'd done both often enough to know what he meant. She thought it might have been different this year, even if Kathleen or Helen turned out to have other relatives who they invited to Thanksgiving dinner. Maybe, in a weird way, the three of them along with Ginny and Emma were starting to *feel* like family. Still...

"Okay," she said. "I'll come."

"You will?" His voice lightened, as if she'd made his day. "Great!"

They discussed airline fares and dates. She hung up, dropped the phone on the end table and then wrapped her arms around her knees. She was going to see her father.

Would she finally be indifferent to him?

Jo let out a huff that was almost a laugh.

Who was she kidding? The minute he walked in the door, she'd revert to a hurt, confused, angry teenager again. And people said time travel wasn't possible.

The upside was, she wouldn't have to fake having terrific fun with Ryan's children.

She could put that off until Christmas, unless she was so lucky as to receive an invitation she couldn't turn down for that holiday, too. Maybe Aunt Julia would long for company on a trek to the Yucatan or for a lazy two weeks in Kauai. Or maybe Jo would lie to Ryan and go to Kauai all by herself.

He was disappointed but philosophical when she told him the next day that she'd be flying to San Francisco for Thanksgiving.

"We'll miss you, but, hey, the kids'll be back for two weeks at Christmas. You can get to know them then."

Her life's ambition. Hadn't he listened to her? she wondered on a spurt of anger. Did he not believe any woman could want to be childless?

She was immediately ashamed of herself. More likely, he loved Melissa and Tyler so much, he couldn't imagine how anyone could feel any different. Well, she thought, brightening, they'd probably hate her cordially.

What self-respecting kids *liked* the woman Dad was dating and might even *marry,* thus making her the wicked stepmother?

No, this relationship would be mutual, if not exactly what Ryan had in mind. She and the kids would be polite and find excuses to avoid being in each other's company. Then they'd be gone. He hadn't said anything about spring break, had he? And what were the odds she'd still be seeing him next summer?

No, she wouldn't worry, not about his children. They lived with their mother. As long as Jo was part of his life, they would be no more than visitors. An occasional inconvenience, from her point of view.

And her father... It might be interesting to see him. To find out whether she'd told Ryan the truth when she claimed to no longer care. Think how liberating it would be to discover she didn't!

Maybe she should use this unexpected family gathering to ask some of those questions she'd always been too cowardly to put to him. She was a big girl now. If he snubbed her, so be it. It wouldn't be the first time. If he was willing to talk about her mother and she didn't like what he had to say, well, sometimes any answers were better than none. It wasn't as if she'd ever kidded herself that her mother, at least, had loved her.

Hoped, maybe. Dreamed. But never really believed.

Jo found now that she was hungry to know more about her mother and the choices she'd made. Ryan was right—Aunt Julia had a bias. What if Jo were to find out now that her mother had never, for a single instant, regretted the sacrifices she'd made to have children?

Would it change her life?

Jo shook her head impatiently and scrambled up from the couch. Ridiculous. She was twenty-nine years old, her character complete.

So why, now of all times, did she feel such a childish longing to know her mother better? Why did she regret having so few memories to which to cling?

Why was she suddenly reexamining her image of Aunt Julia, noticing now that her aunt was not just glamorous, but also lonely?

On her way to the kitchen to relieve Kathleen and Helen of their dish-washing duty, Jo refused to answer her own questions. Wasn't that her prerogative?

She was suffering from curiosity, that was all. A need to understand her roots.

She was certainly *not* imagining herself in love.

CHAPTER EIGHT

RYAN AND HIS CHILDREN CAME noisily into the house the Saturday before Thanksgiving, Ryan calling, "Hey! Where is everyone?" and Tyler and Melissa apparently arguing about what meal they'd eaten on the plane. Kathleen and Emma rushed to meet them, Jo following but hanging back. Only Helen and Ginny were missing, Helen having taken Ginny shopping for new shoes, since her toes were crammed into her existing ones.

"Aunt Kathleen!" The slight boy who looked younger than his eight years had a great smile. With wavy brown hair, brown eyes and a thin face, he must take after his mother. After enduring his aunt's embrace, he studied his cousin with a child's frankness. "Gol, you're even skinnier than I am."

"Skinny?" Emma made a horrid face looking down at herself. "What are you talking about? I'm fat!"

"Fat?" Ryan's son stared incredulously. "Dad! Emma's not…"

Ryan laid a gentle hand on his son's shoulder, silencing him.

Melissa, meantime, was accepting her aunt's embrace, saying hi shyly to Emma, and eyeing Jo with cool curiosity.

Ryan gave Jo a private smile over the family hubbub. Jo returned it with a composure she didn't feel. What she wanted to do was flee.

She was actually scared to meet his children.

The realization embarrassed her. So what if they didn't like her? So what if they did?

They were an occasional inconvenience, she reminded herself, as if it were a mantra. That was all. For Ryan's sake, it would be nice if she could get along with them well enough to enjoy an outing with them now and again. If she could do preschool story times in her library with enough élan to delight three-year-olds, she could manage this modest goal.

Maybe. As Ryan drew his children forward and Kathleen and Emma parted to allow them to face Jo, Melissa's eyes narrowed into a stare that suggested *she* wasn't going to be charmed.

"Jo, my children," Ryan said simply, his

voice resonant with pride. "Melissa, Tyler, my friend Jo."

"That's a boy's name," Melissa said in a deliberately rude voice.

Ryan looked at his daughter and opened his mouth as if to speak, but Jo silenced him with a shake of the head.

Smiling ruefully, she said, "I know. I wanted it that way. I always hated being girly. I sure wasn't going through life as Josephine, I can tell you that."

"You were, like, a tomboy?" Tyler asked. His expression was open and curious. Either he wasn't old enough to understand the implications of his father's friendship with a single woman, or he didn't mind. Not the way his sister clearly did.

"Yep. I still am," Jo admitted. "I hardly own any dresses."

"*I* like dresses." The pretty eleven-year-old had taken after her father in coloring. Her blond hair, partially gathered at the crown with a pink scrunchy, fell to the middle of her back. Her jeans were boot-cut like a teenager's, and her shirt, with glittery script that declared she was a princess, was the kind of baby T fifteen-year-olds wore. She even,

Jo decided after close inspection, wore some sparkly eye shadow.

Jo had an aversion to the idea of children dressing to appear sexy. This Britney Spears look mildly shocked her. But Mom must have okayed it. They'd come straight from the airport, hadn't they?

"I'll bet you look great in dresses," she said neutrally. "Me, I twist my ankle every time I put on high heels."

Melissa rolled her eyes as if to say, *Of course you do.* Actually, she was doing the teenager thing better than Emma, for all of Emma's problems.

"Listen," Ryan said, "we have to get going. I wanted to stop and say hi, but 'Lissa and Tyler want to unpack. You're not leaving until Wednesday, right? Can we do something tomorrow? All of us?"

Jo had been expecting this. From the expression on his daughter's face, the suggestion was not welcome there.

"Why don't you spend the day with the kids?" she suggested gently. "We—Helen and Kathleen and I—were hoping you'd all come here for dinner tomorrow night."

Ryan's brows drew together. "Of course we

can, but we'd like it if you'd hang out with us. Wouldn't we, kids?"

Tyler shrugged. "Sure."

"Um…I guess," Melissa mumbled.

"Come on," Ryan coaxed. "It's your only free day to spend with us."

Feeling trapped, Jo managed a laugh. "You've convinced me!"

"Good." Either not recognizing the resentment emanating from his daughter or choosing to make a statement, Ryan kissed Jo lightly before saying, "Okay, let's hit the road, kids."

After they were gone, Jo looked at Kathleen. "I don't think your niece likes me."

Kathleen shook her head. "I don't think she does, either. And did you see her clothes? She's only eleven!"

"They were cute," Emma put in.

Jo wasn't alone in having forgotten she was there, as they both turned in concert. "For someone your age, maybe," Kathleen said.

Emma shrugged. "Kids like to look like teenagers. What's the deal?"

"It's a big deal," Kathleen said strongly. "Do you remember when I wouldn't let you buy a bathing suit with the legs cut up to your waist?"

"Yeah," Emma fired back, "and I looked so un-cool!"

Kathleen often tiptoed around her daughter. Not today. "You also looked like the girl you were."

Emma sneered. "It was *so* typical of you! *Your* standards are always higher than everyone else's, right? Like, all my friends' moms were wrong!"

For once, Kathleen didn't back down. "I was trying to protect the daughter I love. Is that wrong?"

A zillion complicated emotions stampeded across Emma's face. "I don't know!" she cried. "You're just always so...*good.*" She swung blindly away. "I've got to go do homework."

Kathleen's shoulders sagged as she watched her daughter race up the stairs. "The joys of motherhood," she said, making light of the ugliness she hoped no one else saw.

Jo went along. "This time, I think she's escaping not just you, but *two* women mired in the dark ages."

Kathleen sighed. "Do you have time for a cup of tea?"

"Sure."

"To leave the subject of my charming

daughter," Kathleen said as they started toward the kitchen, "Melissa will get over it. Unfortunately, she's taking after her awful mother." She stopped, so that Jo bumped into her. "I shouldn't have said that, should I? Especially given my own track record as a parent." She sounded stunned. "I'm a hypocrite."

"You're human," Jo said bracingly. "And I'm sure you're aware that Emma is a very nice girl. You can't have done that much wrong."

She hoped she wasn't lying.

Kathleen's laugh was bitter as she grabbed the tea kettle and ran water into it. "That's not what she'd tell you."

"Isn't it?"

Kathleen leaned against the stove. "You notice she never talks about her father?"

Jo chose her words with care. "I assumed that's because she isn't seeing him. Is she?"

"No. His choice." Kathleen looked as if she'd bitten into a lemon, so sour it stung. "But I think it's more than that. I think she blames me, not him."

Jo took mugs from the cupboard and unwrapped bags of Market Spice Tea, an orange-spice blend unique to Seattle for which she had developed a passion. "Maybe. Or maybe she feels safe enough with you to criticize you. She knows you won't reject her if she gets angry. I don't know him, or, um, the whole story, but it sounds as if she can't feel that confident about him."

Her roommate cocked her head, expression startled. "That had never occurred to me." Tears sprang into her eyes. "Jo, I'm so glad you saw my ad in the paper."

Uncomfortable, Jo said, "I'm not that…"

Kathleen gave her a brief hug. "Yes, you are! You've fit in like…like family."

Jo found her own eyes misty. She detested feeling sentimental!

"I'm flattered." She made her smile deliberately light. "Back to Melissa. Ryan told me you didn't like Wendy."

The tea kettle whistled and Kathleen poured the water over the tea bags. "'Awful' is an exaggeration. She's just whiny, clingy and so sweet I always wondered whether any of it was sincere."

Jo was suddenly ashamed of herself for asking about Ryan's ex-wife. He'd married her, after all, which must mean he'd loved her. She shouldn't have encouraged Kathleen, tempting though it had been. She should have let him tell her as much—or as little—as he wanted to.

"In this case," she said, taking the sugar bowl along with her own mug to the table, "I suspect Melissa's reaction is normal. What kid likes a woman Dad is dating?"

Following her, Kathleen made a face. "I dated once, a few months ago. Emma threw a fit."

"There you go. At least Melissa was polite."

Stirring a teaspoonful of sugar into her tea, Jo decided the moment was ideal to find out how Kathleen felt about her dating Ryan. She'd never said a word, never raised her eyebrows. But as his sister she *had* to have opinions, if not feelings, about Jo's suitability.

"Kathleen." Jo stirred her tea unnecessarily. "You've never said what you thought about me dating your brother."

Kathleen reached for the honey. A long golden strand curled around her spoon. "He's an adult. I don't figure it's my business."

"So you don't mind?" Jo pushed.

"Don't be silly! What did I just tell you?" She paused—something about the quality of the silence told Jo it *was* a pause and not a conclusion. "My only worry," she said finally, "is that it will be awkward here if you two break up."

Jo nodded. She'd thought of that, too. "I hope if that happens, the break will be amicable. I don't know why it wouldn't be."

"I hope so, too." Kathleen's eyes met hers at last, and the steel in her character showed. "Fair warning. If I have to choose between you, Ryan is the winner, no matter how friendly we've become. He's my brother."

Read: *You will be out of the house.* Jo hesitated, then nodded again. "I understand."

The conversation moved on, as if both knew they'd said what was important. Kathleen didn't offer more gossip about Wendy or the divorce, and Jo didn't ask. Wasn't even sure she wanted to know.

THE NEXT MORNING, Jo found herself being picked up to go she knew not where with her boyfriend and his two children she'd been pretending didn't exist in any way meaningful to her.

The day was cold and wet, apparently typical for autumn in Seattle. The snow level was probably no more than a thousand feet above, if that. Ski areas in the Cascade passes had opened this week and chains were required to cross the mountains to eastern Washington. She wore a turtleneck and a heavy sweater over jeans, and stuffed Thinsulate gloves in the pocket of her yellow rain slicker.

"Hi, everybody." She hopped into the truck, shook off raindrops and smiled impartially over her shoulder. "Too bad the weather isn't better. I've convinced your dad to take up in-line skating. We could have gone around Green Lake."

The paved path ran the three miles around the pretty lake in north Seattle. Joggers, bikers, women pushing strollers and dog-walkers crowded it whatever the time of day. Ryan ran the circle several days a week already. He'd seemed to enjoy the skating.

"Dad?" his son said in apparent amazement. "In-line skating?"

"Does Dad do *anything* you want him to?" his sister asked Jo, tone snotty.

Jo was oh, so tempted to say cheerfully, *Pretty much.* Her better nature prevailed.

"Are you kidding? You know him better than that."

"What?" He shot her an intimate, sidelong grin that was sure to irk his daughter. "Are you implying I'm stubborn?"

Jo batted her eyes. "Never!"

They laughed. From the backseat came nothing but silence.

"So." Jo shifted to look back at the kids. "Where are we going?"

"The Pike Place Market," Tyler said. "And maybe the aquarium."

"You know, I've never been to the Pike Place Market," Jo admitted. "People keep saying I should."

"It's just, like, shops," Tyler said, sounding disgruntled. He looked even smaller today, hunched inside an oversize hooded sweatshirt. "The aquarium is better."

"I like aquariums," Jo told him. "The one in San Francisco is great. That's where I'm from."

Melissa sniffed and stared out the window. "*We* live in Denver."

"We just moved to Denver," Tyler corrected her. "I hate it there." For a moment he seemed desperately unhappy. "I miss my friends."

Looking at his son in the rearview mirror, Ryan asked, "Aren't you getting together with Chad tomorrow? He was riding his bike the other day when I was going out. He was really excited about you coming home."

"Yeah!" Tyler straightened in his seat, his

voice gaining vibrancy. "We emailed. It'll be really cool to see him."

Jo noticed that Melissa didn't claim to have made all super-cool new friends. Perhaps she, too, was unhappy in Denver, so far from her father. Maybe that was why she didn't like Jo. She might still be imagining that somehow the new stepfather would vanish and Mom and Dad would get together again, making her world right.

Her mother's death had cheated Jo of such fantasies, but she understood them. She had longed so passionately for a way to go back, to before. Before her mother was gone, before she'd had nobody but her distant, irritated father.

They parked in a garage on the waterfront, below the Pike Place Market, which clung to the bluff above. A Seattle institution, the ramshackle structure had started as a modest farmer's market. The top level, open to Seattle streets, still was a farmer's market, Jo discovered. Ryan had suggested they start there and work their way down again, instead of the other way around, so they took a glass-enclosed elevator to Pike Street.

Despite the season, fresh fruit and vegetables filled open stalls, alternating with fish markets and bins of Dungeness clams and huge crabs laid in ice. Farther along, artisans sold their wares, spread out on felt-covered tables. Sterling silver earrings, dream-catchers and stained glass slowed Jo's pace.

"Do we have time to Christmas shop a little?" she asked, when Ryan dropped back to her side.

"Why not?" he said. "Melissa's coveting those hats. I might buy her one."

Jo was agonizing over the dream-catchers when Ryan and his kids joined her, Melissa wearing a new lavender felt cloche. "I want to get one for Emma for Christmas," Jo said. "Melissa, you know Emma. Which of these do you think?"

Obviously torn between being flattered and wanting to snub Jo, Melissa hesitated. Either flattery or her genuine liking for her cousin won.

"That one." She pointed. "Emma likes blue and green."

The leather plaited circlet was decorated with feathers and beads. Jo loved the idea of protecting Emma's dreams.

"It's a perfect present," Ryan said in a low voice, just for her, as she paid.

They wandered on, eventually to the warren

of shops on lower levels. The adults bought espresso and sipped as they browsed South American imports and antiques, a shop that specialized in incense and another that sold unusual musical instruments. Both the kids tried out flutes and drums, even Melissa was laughing and having fun. Her dad declined to pay for her to have her palm read, but her mood revived in a shop full of gifts with a dog theme. All carrying packages by then, they had lunch in a vegetarian restaurant where Tyler and Melissa ordered warily but then ate with hungry satisfaction.

Watching Ryan listen intently to something Tyler was saying, Jo felt a peculiar squeezing sensation in her chest. Nobody so handsome should be so *nice,* she thought. It wasn't fair.

The next moment, he laughed with open enjoyment, the creases in his cheeks deepening and the skin by his eyes crinkling. His gray eyes were suddenly warm.

The waitress paused, studying him with appreciation until she caught Jo's eye and flushed, moving on. But how could Jo blame her? The wretched man was beautiful! Today his hair was tousled, his shoulders broad in a bulky sweater, his hips and thighs lean in worn jeans. Fathers shopping with school-age kids weren't supposed to turn women's heads, never mind shake the determination of a career woman who intended never to be caught in the marriage trap.

And where had *that* come from? she wondered in dismay.

When Ryan paid the bill, Jo suggested they move on to the aquarium. "Fair's fair."

Tyler smiled.

Melissa sneered. "Fish are boring."

He bumped her with his shoulder. "*Shopping* is boring."

His sister whirled. "Don't hit me! And it isn't! You had fun!"

"I did not hit you!"

"You did! Dad!"

"Neither of you are hurt. Quit bickering." He frowned at them. "And she's right. You did have fun, Tyler. And you—" he transferred his gaze to his daughter "—will enjoy the aquarium. Trust me."

He made the mistake then of wrapping an arm around Jo. "Let's get going."

Eyes narrowed furiously, Melissa flushed and stomped ahead. Tyler gave his dad a dubious expression and followed.

"When I miss them," Ryan confided, the

words a low rumble in Jo's ear, "I forget about the quarreling."

Much as she adored the warm weight of his arm, Jo casually moved out from under it. "How could you? You have a sister."

"So I do." Furrows formed in his brow, but he said nothing about her withdrawal. "Did you fight with your brother?"

"Are you kidding? Like cats and dogs." Jo gave a shudder. "After seeing Pirate's eye, I hate that saying."

"Hey, guys!" he called. The kids had emerged ahead of them into the rainy out-doors and run ahead to the elevator. "I forgot to tell you about the kitten."

They clustered close until the elevator came, listening to the tale.

"*She* rescued him?" Melissa asked once, tone suggesting Jo couldn't possibly be so noble.

"Yep. All I did is drive," her dad assured her.

"Like a bat out of—" Jo swallowed the rest. "I held on to the armrest and prayed," she told the kids. "He was screeching around corners and roaring up to stoplights. It's a wonder we didn't end up with a police escort, like a guy driving his wife to the hospital when she's in labor."

Melissa laughed. Tyler instead had an avid expression. "Was his eye really gross?"

"Pretty gross," Jo admitted. She could still picture it all too easily.

Tyler lifted his face to his dad. "Can we see him when we take Jo home?"

"You bet. But his eye looks just about normal now. You missed the gross part."

"Gol." Tyler left the elevator. "I wish *I'd* been there."

Hanging back, Melissa looked at Jo. "Is he your cat, then?"

"No," she said, "I think he's going to be Ginny's. Have you met Ginny yet?" The kids shook their head. "Well, she's only six, but she's really quiet. Her dad died not that long ago, which is maybe why. But for Pirate, she smiles and even laughs, and she's endlessly patient when he wants to play or if he just wants to cuddle. So he's been sleeping with her, and he goes to her first."

"Oh." The walk light turned green, but Melissa went forward only when her father nudged her. "Don't you mind?"

Jo shook her head. "I didn't especially want

a cat. I think Ginny needs him, and he needs her."

"Oh," the eleven-year-old said again, thoughtfully.

Despite the wet wind blowing off the Puget Sound, they paused at a railing to watch a huge green-and-white ferry leave the dock with a blast of its horn and embark on a crossing of the Sound. Across the street, a trolley clanged by. The scent of seafood drifted from restaurants, and Christmas shoppers prowled the warehouse piers turned into malls of boutique.

The aquarium itself was out on a pier. They paid and entered, plunging into a maze of dim rooms lit by the jewel-like colors of aquariums filled with fish so colorful and weirdly shaped, they didn't look real.

Studying a perch-shaped fish striped in black and lemon-yellow, Jo mused, "Imagine snorkeling or diving with schools of these fish around you. Maybe bumping you or nibbling at your fingers."

"Have you ever done it?" Tyler asked eagerly.

Jo shook her head. "My aunt has. She told me about it. I've always wanted to go."

She felt Ryan watching her, but didn't turn

her head. She didn't want him to think she was suggesting an expensive vacation together. Anyway, someplace like Hawaii or the Bahamas sounded like a honeymoon.

Both kids rushed to the outdoor, covered pool that held the otters. Even Melissa's face lit with delight when a sleek brown body shot by, twisting so that big brown eyes could study her briefly before the otter dove underwater.

"Did you see his face?" she asked.

Like a child herself, Jo hung over the railing. "He's darling! Look at those whiskers!"

Ryan watched the other three in amusement as they stayed captivated by the two otters. Occasionally, they'd scramble out onto a rocky landing before sliding back into the cold water. Waddlers on land, when swimming they moved with lithe ease, sleek glistening brown bullets shooting through the water. But it was their faces, intelligent, funny, charming, that enraptured the humans.

Ryan pried them away at last, reminding them that Kathleen was making a nice dinner.

"I *am* hungry," Tyler said with an air of discovery.

"Me, too," his sister admitted.

"Me, three," Ryan murmured to Jo.

She laughed up at him. "You're always hungry."

His eyes glinted. "I just like taking you out to dinner."

Jo stuck an elbow in his ribs. "You're flirting with me, right in front of your kids!"

He nodded ahead. "They're not listening."

"Melissa has eyes in the back of her head. She does *not* like it when you put your arm around me. Haven't you noticed?"

Manlike, he looked surprised. "No. She doesn't? Why not?"

Jo made a sound of disgust and strode ahead, catching up with his kids in the gift shop.

The walk back to the pickup was mostly quiet, as if all had realized at the same time that they were tired. It felt wonderful once Ryan got the heat cranked up, sending warm air pouring over their legs. Jo hadn't realized how cold and damp she was.

"Gosh, are you guys wet, too?" she exclaimed. "You don't have anything to change into."

Ryan shrugged. "We'll be okay. Right, gang?"

Tyler bravely agreed. Melissa mumbled assent.

Jo ignored Ryan. "I have some fuzzy socks you can borrow. And maybe Emma's jeans would fit you, Melissa, if you rolled up the hems."

"How come she's so skinny?" Tyler asked. "You said you'd tell us, Dad."

For the remainder of the drive, Ryan talked about eating disorders and how hard it was for Emma to eat something she imagined might make her fat. "She's seeing a counselor, and she's getting weighed weekly to make sure she doesn't get any skinnier."

"What if she does?" Tyler asked in a hushed voice. "Will she die? Like Duster? Remember, Dad? He quit eating."

"He quit eating because he was really, really old and his kidneys were failing. Emma is different. People can die from anorexia nervosa," Ryan said evenly, "but we won't let that happen to Emma. If her weight falls at all, she'll be checked into the hospital. She knows that."

"Oh."

Right then Ryan pulled into a parking spot only half a block from the house. He turned off the engine, then laid a hand on Jo's seat and turned to look at his kids.

"We don't say anything to Emma. Her

eating is between her, her mother and her counselor. It'll just embarrass her if you comment. In other words…"

"We get it, Dad," Melissa said tartly.

"Tyler?"

The boy nodded. "I won't say anything. Before, I didn't know."

"I know you didn't, and that's okay," Ryan said reassuringly. "But Emma probably won't eat with us tonight, and I just didn't want you to make her uncomfortable about it."

Privately, Jo wondered if it might not be good for Emma to see her peculiar behaviors reflected in the mirror of a normal child's judgment. Everyone always tiptoed around Emma. She was never forced to see how abnormal her eating was.

But then, Jo thought, what did she know?

Inside, the kids left their wet shoes and socks by the door and followed Jo upstairs. When autumn arrived, she'd found the bare wooden floors in the old house so cold, she'd gone right out and invested in several pairs of fleece socks, cozy enough to wear to bed and heavy enough to wear as slippers. She loaned pairs to both kids. While she was changing into jeans, dry socks and loafers, they went off with Emma and Ginny to meet Pirate.

Dinner, which turned out to be spicy baked burritos accompanied by tortilla chips and salsa, smelled delicious.

"I helped with it," Emma announced, carrying a dish of salsa to the table. "Mom and I decided to try a new recipe."

Tyler opened his mouth, met his father's eyes and shut it.

Emma actually had set a place at the table for herself. She even ate a tiny mouthful of burrito, which earned her a glowing smile from her mother.

"It's good," the teenager pronounced, before pushing her plate away.

When Ryan rounded up the kids later to leave, he drew Jo aside.

"You're flying out Wednesday?"

"Right after my last class."

"Can you come to dinner tomorrow or Tuesday?"

"Tomorrow night is my night to cook, and I hate to keep cutting out on it." She hesitated. "Ryan, today was great, but I think the kids would rather be with you. If you keep having me join you, they're going to think…um…"

"That I'm trying to make you part of their lives as well as mine?" His eyes were enigmatic.

She nodded.

He ran his knuckles lightly over her cheek. "Would that be so bad?"

Curiously breathless, she tried to sound firm. "I'm not stepmother material."

"Aren't you?" Ryan murmured, before smiling crookedly. "I'm not so sure," he added, before turning away and saying his goodbyes to Kathleen, Emma and Helen. Hummingbird's shoulder he squeezed. Pirate, wrapped in her thin arms, purred contentedly amid the bustle.

Jo, deeply disturbed, was glad to see them go.

Washing dishes a few minutes later, she brooded.

He didn't believe she wasn't interested in marriage. Or he was so arrogant, he was sure her convictions would crumble in the face of his assault.

She should quit seeing him.

Jo went still, hands deep in soapy water, unconscious of Helen quietly drying the dishes beside her.

She didn't want to quit seeing Ryan.

She didn't even necessarily want to quit seeing his kids. They were okay. A little bratty, but smart and...well, fun. She wouldn't mind them that much, not if they were just here for a couple weeks—or a couple months—at a time. She didn't have to live with them, after all. Like now. She could say, *No,* and avoid them for two days when she got tired of them.

Marriage, being a stepmother... That was another story. Definitely not for her.

She just had to convince Ryan, before he became so insistent she *had* to quit seeing him.

An eventuality, she realized with dismay, that would make her very, very unhappy.

CHAPTER NINE

JO STOOD BACK and contemplated her brother's kitchen. Kathleen would have a heart attack if she saw it. Half-unpacked shopping bags mingled with dirty dishes, damp crumpled dish towels, a vase filled with flowers that had long dried up and a towering stack of untouched catalogs and credit card come-ons that Boyce hadn't bothered to sort. The kitchen wasn't precisely dirty—the unwashed dishes were all from today, from their looks—but it was definitely cluttered.

What's more, nothing was where it seemed to Jo it should be. Pans were in a cupboard up high by the refrigerator; canned goods down low beside the oven. Cereal—well, that was in the cupboard with the bowls, which Jo supposed made sense of a sort.

"Where's the sugar?" she called, pouring hot water over a tea bag into the mug she had located with some effort.

"Uh…" Still pulling a sweatshirt over his head, her brother appeared in the kitchen.

He'd picked her up at the airport straight from work, dressed in a well-cut gray suit. "I don't have a sugar bowl. You'll have to get it out of the canister."

"Which is…where?"

"It's on the counter." He strode over and shoved grocery sacks aside. "Right here."

"Oh. Well." Jo dipped her spoon into the canister before shoving it back. "I don't know how I could have missed it."

Boyce stepped back and eyed the counter-top ruefully. "Yeah, it's kind of a mess, isn't it?"

"It reminds me of your bedroom, when we were kids."

He groaned. "Remember the wars?"

"How could I forget," she said with a shudder.

Their father had intermittently decided that Boyce's room should be clean. Unfortunately, Boyce had genuinely seemed not to know how to tidy his possessions. He'd end up shoving everything under the bed and into the closet, which worked until Dad caught on. Sometimes, when she had still thought she could please their father, she had helped Boyce straighten his room to avoid the fights.

Shaking off the memory, she said practically, "We'll have to clean up to cook Thanks-giving dinner."

"Yeah." Her too-handsome brother rubbed his hands on his denim-clad thighs. "Hey, Jo?"

She knew that tone of voice. He wanted something. He intended to wheedle her into giving it.

Eyes narrowed, she faced him. "What?"

"See, here's the thing." His smile was sheepish but charming. "I don't know how to cook Thanksgiving dinner. I bought a turkey, but, uh, do I just stick it in the oven the way it is? I mean, I guess I take the plastic off first, but there's supposed to be stuffing inside it, isn't there? Except…I looked! There isn't any inside."

Hiding amusement, Jo said sternly, "Are you telling me that you expect me to cook the Thanksgiving dinner that you invited me to?"

"You don't have to cook. I mean, if you can just tell me what to do, I'll manage. Or maybe there's a Cooking Thanksgiving Dinner For Dummies book. Yeah, that's what I'll…" He stopped, eyeing her suspiciously. "You're laughing at me, aren't you? Jo! You made me feel guilty!"

She laughed aloud at the ring of accusation in his voice. "You should feel guilty."

"Yeah." He screwed up his face in apology. "I should. But…you will help?"

She crossed the kitchen and kissed his cheek. "You know I will. Just let me drink my tea and then we'll make a grocery list. If we buy everything we need tonight and get the kitchen clean, we'll be set for morning."

His face brightened. "Cool! Hey. How'd you learn to cook a turkey?"

"In college, a roommate and I decided to try one Thanksgiving. Neither of us had anyplace to go. Anyplace we wanted to go," she amended. "I made this elaborate stuffing. Cooked the giblets—that's the neck and organs that are filling the cavity inside the turkey, by the way. Chopped 'em up in this stuffing and discovered, after hours of labor, that I hate giblets." She made a face, remembering. "But the turkey was good. I've had friends over for a couple of Thanksgiving feasts since."

"You're amazing." He sounded like he meant it. "Of course, you're my sister, so you have to be, right?"

Jo laughed again. She forgot how much she enjoyed Boyce's company. Twenty-four now, he had added a man's muscles in the past couple of years, filling out his tall, rangy body. With his dark, straight hair long enough to pull into a stubby ponytail—which Dad would hate, she thought with relish—and eyes the color of whiskey, Boyce must have women flocking around. But to her, he didn't seem arrogant. He was his same old self: smart but bumbling, funny and humble, ready to laugh at himself.

She could have done a lot worse in the family department, Jo surprised herself by realizing. Plenty of people didn't have a brother and an aunt as special as hers. As for Dad, well, maybe she really could feel indifference toward him this time.

Her tea downed, she and Boyce talked about friends, school and work while they cleaned the kitchen, working together with the comfortable familiarity of family. He sorted the mail, recycling most, while she washed dishes. The groceries got put away, the dish towels into the wash and the burner pans scrubbed. She sent him to the store with a new list while she mopped his kitchen floor. On the way out the door, he was still protesting.

"Why am I getting the good part of this deal?"

"Because you don't know how to clean!" she called after him.

"Hey!" he said indignantly.

"Go!"

"All right, all right!" The front door slammed.

Jo set the alarm so that she could put the turkey in the next morning. She dragged her sleepy, reluctant brother out of bed so he could watch if not contribute.

"Gross!" he proclaimed, when she wormed the giblets out of the still icy cavity under warm running water. "People actually eat those?"

"I truly do not know why," she said. "Friends of mine cook them for their cats. Speaking of which…" While he chopped onions, she told him about Pirate's rescue. "He is such a kick, now that he has the Elizabethan collar off. Even Kathleen enjoys him, except when he decides to scale the living room drapes. Or her bare leg beneath her bathrobe when she's eating breakfast."

Tears in his eyes from the onions, Boyce laughed. "Yeah, well, I can see how the drawing of blood might dim her enthusiasm."

"You should get a cat," Jo suggested.

He raised a brow, an effect killed by red-rimmed eyes and a veil of uncombed hair. "To fill the void left by Jennifer?"

"Don't be sarcastic."

"Wouldn't dream of it."

Jo scraped the celery she had just chopped into the biggest bowl she'd been able to find in her brother's kitchen. "To keep you company. To make you smile. To warm your toes at night."

"Gee." He leveled a look at her. "That sounds like—I repeat—you think a cat would take Jennifer's place."

"You're still sulking, I see." Jo took the cutting board from him and added the onions to the celery. Ripping open a package of dried, herbed bread chunks, she dumped it into the bowl.

"You mean, I'm still nursing a broken heart, don't you?"

"Are you?" she asked, spooning margarine into a saucepan to melt over a warm burner. "Brokenhearted, that is?"

He scowled. "No. Yeah, maybe. I liked her."

Jo cracked an egg into a smaller bowl. "But did you love her?"

Frowning, he shrugged. "I don't know. I wasn't ready to start a family or anything like that, and some things she did irritated me, but…sometimes she'd have a moment where she'd smile so sweetly, I'd feel something, oh, just kind of twist inside." For a moment, pain carved lines in his face. "And I'd think, I want her smiling like that at me for the rest of my life."

"I'm sorry," Jo said softly.

"Thanks." He let out a deep breath and jerked his shoulders in resignation. "She didn't love me. She thought I was incredibly 'establishment' because I wouldn't pierce my eyebrow." He cleared his throat. "What seemed free-spirited when I met her was beginning to bug me, which I guess means we weren't meant for each other."

But what if they'd thought they were? Jo wondered. Just long enough for one to make the ultimate sacrifice of career or self?

"Do you think Mom and Dad loved each other?" she asked abruptly.

Boyce shoved his hair back and stared incredulously at her. "What brought that to mind?"

"Just…wondering. If Mom and Dad were meant for each other, or if they only thought they were and then found out they'd been wrong."

He swore. "How would I know? I hardly remember her. You're older!"

"I...don't remember her well, either." Jo busied herself mixing the stuffing. "You know that."

"You should. You were, like, seven when she died."

"I know," she said quietly.

"But you've forgotten."

Her eyes stinging with tears—from the onion, she told herself—Jo grabbed the slippery turkey and maneuvered it into the roasting pan. "Not everything. But I should remember more." She heard her own fierceness. "I think I just missed her so much, I didn't let myself remember."

"And Dad didn't like to talk about her."

"No." She saw herself, no more than eight or nine, quailing from her father's frightening anger because she'd asked...what? Something about her mother, that's all she remembered. He'd shouted. *She's gone! What difference does it make?*

How odd that she could remember what he'd said, but not her mother's face when she tucked her daughter into bed at night.

"Why did you invite him?" she asked her brother. She didn't look at him as she spooned stuffing into the turkey.

"He's our father. He could have been worse."

"Could he?" Her jaw muscles hurt.

"He picked me up from wrestling and track practice at the high school every day for four years, even though he had to rearrange stuff at work. He even came to some meets. Did you know that?"

Jo shook her head, wordlessly.

"Do you remember him driving you to that spelling bee, when you reached state?"

Her hands went still as she plunged into her memories. Nervous. She was nervous, sitting in the front seat of the car. The dictionary was open on her lap, but she was getting car sick from trying to read the small print. Her father… She saw his hand reach out to gently close the dictionary. "You know what you know," he said.

"I'd forgotten," she confessed to Boyce, her throat tight.

"He got stuck being mom and dad both, and he wasn't very good at it. I wished…" Boyce cleared his throat. "Sometimes I wished he'd pat me on the back and say, Good going. Something. But he did drive me. He was there. Which is more than Tony's dad was. Remember Tony? His dad walked out when he was four or five, and he said he'd take the kids weekends, but then he never showed, and I used to hear Tony's mom yelling on the phone trying to get child support. So, you know, our dad could have been worse. Lots worse."

Moved despite herself, Jo fought to shore up her anger. "That's why you invited him? Because he could have been worse?"

"I like to feel connected," her brother said simply. "Is that so bad?"

Her shoulders sagged as her anger drained uselessly away. "No. Of course not."

"You'll be nice?"

She gave him a crooked, painful smile. "Maybe."

"Ask him about Mom. Why she never sang."

"He won't answer. He never would."

Boyce's gaze held hers. "Try."

"All right. I will." Of course she would, she realized; why else had she come? She shouldn't have spent the money for the airline ticket, as tight as her budget was these days. She'd wanted to see Boyce, of course, but he wouldn't have been alone if she hadn't come. They might have ended up with a very odd Thanksgiving meal, given Boyce's cooking skills, but he wouldn't have been alone.

No, she had wanted, needed, to see her father. She was due, she thought wryly, for her every-other-year pilgrimage, to see if he had changed, or she had changed. If something was different.

This year, she had the strangest idea that something was.

IT BOTHERED Jo every time she saw her father to realize how much she and Boyce looked like him. A Frenchman, born to immigrant parents, he had passed on more than the name Dubray to his children. They shared his dark eyes and hair and lean physique. Boyce, who had gained height from his maternal genes, was taller than his father, who stood a couple of inches under six feet. Jo knew very well that her petite stature was inherited from him.

She hated to think any of her qualities but the external ones came from her father.

He had aged well, she had to concede, when he arrived. His temples had grayed but the rest of his hair was still dark. The lines on his face almost made him more handsome.

He must be…fifty-four, she decided, after a quick mental count. For the first time, it occurred to Jo to wonder whether he dated or considered remarrying.

She didn't remember him ever dating while she and Boyce lived at home. He went out sometimes without telling them where, and it might have been to see a woman. She had never once thought of him as a man, rather than as her father.

"Dad!" Boyce shook his hand. "Look who's here."

He hadn't told Dad she'd be there? She shot him a glance before going forward.

"Dad." She politely kissed his cheek, felt his hand press her back as if he had almost hugged her. "How are you?"

"Well." He stepped back. "And you?"

"Just fine." Already, she couldn't think of anything to say. "Um…come in. Would you like a coffee or tea?"

"Coffee. Thank you." He let Boyce take his coat and followed Jo to the living room, which her brother had spent the morning straightening. "Is it just the three of us?" he asked, as if the answer didn't matter.

"Yeah, Jennifer and I broke up."

Jo's father sat in the armchair. "And Jo? You don't have anybody important?"

No, Dad. You taught us so little about intimacy, neither of us is apparently capable of finding true love.

"Afraid not," she said carelessly, then had an odd moment of shame, as if she'd denied something—someone—she shouldn't. She tried to send a silent message: *I'm sorry, Ryan.* The moment she did, she frowned, trying to understand the shame. He wasn't that important. Was he? She'd never let anybody be that important.

Conversation remained stilted, Boyce talking more easily than either Jo or her father. A feeling of disbelief or perhaps disorientation kept sweeping over her. She'd look across the room at her father listening attentively to something Boyce said and think, *He's a stranger.*

Her more typical anger and resentment and disappointment seemed absent. There had to be some kind of connection before she could feel anything so turbulent.

Jo stood abruptly. "I'd better check the turkey."

An expression of faint relief crossed her father's face. "You did the cooking?"

"Hey!" Boyce exclaimed. "I think I'm insulted."

Their father cleared his throat. "The last time you had me, your friend, Jennifer, made something rather odd. Spicy, too. Indian, I believe. I didn't know what to expect today."

"Well, Boyce had no idea what to do with the turkey," Jo said frankly, "so I took over the cooking. Excuse me for a minute."

She managed to spend much of the next hour in the kitchen, putting potatoes on to boil, snapping green beans, mashing the potatoes, opening a can of cranberry sauce. Boyce intermittently appeared to help her, and she popped back into the living room a few times to look sociable.

Ask Dad about Mom, she ordered herself, watching him talk to Boyce about football. *Now. Interrupt. Just say, Dad, did Mom ever sing?*

"You a Seahawks fan yet?" her brother asked her.

"What?" She stared at him, before the sense of his question registered. "Oh. No. I've been to a couple of Mariner games, but not the Seahawks. Ryan—" She stopped.

Her brother raised his brows. "Aha! Ryan...?"

"A friend. The brother of one of my room-mates. He enjoys baseball and I've gone to games with him twice. He's never suggested football."

"A friend." Boyce made the innocuous word sound as clunky and unlikely as a chunk of concrete rolling across the berber carpet. "He's a friend."

"We're dating." She shot to her feet. "I'll bet the green beans are done."

"You can run but you can't hide," he called after her.

Cheeks blazing, Jo escaped to the kitchen. She fumed, why was she embarrassed? She dated. So what? She was an adult. And she wasn't ashamed of Ryan.

During dinner, she came to the conclusion that she was, once again, chickening out of asking her father about her mother. History was repeating itself. He'd gotten mad at her when she was eight years old because she wanted to talk about Mom, and she was still scared to ask.

Well, she had a right! But not during dinner, she amended, catching her brother's eye. He wanted to have his family here, all together. She could give him that much.

"Your aunt Julia," her father said unexpectedly, while dishing up a second helping of stuffing. "Do you hear from her?"

"Yes, she stopped overnight in Seattle last month. We had dinner," Jo said.

"She's well, then?" Finding a place to set the serving bowl back down, he seemed to be careful not to meet Jo's eyes.

"She looks wonderful. We should all age so well."

"Yeah, she's hot," Boyce agreed. "For her age."

"Careful." Their father gave his son a look. "That's my age you're talking about."

Was that a glint of humor in his eyes? Jo studied him surreptitiously. No. Surely not. He had no sense of humor.

Dinner was almost over. A pumpkin pie waited on the counter. Jo set down her fork, lifted her chin, and said, "Aunt Julia was telling me that Mom had a pretty successful singing career before you got married."

He glanced her way, gaze cool. "I believe she had some attention locally. She played coffeehouses. That kind of thing." His tone was dismissive. "Recording was out of the question."

"Why?" She sounded, and felt, pugnacious. If he could deny that her mother had had any real talent, did that free him from guilt? "If she was that popular, who's to say she didn't have what it takes?"

"She had nodes on her vocal cords," he said dispassionately. "The doctor recommended that she stop singing."

Jo opened her mouth, then closed it. That was why her mother hadn't sung?

Not because she couldn't bear to, but because her voice had begun to scrape her throat?

"You never told me that."

"You never asked." He pushed away his plate with an air of finality. "That was very good, Jo."

"I...thank you." She looked down at her plate, saw that it was half-full, and used her fork to squish mashed potatoes into a smaller heap.

"Are you ready for pie?"

Unrelentingly civil, her father said, "I think I am. Pumpkin?" He swiveled to look toward the counter. "Ah. Good. I'd love some."

Frowning fiercely, Jo carried her plate to the sink. Her brother followed suit.

"Told you so," he murmured in her ear, before pouring coffee for all of them.

Jo dished up the pie and carried the dessert

plates—well, actually, the saucers that went with the coffee cups but had been pressed into service for pie—to the table.

She gave them to her brother and father and sat down with her own. Instead of reaching for her fork, she said loudly, "You never liked to talk about her."

He lifted his head. "What?"

"I didn't ask about Mom because you used to refuse to talk about her."

Outwardly she was…not calm, precisely, but composed, determined. Inside, she shook, as scared of him as she'd been when she was a small child.

His nostrils flared, but that was the only sign that she had disconcerted him even slightly. Instead he wore his usual mask. "I may have found it upsetting when she first died. I don't recall you asking about her at all."

I was afraid to.

Old resentment tumbled in her chest. How she had always hated that expression, the distant "Do I know you?" way he looked at her.

For the first time ever, she didn't back down. "Why didn't you talk about her? Why did I have to ask? You must have known we were curious about Mom."

He carefully set down his fork, as if finally noticing that she was serious.

"It…didn't occur to me." He cleared his throat. "I knew nothing about raising children. I never knew how to talk to you. What to say, or not say." He looked from one to the other of them, seeming to struggle for the right words. "I'm just not much good at things like that. Or with people at all. I never understood why your mother was interested in me." He stopped, brows drawing together as if he had surprised himself, or was annoyed with his frankness.

Jo felt an inner quake she chose to ignore in favor of her familiar anger. "Did you love her?" she challenged him.

His frown deepened as his irritation became directed at her. "What a ridiculous question. She was my wife."

Jo could hardly breathe, so tight did her chest feel. "That doesn't mean you loved her."

"I'm not sure it's any of your business," her father said quietly.

Jo fought an impulse to shoot to her feet. "She is my business. She was my mother, and I know almost nothing about her!"

"You were old enough to remember her."

"But I don't!" she shouted. "You wouldn't talk about her, and I forgot her!"

Somehow she was standing, stumbling over the chair, tears coursing hotly down her face. Anguish filled her even as a part of her felt ridiculous for the scene she was making. *Poor Boyce!* that part of her thought, seeing him gape. But the rest of her, the child who blamed her father for so much, remained fiercely focused on him.

He simply sat, very still, and said, "I didn't know."

"You yelled at me when I asked about her."

He closed his eyes. "Talking about her would have made us all sadder."

Jo swiped at her cheeks. "I tried to forget her to please you."

Bleakly she wondered why she was telling him this. What possible good did it do now?

He looked up at her, and for just a moment she saw grief in eyes that usually looked remote. "I didn't know."

That was it. He hadn't known how much his small daughter missed her mother, how desperately she had wanted to cling to her memory, how much she had needed him to help her.

"I tried to tell you," she whispered.

Years seemed to settle on his face, making him less handsome, more worn and human. "I wasn't a good father," he said with difficulty. "I'd have done better if I'd had your mother to...nudge me. As it was, I was angry at her for a long time. For leaving us."

Boyce spoke up for the first time. "She didn't choose to die."

"Of course not. But I was angry anyway. How could she do this to me?"

"Stick you with us?" Jo asked harshly.

This time when he looked at her his eyes appeared blind. So quietly she could barely hear him, he said, "Leave me."

Anger left her like helium from a punctured balloon. She sagged into her chair. All this time, and she had never understood that he was only grieving, too.

"You did love her," she murmured.

Face ravaged, he said, "Of course I did. Why would you doubt that?"

"Because you never said. Because you seemed to forget her so quickly."

"I am not a man who expresses emotion easily."

"Or willingly," Boyce muttered.

His mouth twisted. "It may even be that I don't feel what other people do. But in my own way, I did love your mother. I have… never considered replacing her."

They sat silent for a long moment. Her father was the first to speak. Pushing back from the table, he said, "Perhaps I should go now."

"No!" Boyce protested. "No. Please, Dad. Let's have pie and coffee. Don't go."

"No." Jo drew a ragged breath. "No, don't go, Dad."

He hesitated, then inclined his head. One by one, awkwardly, they all reached for forks or coffee cups.

"I am dating Ryan," Jo heard herself say. "My roommate's brother. He has children."

Her father raised his brows; her brother looked startled.

"They live with his ex, but they're with him for Thanksgiving."

"You're not thinking of marrying him, are you?" her brother asked.

"No, of course not!" she denied, too vehemently. "He hasn't even asked."

"Is he going to?" Boyce asked.

"I don't know." She felt herself frowning. "We're not that far along. No. He won't anyway. I told him I wasn't interested in marrying."

"You sound like Jennifer." Her brother looked at her with near dislike.

Stung by the comparison—what did she have in common with his tattooed, pierced, sneering ex-girlfriend?—Jo snapped, "You don't know anything about it."

Boyce snorted. "And they say it's men who are afraid of commitment."

Now their father watched them, head turning, as if he were compelled to observe a particularly bizarre match where opponents lobbed words instead of balls.

"I'm not afraid of anything! I just don't want to be trapped, like—" Stunned, she bit off the rest. Trapped like her mother, who had not sacrificed a glorious career? Like Aunt Julia, who had never tried marriage herself, insisted all married women were?

Her brother's eyes narrowed. "Like who?"

"My career is important to me."

"Uh-huh. And that has…what to do with anything?"

"It's different for women." She glared at him. "They still do most of the cooking and housework and childcare. They're the ones who sacrifice in a marriage."

Infuriatingly, he laughed. "You've been listening to Aunt Julia. I did most of the cooking, not Jennifer. She was awful at housework."

"Most men aren't like you."

"This Ryan wants a wife so he'll have a housekeeper?" Boyce shrugged. "Good decision, then. Marrying him would be stupid."

"Ryan doesn't…!" Jo let out an angry huff of breath. Her brother was being deliberately obtuse. Anyway, what difference did it make if her brother got it?

She turned in her seat to face her father. "Did Mom want children?"

For a moment, his face softened. "Yes. She was so excited when she was expecting you, and then Boyce."

Tears stung Jo's eyes. She blinked, trying to stop them stillborn. Inside, she welled with both intense grief and exultation. Mom had wanted her!

Her voice sounded scratchy when she asked, "Did you want kids, too?"

"Once I met your mother, I assumed we'd have them. It seemed…not my business." He frowned. "I mean that only in the sense that I thought women took care of children. I suppose, in a way, I had the attitude of another generation. I was the breadwinner, she was the homemaker. I was completely unprepared—"

He didn't have to finish. For her death, he would have said. To braid your hair for school, or do multiplication flash cards with you, or to nurse you through chicken pox.

None of them said more about her. They ate their pie, and Dad insisted on helping clean the kitchen. Working with the two men felt extraordinarily awkward to Jo. "Excuse me," she said too often, being careful not to bump either or intrude on their tasks. They did the same, she noticed, as if all of them were on their best behavior.

Yet it was nice, too. Jo couldn't remember the last time they'd all been in the same kitchen. Probably not since she'd roared out of the house when she was eighteen.

Today, the air was cleared. Even a new beginning made, although she couldn't imagine ever being close to her father. She had too many bitter memories. Would forever suffer from bafflement that he could have been so unaware of the needs of his children.

Still, something had started today. She was washing dishes, he was drying them right beside her while Boyce worked on the turkey carcass, and she felt no anger at all, no desire to escape.

When he finally did leave, she and Boyce walked him out to his car. Fog had rolled in, swirling down the steep hill from the bay, muffling their footsteps and voices.

"Thanks for coming," Boyce said.

Their father looked across the roof of his car at Jo. "I have things of your mother's," he said abruptly. "In a box. Some jewelry, some pictures. I'll send them...if you'd like them."

This time, she let the tears fall. "Yes." Her smile wavered. "I'd love them. Thank you."

Her father nodded, said, "Good night," and got into his car. Side by side, Jo and Boyce stood watching until it disappeared into the fog.

Then her brother laid a comforting arm over her shoulders and turned her toward the stairs up to his apartment. "You worked miracles, Josie," he said, using Aunt Julia's pet name for her.

She smiled, sniffled and said, "I did, didn't I?"

CHAPTER TEN

"I CALL THE FRONT SEAT!" Tyler called, racing ahead of his sister.

"Oh, yeah, *right!*" she snapped. "It's my turn and you know it."

Going down the walk behind his children, Ryan grimaced. He was getting sick of this particular battle, waged every time they headed for the pickup. He'd mercifully forgotten their power struggles, a gauzy curtain having settled over his memory.

Ahead, Melissa shouldered her little brother aside. He howled with rage and clung to the door handle.

Wearily, Ryan said, "Enough! Okay, who rode in the front yesterday?"

"You did!" his daughter exclaimed in triumph.

"You did!" Tyler argued. "When we went to see—" He stopped, eyes widening.

"We went to the movie yesterday *afternoon,*" Melissa reminded him with an air of superiority. "Last *night,* you rode in front when we went to Pagliacci's. So there."

Tyler sagged.

Ryan put Melissa's suitcase in the back, closed the tailgate and canopy door, and came forward to unlock. He laid a hand on Tyler's shoulder, but the boy didn't even look up.

All the way to the airport, Tyler slumped in back with his chin resting on his chest, while Melissa, once settled with a wriggle of satisfaction, fell into a brooding silence, her face turned away from Ryan.

Why did Wendy have to move? he thought viciously. Things had been bad enough before, when they'd traded the kids every few days. This felt like a form of death to him, even though he knew rationally that they'd be back in a month for the Christmas holidays. From their unhappy silence, he guessed they felt the same. They'd both been crabby since they got up that morning.

Worse, he kept wondering whether they'd missed their mother at all, or whether they were dreading going home. Tyler, more open than his sister, had said enough that Ryan knew he wasn't happy in Denver. Melissa hadn't talked as much. She'd never altogether relaxed with Ryan. When he asked how she and her mom were getting along, all she would say was a bright, "Fine!" that he wasn't sure he believed. Neither of them spoke about their mother the way he'd expected, the "mom said this, did this, made me do this" kind of thing.

He kept remembering Wendy's reluctance to have children at all. She'd wanted to wait, even though when he suggested they start a family they had been married five years. "I'll be fat!" she'd wail, or make a pretty moue and complain, "You know once we have a baby we'll never be able to go out again."

As if he cared. He was a family man. He'd always wanted children, and he didn't much like to party. Wendy had been good for him in that respect, forcing him to be more sociable than came naturally. But after five years, he'd been *ready*. He looked forward to wondering smiles and building blocks and bikes with training wheels.

Wendy had given in, and even seemed to enjoy the excitement of pregnancy. She'd spent what seemed a small fortune at the time on maternity clothes and on decorating the baby's bedroom. But she decided not to nurse, which disappointed him, and she wanted to put Melissa in a morning day care by the time she was six weeks old.

"You could drop her off on your way to work and I could get some sleep," she'd said, her smile coaxing. "Then I could pick her up and she and I could have a lovely day together, and I'd feel like a human being when you came home from work."

Actually, Melissa had napped in the afternoon, and Wendy had still been frazzled when he got home, eager for him to change their baby daughter's diaper or give her a bath or a bottle or tuck her in.

Ryan frowned out the windshield of his pickup as traffic slowed on the freeway north of Southcenter Shopping Center and the exit for the airport.

Of course Wendy had loved Melissa. But her love, he had sometimes thought, was like a child's for a doll. She'd coo and kiss and get down and play like another toddler, and then abruptly lose interest and announce in a brittle voice that, "I have to get out of here for a while or I'll go crazy!" She'd snatch up her keys. "I'm just going to the mall. *You* can babysit."

She'd loved Tyler in turn, but even less patiently. Ryan's feelings for her had eroded when she went out with girlfriends and was late picking up the kids at day care, screamed at Tyler because he wouldn't go down for a nap and pouted when Ryan balked at hiring babysitters every Friday and Saturday night.

She'd been right, he concluded finally. She wasn't ready to be a mother. Maybe she should have waited. Maybe she should never have had children. But when the divorce came, she wouldn't admit she was overwhelmed by them.

"I'm their mother!" she announced fiercely. "Of course they'll live with me. You work, you're never home." A more than slight exaggeration, but he let it slide. After all, she was staying in the house and he had rented an apartment not half a mile from his family. He could keep an eye on them. Run over if either of the kids called. They spent every weekend with him, so Wendy didn't have to worry about affording babysitters. He took Melissa to T-ball games and Tyler to soccer, biked around Green Lake with them, knew their friends.

He hadn't considered one thing. Wendy wasn't going out alone. She was dating. And with stunning speed, she announced she was remarrying.

Only months after her marriage came the bombshell, she, her new husband and the kids were moving.

Melissa's small voice jarred Ryan out of his reverie. "Are you okay, Dad?"

They were slowing again, this time to join the backup to grab a ticket for the airport parking.

"Yeah." He found a grin for her, if a sad one. "I'm just missing you guys already, even if you're not gone yet."

Her mouth pinched. "I wish we could stay longer."

"Yeah. Me, too. But you'll be back in less than a month. Twenty-eight days."

Her anxious gaze met his. "You don't think Mom will change her mind?"

Hiding his anger, Ryan smiled reassuringly. "Nope. She can't. We have a parenting plan that's court-approved. This Christmas is my turn."

"Oh." She visibly relaxed. "Okay." Silent while he began the spiral upward in the parking garage, the eleven-year-old said suddenly, "Sometimes I wish…" before stopping just as abruptly.

He shot her a glance. "You wish?"

She shook her head. "Nothing."

From the back seat, Tyler said loudly, "*I* wish we could live here."

"But then we wouldn't see Mom."

"But now we don't see Dad hardly ever."

Melissa had no rejoinder.

Ryan said heartily, "A month. You'll be back in a month. And then for the whole summer."

Neither said anything.

He hated putting them on the airplane. They were too young to be flying halfway across the country, shuttling between parents for the convenience of the two adults, with no reference to what they preferred or needed.

He watched the plane take off, diminishing into a late November sky. Then he hiked back to his truck, paid the outrageous parking fee and wished he knew what flight Jo was coming in on.

DING DONG.

Sunday night, eight o'clock, and somebody was ringing his doorbell?

Ryan put down his book and left his easy chair to go to the door.

Jo. Jo stood on his doorstep, bundled in a parka, looking small and uncertain. "I should have called, but…"

Exultation swelled in his chest, hurting like he guessed a heart attack might. Without a word, Ryan snatched her off the doorstep and into his arms.

It was a good minute before she emerged from his kiss, her cheeks pink. "Do I take it you missed me?" she asked, voice breathless.

"Yeah." Belatedly, he reached past her and closed the front door, shutting out the cold air. "You could say that."

"I missed you, too," Jo said simply. "When I got in, I went home, and I almost called, but then…I just thought I'd come."

"I've been waiting by the phone." Which, he realized, was exactly what he'd been doing. He couldn't remember a thing about the two chapters he'd read in the past hour; he'd been reading with only half his attention while he waited.

"Really?" Her dark eyes were shy.

"Really." He cupped her face in his hands, threading his fingers through her thick, silky hair. He loved her hair, the texture and the rich glow when light shone on it. His voice thickened. "You're beautiful."

"No," she protested. "You know I'm not."

He nipped her lower lip. "Don't argue," he

murmured against her mouth. "I'm the expert. You're beautiful."

Her laugh was joyous, her mouth soft when he kissed her again. Lifting his head at last, Ryan sucked in a shaky breath.

"I want to hear about your weekend. Here." He reached for the zipper of her parka. "Let me take your coat."

He laid an arm across her shoulders and steered her companionably toward the kitchen. "Coffee?"

"I'd love some."

He put it on to brew and leaned back against the counter, savoring the sight of her in a red turtleneck sweater and jeans. "Did you enjoy seeing your brother?"

Jo sat at the long kitchen table, one foot tucked under her. "Actually, I did." She had an oddly pensive expression. "My father came to Thanksgiving dinner."

Ryan raised his brows. "You didn't know your brother had invited him?"

"I knew. I'm not sure why I went, but… it actually turned out to be…nice. Oh." She made an impatient gesture. "That isn't right. But better than I would have expected. I said things I should have said years ago, and he opened up a little. As much as he's capable of, I suspect."

Watching her face and the flicker of expressions crossing it, Ryan made no move to reach for mugs. "What did you say?"

"I told him I was angry that he'd never talked about my mother. That I blamed him for how little I remember about her. How little I even *know*."

"You have your aunt."

Wryly, Jo said, "I'm realizing how much of what Aunt Julia tells me is filtered through her biases. Much as I hate to admit it…you were right." She hesitated. "For example, she always said Mom gave up a singing career to marry Dad and have children. That she could have been a star."

"And?" he nudged, when she fell silent.

"Dad says she had nodes on her vocal cords. That the doctor wanted her to quit singing."

"Couldn't they do surgery?"

"I don't know. Maybe not then. Haven't I read that Julie Andrews can't sing anymore after some kind of surgery like that?" She shook her head. "Maybe Mom just didn't care enough about making it. Maybe she *wanted* to be a wife and mother, and Aunt Julia just didn't believe she possibly could."

He knew this was important, knew it all figured in why Jo herself was so determined never to marry. Quietly, he asked, "Why is she so antimarriage?"

Jo shook her head. "I have no idea. No, that isn't quite true. I guess their parents— my grandparents—had a horrible marriage. My grandmother was a teacher until she got married, but she was expected to give it up afterward. I think maybe she was bored as a housewife, and she infected Aunt Julia. Or maybe Aunt Julia fell in love with someone who assumed she'd give up going to law school for him. She's never said." Jo paused, then smiled reminiscently. "She always told stories about these men she had dated. There was a senator and a Pulitzer-prize-winning journalist and judges and even a movie star." She named him. "Her life always sounded so glamorous. So much better than if she was married to one guy settling into stodginess." Jo looked at him in appeal, as if asking for agreement.

He nodded to show his understanding even though he didn't like knowing that *he* was "the stodgy guy" competing with Jo's vision of a lifestyle that would have her appearing in *People* magazine's "Star Tracks" on the arm of some celebrity or another.

"I always wanted to be like Aunt Julia," Jo concluded softly.

Wanted. Past tense. Trying to quell the hope that insisted on rising like flood waters, Ryan turned and opened the cupboard.

"And now?" he asked casually.

"Now?"

"Do you still want to be like her?"

She didn't answer. He stole a look over his shoulder to see her staring into space with the intense, frowning concentration of someone searching a website for one magical nugget of information.

At last she let out a giant sigh. "The last time I saw her—when she stopped overnight last month—I suddenly realized that she's lonely. She won't admit it. She may not even know she is!" Another gusty sigh followed the first. "But I could tell. All the charming, successful men her age have wives now. And children. Her judge…" Jo looked up. "She's been seeing him forever. I actually thought they might end up getting married. But instead he married someone else, and now he's pushing a baby carriage. Aunt Julia curls her lip, but I wonder…" Her voice trailed off.

"You wonder?" He'd been doing a lot of prodding tonight, but he wanted her to admit to a change of heart. He wanted her to say, *I've realized that I love you. That I want to marry you and have your babies and be a librarian in Seattle.*

Because he was in love with her.

Apparently, he was a stodgy guy to his core.

"I wonder if she hasn't realized that she's going to end up lonely." Jo sounded sad herself. "I wonder if she wasn't jealous when she saw him with his pregnant wife, even though I expect he asked her to marry him and she turned him down."

Ryan thought it was possible she was reading her own feelings into her aunt's life, but he sure wasn't going to say so. Maybe he even hoped that's what Jo was doing, because it would suggest that she was starting to realize that *she* would end up lonely if she never married.

Specifically, *him.*

"Why don't you ask her?" he suggested.

"I tried. Well, in a roundabout, gentle way. She sneered at the idea."

"Ah." He set a mug of coffee in front of her. Jo reached for it. "But she would, of course."

"Yeah, I suppose she would."

She stirred sugar into her coffee. "Boyce's girlfriend left him, so he's feeling down. I met her once and wasn't impressed, but he was halfway to being in love with her."

"Why'd she leave him?" Ryan didn't much care about her brother's romantic troubles, but he did care what she thought and felt, and he was enjoying watching her face, seeing it brighten and shadow, her mouth pucker when she thought, the small creases form between her high arched brows when she was momentarily disturbed. She had a delicacy about her bone structure, a fineness to her porcelain skin, that her personality belied. The contradiction was one of the many fascinations she held for him.

"According to him, because he's too 'establishment.' Even to please her, he wouldn't pierce his eyebrow." Now her face lit with laughter. "Which sounds yucky, doesn't it?"

"I would use a word considerably stronger than 'yucky,'" he said with feeling.

Her laughter fled. "All I've done is talk about my family. How was *your* week with the kids?"

Seeing real interest in her eyes, Ryan told her. He didn't sugarcoat the visit. If she was to be a real part of his life, she'd see his kids at their worst as well as their best.

She encouraged him to talk about his worries: Melissa's premature adolescent behavior, Tyler's depression and their stiff mentions of their mother.

"Do you have any reason to think she isn't a good parent?" Jo asked.

"I'm not sure she wanted to have kids at all." He'd never told even Kathleen about Wendy's reluctance, not wanting his sister to judge his wife. "I'm the one who wanted them. Sometimes I feel guilty, wondering if I pushed too hard…."

Softly, Jo finished his thought. "But if you hadn't, you wouldn't have Melissa and Tyler."

"Right." He rubbed the back of his neck. "I know she loves the kids. I also know she loses interest in the day-to-day demands they place on her. I think she did better when she was first married, probably because she was trying to impress Ronald with how devoted she was. I'm guessing, from things they let slip, that she's quit trying. She's got him sewed up, right?"

Jo expressed another of his fears. "Or maybe he wants more of her attention."

Ryan shoved back his chair and rose, suddenly unable to bear just sitting. "I wish I had some grounds to demand custody."

"Did you try, after the divorce?"

"No." He gripped the back of the chair. "I thought it was better for the kids if we worked everything out amicably. They were young enough that it made sense for them to be with their mother. Tyler was still coming home at lunchtime. Living with me, he would have had to be in before-and after-school care." He grunted. "Maybe I was a coward. I didn't want to start a war."

Jo stood and came to him, sliding an arm around his waist. "Keep talking to them. Find out what life's like before you make a decision. Remember, they'll be back for Christmas. This time, they won't be wary of you. You'll just be Dad."

"Yeah." He made himself relax, rotating his shoulders, then faced her. "You're right. Like I said, you have good instincts."

"I sure didn't inherit them from my father," she said.

"If he was such a bad parent, how did you

turn out so well?" Ryan asked, wrapping one hand around her nape and gently massaging.

She gave a laugh that was more than a little sad. "Sometimes I think I'm a bundle of neuroses. What you see is facade."

"I'm betting that's not true." With his other hand he smoothed her hair from her face. "Our choices, our behavior, our relationships with other people, that's a big part of us. The things we fear, those are just a facet."

Her sigh was tremulous. "My relationships with other people stink. Do you know how few truly close friends I've ever had? I see my father every few years and wish it wasn't even that often. Boyce and I go a year at a time without getting together. I've never stuck with a boyfriend for any length of time. Aunt Julia was my…" She hesitated. "My lodestone, I guess, and now I'm questioning her. You don't know me, Ryan."

"Then let me," he said with sudden ferocity. "Show me who you are."

Her eyes were wet with tears when she looked up. "I'm trying," she said in a choked voice. "I am. I promise."

He pulled her tight against him and buried his face in her hair. "That's all you can do.

That's all I ask. Whoever you are, I love you, Josephine Dubray."

She shook her head wildly. "You don't. You can't."

"I can," Ryan said patiently.

"But…it's too soon," she muttered into his chest.

She didn't love him.

Ryan closed his eyes on a surge of agony. No! She was afraid, that was all. Afraid to admit she did care. He had to believe that!

"Maybe. But I love you anyway." He nuzzled her hair. "I'm not asking for some kind of declaration in return. I just thought you should know I'm in danger of violating our agreement."

She mumbled something.

He went still. "What?"

Jo drew a deep, shaky breath. "I'm in danger, too," she whispered, before pressing her face against his chest again.

Jo WENT HOME late, having dragged herself unwillingly from Ryan's house. She had a nine o'clock class in the morning.

The house was dark. Jo was grateful to find a parking spot across the street but only a door or two down. Shivering from the cold night, she hurried in.

A wonderful, powerful fragrance filled the entry. She breathed it in, thinking, *Vanilla. No, cinnamon. Or even lemon and thyme. Or cocoa. Or...was that a whiff of mint?*

Kathleen had been cooking in the kitchen earlier. What on earth had she been making? Curious, Jo turned that way, switching on the light as she went.

The kitchen counter was covered with rows of...soap bars. Some sat in molds, while others were laid out on sheets of cardboard. Wonderful, intriguing soap bars, some clear with what might be rose petals captured inside as if in amber, others the color of oatmeal that had been molded into ovals. They were lined up like fresh-baked cookies set out to cool.

Wonderingly, Jo picked up a bar that had layered colors like a fancy dessert and sniffed. Definitely peppermint and a hint of...chocolate? Was it possible? It felt a little soft, and she quickly set it down.

A clear, square bar with petals frozen inside did smell like roses, while a smooth, oatmeal bar flecked with darker colors exuded cinnamon and nutmeg.

How extraordinary, she thought finally, backing away. Imagine, Kathleen making all these! Practical, brisk and sometimes entirely too regal, she of all people was unlikely to have such a...frivolous, if creative, hobby.

The potpourri of scents followed Jo upstairs, seeming to have soaked into the very woodwork of the house.

She was still smiling when she went to bed, feeling absurdly as if something magical had happened.

Turning in bed, she rubbed her cheek against the pillow. Perhaps magic *had* touched her tonight.

He loved her. Despite her prickliness, her contradictions and warnings and independence, Ryan loved her.

If that wasn't magic, what was?

And no, she wasn't going to think about the future, not right now. She wouldn't think about whether she loved him despite her best efforts not to, whether she *wanted* to love him, whether she could imagine marrying him. Becoming Mrs. Somebody instead of forever being Ms. Dubray, a woman entirely unto herself.

She would just think...he loves me, and hug herself like a teenage girl who has joy-

ously tossed the last daisy petal into the air.
He loves me not.

He loves me.

CHAPTER ELEVEN

WHEN JO GOT UP the next morning, the soap bars had vanished from the kitchen counter, leaving only their fragrance behind. Kathleen must have gotten up extra early.

After her one o'clock class, Jo lurked downstairs until Emma arrived home from school to ask her about the soap-making.

The teenager sank onto a kitchen chair as if she were too tired to stand. She looked even paler today than usual, her skin milky and tinged with blue.

"Yeah, she makes soap sometimes." Her shrug would have been insolent if it hadn't also been so weary. "It was, like, one of her 'See what an incredible homemaker I am' deals. She can't just do things like other people. She has to be, like, a *pro* at it."

"I couldn't believe how wonderful the house smelled last night when I got home." Jo carried a glass of milk to the table. "You want this?" she asked casually. "It's non-fat. I can pour another."

Emma fixed a hungry gaze on the milk, as if it were a chocolate mousse or a billowing lemon meringue pie. But she averted her face and shook her head. "Thanks. I'm not thirsty."

Jo sat down, too, and sipped, feeling as if she were cruelly eating a four-course meal in front of a starving refugee.

"Did you have a nice Thanksgiving?" Emma asked.

"Actually, I did." Jo smiled at her. "You?"

Emma jerked her shoulders again. "Mom and I fought all weekend. She just won't let up!"

"Let up?"

"I do eat, but she wants me to stuff myself! I can't!" she exclaimed in agitation. "I won't!"

Jo hesitated. "We're all worried about you."

The teenager pushed back. "Don't you start!"

"I won't." Not a toucher by nature, Jo reached over and laid her hand on Emma's. It was not only bony but icy cold. Hiding her shock, she said, "I promise."

"I thought I could talk to you!"

"You can." Jo kept her voice soothing. "I promised."

Emma's blue eyes were wild. "I know what

I'm doing. I feel fine. Why is Mom so determined to…to fatten me? It's like I'm a beef calf or something, and she's going to lose money if I don't put on enough weight."

"Do you really believe that?"

"Yes!" She stood, swayed, then straightened with an air of determination. "I wish I were older and I didn't have to listen to her!" Hefting her book bag as if it weighed a hundred pounds, Emma left. A moment later, the sound of her slow footsteps on the stairs came to the kitchen.

Jo wanted to go help her, but knew better than to offer.

"Oh, Emma," she said aloud, quietly, sadly.

Ginny came home an hour later and did join Jo at the kitchen table for milk and a peanut butter sandwich. She carried Pirate into the kitchen with her, and he leaped onto her lap when she sat down.

She shook her head vigorously at the suggestion she add jam. "I like just peanut butter."

"How was your Thanksgiving?" Jo asked. For some reason, she truly did want to know what this Thanksgiving day had been like for her housemates.

Head down, Ginny murmured. "Okay."

"Emma said she fought with her mom."

The six-year-old nodded.

"Did you have other family to Thanksgiving dinner?"

The mouse-brown braid swayed when she shook her head.

"Did you miss your dad?"

Without looking up, Ginny said softly, "No."

Understanding, Jo said, "He'd been sick a long time, hadn't he?"

She nodded.

"Did Pirate get some turkey?"

This earned her a quick, mischievous smile. "He liked turkey."

"I'll bet he did," Jo said dryly.

"Mom didn't want me to give him any, but I sneaked it. I saw Auntie Kathleen sneak some, too." Her forehead puckered. "She told me to call her that. Do you want to be Auntie Jo?"

Jo's heart gave a bump, skip and squeeze. "Yes, I think I'd like that a lot."

"Okay." Ginny munched contentedly.

Jo returned upstairs to her computer and to the research paper she had been writing—and making excuses *not* to write. But when she heard first Helen and then Kathleen come home after 5:30 p.m., she wandered back down to the kitchen to lurk again.

Tonight, unless she'd lost track entirely, was Kathleen's turn to cook. When Kathleen did appear, she looked as exhausted as her daughter, if healthier in color. Hair that had probably started the day braided was slipping loose and fluffing around her face. She had a spot of what looked like mustard on the blouse that was half pulled out of the waist-band of her skirt. One stocking had run, and she was limping although she wore slippers instead of pumps.

"Bad day?" Jo asked from where she sat at the kitchen table with a book open in front of her.

"Awful," Kathleen said briefly, opening the refrigerator. Eyes squeezed shut, she closed it.

"What's wrong?"

"Forgot to defrost the chuck steak." She rubbed her temple. "I guess I can do it in the microwave."

"You look like you need a nap. Why don't I cook tonight?"

Hope briefly lifted Kathleen's head before she sagged again. "That's not fair. You haven't had a chance to plan anything. And you just got in last night."

"I could make homemade macaroni and cheese. Ginny loves it. And we have plenty of broccoli. Seriously. Why don't you lie down for an hour? I'll aim dinner for 6:30 p.m."

"If I can just take something for my headache, I'll be fine," Kathleen said stoutly before offering a weak smile. "I'd be thrilled if I could watch you cook instead of doing it myself, though."

Jo smiled in return. "Done. Can I get you a cup of tea first?"

"Oh, yes, please!" Kathleen sank onto the same chair Emma had sat earlier. "What a day."

"Did you hurt yourself?" Jo asked above the water she was running into the sink.

"Hurt…? Oh. No. I wore a pair of shoes I've always hated just because they go with this skirt." She waved at the navy-and-green tweed. "I have blisters you wouldn't believe. I swear, I'm throwing those dumb shoes away this time!"

Jo handed her a bottle of pain relievers and a glass of water. "We could have a ceremony. We'd each offer the shoes that have caused the most agony. Maybe burn them. Or—

wait!—we could torture them first. Smash them against a concrete wall."

Kathleen chuckled, sounding almost like herself. "How was your holiday?"

Was the question genuinely curious, or polite? Jo wondered. "Good."

"We missed you."

"How could you? You had Ryan's crew, didn't you?"

"Mmm. But Emma was in a sulk, Helen burst into tears in the middle of dinner and the turkey was dry."

"Oh, dear." Jo poured boiling water over the tea bag and carried the mug to the table, knowing her offering was inadequate. "I hear Pirate liked it anyway."

Kathleen laughed. "He did. And Ginny caught me redhanded, sneaking him some."

"She told me." Jo brought her own tea to the table. "Now, tell me about the soap. I couldn't believe the glorious fragrance when I got home last night!"

Her beautiful blond roommate grimaced. "When I'm upset, I have to *do* something. I hadn't made soap in ages, I've been buying it at the grocery store, so I thought, *that's* what I'll do. I got carried away. And we won't even be able to use it for weeks."

"Carried away over what?" Helen shuffled into the kitchen in a pair of baggy sweatpants, a flannel shirt and down booties.

"Cold?" Kathleen asked.

Helen glanced down at herself. "Comfortable. My feet killed me all day."

The other two women laughed, which required explanation. After they further plotted the demise of their most elegant and therefore excruciating dress shoes, they went back to the subject.

"The soap?" Helen prodded, adding honey to the tea she'd poured herself. "Were you making Christmas presents for everyone on your list for the next ten years?"

"Christmas presents." Kathleen's face brightened. "That's what I'll do with it!"

Thinking of the rows and rows of bars, Jo said, "Some of it."

"Oh, we can use it, too." She frowned. "Maybe I'll take some over to the women's shelter once it cures."

Sounding tentative, Helen suggested, "You could also sell some."

"Sell it?" Kathleen lifted her brows.

She looked, Jo thought, faintly amazed and even disdainful, as if the idea of selling the products of her hands was foreign to her.

"Was that your soap in the bathroom when I first moved in?" Helen asked.

"I guess it must have been. Oh, I remember finding a couple of bars and putting them out." Kathleen smiled wryly. "I was trying to be welcoming."

"They were wonderful!" Helen said with more spirit than Jo often credited to her. "That soap left my skin so soft. And there was this one day especially, when I felt really low. But I kept catching these whiffs of cinnamon. This probably sounds weird, but the smell is so...homey, I guess, it raised my spirits. If money wasn't so tight, I'd buy handmade ones more often. Yours smelled better than any I've ever looked at in stores."

"You really think so?" Kathleen asked doubtfully.

Jo chimed in. "Last night I came in the kitchen to see what you'd made that smelled so great, and I felt as if I'd discovered something magical."

Kathleen paused with her mug halfway to her mouth, seeming to take the idea seriously. After a moment, she shook her head. "I'm just not a salesperson. I mean, where would I sell it? On street corners? I can't imagine approaching shop owners, hat in hand. And do you know how many lines of handmade soap are already available out there? Just look at Whole Foods! They have dozens! Why would they, or anyone else, add one more?"

"Why did they add the last one?" Helen asked stubbornly. "Because someone approached them, and they liked the product."

"But I don't have a product! I have a few extra bars with no packaging! They haven't even cured yet."

"We could come up with packaging by the time they do. Something simple." Helen frowned into space. "Your soaps are so gorgeous, we wouldn't want to hide them in paper wrappings. Clear, I think, tied up with coordinating ribbons in casual bows. Or the molded ones with the more intricate designs could be boxed in sets of two or four."

Kathleen set down her mug. "You're serious."

"Well, of course I am!" Helen looked surprised. "You hate your job, right?"

"Well, sure I do, but…"

"I'm not saying you could quit, but you could supplement your income. Make enough to remodel this place. And who knows, down the line? Unless you don't enjoy making the soap, either?"

"I do enjoy making it, but…"

Showing rare determination, Helen continued. "All you have to do is nerve yourself to find a few outlets. How hard is that?"

The two women seemed to have forgotten their tea, their tiredness and Jo. Both sat up straight, elbows on the table as they talked intensely.

"Hard," Kathleen admitted. "I was good at being a businessman's wife, if I do say so myself, because all I had to do was please people with conversation and food. I didn't have to ask for anything, or try to influence anybody. I sure didn't have to try to sell *myself*."

"Well, *I* could sell you." Helen gave a small nod. "I don't mind. Let me try, if you're willing to supply any orders."

"You want to go into business with me." Kathleen sounded stunned but intrigued.

"No, I'm offering to help *you* go into business."

Jo watched with interest as Kathleen shook her head firmly. "Nope. If we do this, it's as partners. We can design packaging and a name together, I'll make the soap and you can sell it."

Helen went very still. "You mean that?"

Her voice was almost…hushed. As if hope was such a tiny flicker, she might blow it out.

"Sure I mean it." Kathleen leaned forward, enthusiasm lighting her face. "We could start with half a dozen of the soaps I already make, but I'd love to experiment with others. I could aim for some that were really distinctive."

"Like the chocolate one."

"Right. Go for the unexpected, the…the…"

"Sybaritic," Jo contributed.

Both heads swung toward her.

"Luxurious," she said helpfully. "Sensual. Voluptuous."

"Yeah. That," Helen agreed, turning back to Kathleen. "Instead of just the citrus scents or the lavender that everybody does—although I like both—we could market you more effectively if your soaps are unique."

"Market *me.*" If she still had a headache, she'd forgotten it.

"Your skill."

"You really think we can do this?"

For the first time, Jo realized that Helen was pretty, perhaps even beautiful when she glowed with purpose and enthusiasm.

Cheeks pink, eyes sparkling, she radiated excitement. "I do."

"It'll mean more work. After we get home from our actual paying jobs."

"Yes, but just think. What if we built a real business? If we started selling through a website, or talked one of the major catalogs into carrying your soap, or started our own catalog…?"

Kathleen threw back her head and laughed. "Do you have the slightest idea how to do any of those things?"

Helen laughed merrily, too. "No, but I can learn."

Jo stood and started work on dinner, leaving her two housemates to plot. Soon they were passing a notebook back and forth with scribbled designs for a label even as they talked about ways to expand into baby soap, bath herbs, pet shampoo for the indulgent owner and laundry soap that would leave hand-washables delicately fragrant for weeks.

Kathleen explained the process of soap-making and the difference between cold-process, hand-milled and melt-and-pour soaps. "The hand-milled is made from already cured cold-process, so of course I didn't make any last night, but it makes a harder bar with a smoother texture than either of the other methods." She talked about why it had to "cure" for anywhere from two to eight weeks, depending on the recipe. "We'd have to have room for huge quantities to be curing," she worried. "I don't know about the temperature in the garage...."

"We could heat it," Helen suggested. "Or, for now, clear out the den, put in makeshift shelves and use it. If Jo doesn't mind," she added scrupulously.

Both turned to look at Jo, who was draining macaroni into a colander.

"Nope," she said. "Never use it."

"The kitchen would be tied up a lot, too," Kathleen said.

"We can work around you," Jo assured her. Or not. They could order pizza, Chinese takeout, fast-food burgers... Personally, she wouldn't mind if she cooked dinner only once a week instead of twice.

"The other thing is..." Kathleen sat back, new anxiety tightening her face. "Well, this will cost."

Helen nodded. "We'll have to get printing done and buy stuff for packaging and probably letterhead and business cards...but we can do that at Kinko's."

"Not just that. I'll have to make lots of soap. I should experiment, try to develop recipes that are mine alone or find ones that we're all agreed are the best. And the ingredients can be expensive. Lye, of course, cocoa butter, glycerin, fats—and the oils! I can't just snap them up at the grocery. Olive oil, for example. Unless I buy pomace, the soap would smell of olives." She wrinkled her nose. "Coconut oil, castor oil, palm oil, jojoba…not to mention the essential oils that provide the scents and the therapeutic qualities. And I'll need more molds and a food processor or spice grinder. I've always done without, but…" She shrugged. "You see? We'll have to invest. And I don't know if I can afford to."

Helen sat silent for a moment. "We could start small," she said at last. "Try to sell in just a couple of stores, then use any income to buy more supplies."

"I guess we'll have to," Kathleen agreed, "but that will mean not experimenting as much, and keeping the packaging really minimal. No boxed sets, for example."

Jo put the casserole dish in the oven, closed the door and turned to face her housemates. "I have a better idea."

They looked at her in surprise. "You do?" Kathleen said.

"Borrow from your brother. He'd love to

help. He'd *give* you money—" she waved off objections before Kathleen could voice them "—which I know you wouldn't take. But this is different. Pay him interest. Offer him a small percentage of profits. Make it business. You'll need an investor if you're going anywhere with this. Why not Ryan?"

Kathleen stared at her with a blank, almost dazed, expression. "Why not Ryan," she echoed. She gave herself a shake. "I just don't want charity."

"We'll find a way to pay him back even if we fail," Helen said strongly. "I could put in more overtime at the store if I had to."

"Look at it this way," Jo suggested. "You could keep him in soap for the rest of his life."

Kathleen rolled her eyes at the frivolity of this idea. But she looked as if she was seriously thinking about Jo's advice. "You really think he'd be interested?"

"I think he'd be thrilled," Jo assured her.

She cut up broccoli and put it in the steamer while the other two women continued to talk and scheme and dream. With her back turned to them, she was more aware of their voices, vibrant in a way they hadn't been before. At night, after a day of work at jobs they disliked, both tended to sound tired, heavy. Jo had never heard Helen crackle with this kind of energy and excitement and hope.

Let this work, she thought. She wanted very badly for their hope not to be false, their dream dead-end. Because if they failed, they'd be more discouraged than they'd been before they started.

Ginny slipped into the kitchen and went to her mother, pressing up to her side and laying her head on her mother's chest as Helen automatically wrapped an arm around her. As was her habit, she said nothing, becoming invisible, only listening as the women talked, her eyes alive and aware in her small face.

"I could ask my brother-in-law, too," Helen said suddenly. "He's offered to help before, but I didn't like to feel…dependent."

"I didn't know you *had* a brother-in-law." Kathleen sounded startled. "You've never mentioned him."

"I don't think he ever liked me." Helen glanced down at her daughter, then said quickly, "No, that isn't right. We always got along fine. It's that…I think Lyman admires women who are go-getters. Women who are smart and ambitious and capable. I was just a housewife. He didn't understand why Ben loved me."

"But he offered financial support after your husband died?"

"Yes, but with an air of…irritation. Duty. His brother might have chosen foolishly, but he felt obliged. You know?"

Kathleen nodded, her lips thin. Jo felt a spurt of rage. How dare that…man have made this kind, gentle woman feel inadequate, and at a time when she grieved so terribly for his brother?

"But I could ask now. He'd loan us money, I'm sure."

"You know what?" Kathleen said. "Let me ask Ryan first. I'd much rather tell your brother-in-law to go to…" her gaze flicked to the little girl listening, "um, where to go."

Relief lightened Helen's face again, restoring her prettiness. "Okay. I like Ryan better."

"Then we're agreed? We're going into business?"

"As partners." Helen held out a hand.

Kathleen took it and they solemnly shook.

"I wonder," Kathleen said, "what Emma will think."

EMMA WAS POUTING when she opened the door to Ryan. "Uncle Ryan," she said unenthusiastically. "Mom's in the kitchen."

"Hey! Wait." He put a hand on her arm to stop her and had quite a time not recoiling. Wow! She was nothing but bone.

"What?" she snapped.

"Is something wrong?" he asked.

"What would be wrong?"

"You don't seem to be in a very good mood."

She shrugged.

"Okay," he said, letting her go. "Talk to me when you're ready."

His niece went up the stairs without looking back. He couldn't help noticing how slowly she went, as if she had to drag herself up each step.

In the kitchen he found all three women clustered around the table, so intent on their conversation they didn't see him right away.

"Aroma, fragrance, essence," his sister said.

"Attar," Jo contributed with satisfaction. She sat as she often did with one foot tucked under her, the baggy sleeves of her shirt pushed up. "I always loved that word."

"Bouquet," Helen said. "Or how about 'natural' or some takes on that?"

"Pure," Kathleen said thoughtfully. "But

that sounds more like a description of ingredients than a name."

"What's in a name?" Ryan asked rhetorically. "'That which we call a rose, By any other name would smell as sweet.'"

Laughing, his sister said, "Thank you for that contribution."

His eyes meeting Jo's in a silent greeting, Ryan pulled a chair up to the table. "Contribution to what?"

"Well." Kathleen glanced at the other women, who started to push their chairs back. "I wanted to ask you something."

That zeroed his attention in on his sister. "Is this about Emma?"

"No, it's…um…" She took a deep breath and clasped her hands together on the table. "I actually wanted to ask you…"

With a last look at him, Jo followed Helen out of the kitchen.

"I'm starting a business," Kathleen said in a rush.

"What?"

"A business!" She scowled. "Is that so unlikely?"

"It's just…not what I expected." He'd been waiting to hear that Emma had collapsed, or that Ian had decided to quit paying child support, or that… "What kind of business?"

"Soap." She looked defiant. "I'm going to make it and Helen will sell it."

"Helen?" He felt guilty raising doubts, but felt obligated. "She's so timid. How is she going to sell anything?"

"That's what she does, you know. She works for Nordstrom on commission."

He shook his head. "It's a long ways from smiling at women shopping for clothes and telling them how wonderful they look in puce to convincing store owners to carry a product."

"Yes, but I think she can do it. When she suggested the idea, she came alive." Remembered amazement crossed Kathleen's face. "She's the one who pushed me into trying to sell my soap."

Frowning, Ryan considered. "I like the soap you've given me. It smells nice, and it lathers better than the stuff I buy at the grocery store." He hesitated, not wanting to rain on her parade, but not wanting to see her stumble and fall, either. "The question is, can you make better soap, or package it more appealingly, than all the other noncommercial ones already available?"

She didn't like being doubted by him, that was clear, but she was a fair woman. "That's the question, isn't it?"

"And?"

She tilted up her chin in pride. "I make extraordinary soap. Whether we can get it out there to compete, I don't know. Helen believes we can."

Ryan smiled and tilted his chair back. "Okay. What did you want to ask me?"

Now she twitched and fidgeted, a sight he thoroughly enjoyed. His big sister hadn't had to ask many favors of him in her life, and she was clearly wishing she didn't have to ask this one, either.

Finally she spit it out. "I need an investor."

"You want money."

She flushed. "I don't *want* money! I need equipment and supplies to make soap on the scale we're envisioning. Plus we'll have costs for printing labels, invoices, business cards and so on, as well as buying the material for packaging. This is strictly a business proposition." She was getting madder as she went. "I'll pay you interest or a percent of my profits so that you're essentially a minority partner. But if you're not interested, I can find someone else!"

He crossed his arms and grinned at her, going for infuriating. "What makes you think I'm not interested?"

His sister gritted her teeth. "Are you?"

"Maybe." He drew the word out. "Now, let me think…"

She let out a huff of rage.

Ryan let the chair legs drop to the floor, hard. "Kathleen! How many times have I offered financial help? If you just asked me for money, I'd give it to you! It insults me that you're doubting for a minute that I'd be there for you."

She wrung her hands in agitation. "I don't want 'help'! You know how I feel about that! I'm asking you to risk money because you have faith I can pay you back. That's not the same thing."

Ian had done a number on her, Ryan thought not for the first time, but with new anger. Yeah, his sister had always been independent, but at eighteen or twenty she wouldn't have been terrified by the idea of depending on someone else.

He reached across the table and gripped her hand, feeling it quiver in his. "Kathleen, I have always had faith and pride in you. You've never set out to do anything and gone halfway." He didn't add that he'd spent much of his life feeling inadequate in comparison. "You can count me in. I'll enjoy watching 'Kathleen's Soaps' burgeon into an empire."

Cheeks flushed again, but this time, he thought, with pleasure, his stubbornly self-reliant sister made a small sound of protest and tugged her hand free. "I'm not hoping for an empire. Enough success so that Helen and I could quit our day jobs would satisfy me."

"Then," he said, "let's celebrate a beginning."

CHAPTER TWELVE

"WANT TO STUDY at my house?" Ryan asked.

"Sure," Jo said readily. "I've got to feed everybody first, though."

He shifted his cell phone to his other ear as he climbed the stairs in a client's home to inspect the tile work a subcontractor had done in the bathroom. "Are you cooking?"

"Kathleen has commandeered the kitchen." Jo sounded remarkably cheerful about it. "We're doing Chinese tonight. You want to join us?"

"I'll do even better. I'll pick it up if you call in an order." He crouched to get a better look at the work around the tub. "Oh great," he muttered. "I wish you worked for me." The simplest job, no elaborate pattern, just a plain, muted peach-and-white checkerboard, and Jacobson had screwed up just because he was in a hurry.

"*What?*" Jo asked.

"Tiling. You should see the size of the gap between the outlet pipes and the cut edges of the tiles." He whipped out a tape measure and laid it across the hole, shaking his head at the result. "The fixture isn't going to cover it."

"What will you do?"

"Call my subcontractor back and make him redo as much of the job as necessary. I get the clients I do because I set high standards. We don't hide mistakes."

"Oooh," she teased, "a hardnose."

He grunted and eyeballed the work around the sink. Better. "That's me."

They agreed on a time and he stuck his cell phone back in its case on his belt.

Things were going well with Jo. Better than before Thanksgiving. She'd relaxed in small ways, as if she were more willing to let him get closer to her.

Earlier in the fall, she hadn't liked to bring her books over to his place, for example. Dates had to be just that—planned, definable occasions, after which he was to bring her back to her house. Now she seemed content just hanging out at his place as well, or letting him hang at hers.

It was also true, though, that she'd never said a word about his declaration of love. He hadn't repeated it—she hadn't asked him to—

and she sure hadn't echoed it. She'd chosen to pretend he'd never opened his mouth.

Ryan told himself he was willing to pretend, too. He'd known it was too soon, that she wasn't ready, that he might even scare her. He was lucky she hadn't pulled back, or sent him packing. She'd warned him she wanted neither his heart nor his hand. And what had he done? Fallen in love anyway and been stupid enough to tell her, that's what.

For a couple of weeks, he didn't push, he didn't demand, and he demonstrated his passion when they kissed but bit back the words. In one way, he was content with the results: she was becoming more open, more likely to tease, to tell him a secret from her childhood or about why she'd isolated herself the way she had. But he also knew his frustration was growing.

If she hadn't changed her mind, was he doing himself any favor to spend this kind of time with her? More of his heart seemed to crumble off every day, every time she smiled just for him, every time she came to him for a kiss or argued with him because she held so many strong beliefs, every time he saw how gentle she was with Hummingbird. Maybe he could still save himself now, if he didn't let her keep shattering him with the way she moved and laughed and thought.

There were days when he had hope, when he'd swear she felt the same as he did, words or no, when she smiled at him with her eyes dreamy and her mouth so soft, or when they were walking down the street and she laughed and elbowed him and then laid her head on his arm as if doing so came as naturally as breathing.

That evening was one of the times he could believe marriage was in their future. When he showed up with the food, everybody gathered in the living room, where they passed around cardboard containers of rice, spring rolls, sweet-and-sour pork and chicken with snow peas, dishing up onto paper plates. Ginny sat on her heels using the coffee table to dine, while the adults sprawled on the sofa and comfortable chairs with their plates balanced precariously and their cans of soda near to hand. Jo settled next to Ryan on the couch as if her place was a given.

Tonight the house smelled like peppermint, so pungent it made Ryan's eyes water. Kathleen had stripped off goggles and rubber gloves when she came from the kitchen. Helen, meantime, had been working on the computer in the den, apparently designing order forms and practicing introductory letters. Both were preoccupied—Kathleen distracted enough to look as if she didn't know who Emma was when he paused before seconds to ask where his niece was hiding.

"Oh, she's upstairs somewhere," Kathleen said vaguely. "She wasn't hungry."

Ryan swore. "She's wasting away, Kathleen. When are you going to do something?"

That got to her. Her chin shot up and her eyes narrowed. "We go to counseling weekly. She sees a dietician on her own. What do you want me to do? Stick a tube down her throat?"

"Maybe the time has come for that," he said grimly. "She looks sick."

Speaking of timing—his stank. Ginny listened with anxious eyes, Jo stirred beside him as if to send a message and Kathleen's expression was less than receptive. She didn't like criticism, and she'd like it even less in front of others. But he could see his niece wasting away, and not much being done about it.

"We've agreed—*all* of us, including Emma—that if her weight falls below eighty pounds, she'll be hospitalized. She's managed to keep it above that."

"Eighty pounds." Shocked, he shook his head. Sixteen-year-old Emma was five-four or five. How could a human being survive weighing that little?

"They do check her bloodwork regularly. I'm not entirely negligent, Ryan."

"I didn't mean to imply that you were." He grimaced. "She just scares me. She went up the stairs the other day as if every step was a gigantic effort. You'd see more spring in the step of a mountain climber at 20,000 feet above sea level without oxygen."

Kathleen wasn't in a forgiving mood. "You think *I'm* not scared?"

"No…"

Beside him on the couch, Jo spoke up in his defense. "We've all noticed that she doesn't look good, Kathleen. You're better informed than the rest of us. You know what's worrisome and what's not. All I see is that Emma's cold most of the time, and she's quit taking Ginny for walks."

"But she always exercises," Kathleen protested. "She wouldn't quit!"

"I think she has. She goes straight to her room when she comes home from school."

Kathleen grabbed for straws. "Maybe she's doing calisthenics there."

"Maybe." Jo kept most of the doubt from her voice, returning her attention to her food, as if she'd said all she meant to.

Forehead pinched, Kathleen set down her plate as if her appetite had deserted her. Sounding defeated, she said, "I'll talk to her counselor this week. What else can I do? They tell me not to try to monitor what she eats or to comment on how much time she spends exercising. If I ask questions or say anything, she blows up." She lifted her hands and let them fall helplessly. "She's my daughter, and I have to watch her starve herself to death."

"Maybe she's like an alcoholic who has to reach a crisis." Ryan felt as though he were offering a pat on the back to someone who needed a wheelchair. He couldn't blame her for being angry at him.

"Maybe." Eyes blind, Kathleen stood up. "Excuse me. I'll check on her and then I'd better get back to work. I shouldn't have taken a break." She walked out with her head high, but he wondered if she was going to her bedroom for a quick cry.

In the silence after she was gone, he felt like a heel. But later, after they'd left the house, when he said as much to Jo, she shook her head firmly.

"No. You love Emma, too. You have a right to say something. She does look awful, and I'm not sure Kathleen lets herself see. She wants so desperately to believe Emma is doing better."

"But she's not, is she?"

The night was clear and frosty, stars distant and brilliant. Fallen leaves crunched underfoot on the uneven sidewalk. Their breath lingered in white plumes when they passed under a streetlight.

Jo shook her head, then hunched into her parka. "She gets dizzy when she stands up. And have you touched her?" She shivered. "She's not just moody, she's shutting us out. Even Ginny."

He nudged her to cross the street to his parked pickup. "Do you think Kathleen *should* do something?"

Tone subdued, Jo said, "I don't know. How can I? Maybe she can't help Emma beyond offering her the resources she already has. Maybe only Emma can help herself."

Anger rasped in his voice. "But if she's not…"

"Like Kathleen said, do you stick a tube

down her throat, as if she were a turn-of-the-century suffragette?"

He made an impatient, choppy gesture. "That was political, a different thing."

"Was it? Force-feeding those women stole their autonomy, made them children who could be compelled to do as their betters— men—thought they should."

"But Emma isn't trying to *say* anything with her refusal to eat!"

Jo stopped beside the truck and faced him. "Isn't she?"

Devastated by the small, simple question, Ryan tilted back his head and looked up at the black velvet of the sky, spangled with million-year-old stars. What if Emma had been trying to tell them all something, only they weren't listening?

What if her last sob was her death?

Jo's gloved hand crept into his. "I don't know anything," she repeated. "I'm not saying anyone has neglected Emma. I'm only guessing that Emma is expressing some huge, all-consuming need or fear through starvation. If she could find another way to say it…"

He made a ragged sound.

"She's only sixteen." Jo wrapped her arms around him and they embraced in the cold.

"She hasn't been anorexic long. She has a good chance of recovering, from what I've read."

"You've been reading about it?"

"Haven't you?"

"Yeah, but I've learned nothing." Frustration choked him. "I can't find answers."

"I know," she whispered.

He gripped her tightly, his cheek against the fleece cloche hat she'd tugged on as they went out the door. With his eyes closed, he smelled peppermint.

After a long minute, he was able to relax and let her go, turning away to open the truck door. They drove to his house in near silence.

There she divested herself of parka, hat and gloves, kicked off her clogs, then in stockinged feet carried her pack into the living room and sank cross-legged on the wood floor. Unzipping her bag, she took out books and binder and spread them over his coffee table.

"You look like a kid," he said.

She glanced up in surprise.

"A kid?"

"Are you really comfortable?"

"Sure. I wouldn't be sitting here if I weren't."

He shook his head, smiling. "Want something to drink?"

Reading already, she flapped a hand but didn't look up. "Not right now, thanks."

He left her for a while, writing up a bid for a job that would be very welcome come mid-January or early February, when construction work suffered an inevitable slowdown given Northwest weather. He didn't believe in laying off his crew if he could possibly prevent it, even to the point of working for ridiculously low prices. If he could just make expenses on this one, it would be worth doing, to keep them from an idle month.

Satisfied at last, he printed the bid and a cover letter as well as copies for his own files, then wandered back to the living room, where he found Jo scribbling furiously, gaze darting between her writing and her open book.

She didn't seem even to notice his presence, so he went to the kitchen and made coffee. When he set a cup in front of her, she grabbed it gratefully.

"Read my mind."

"I doubt it," Ryan said with amusement. "What are you working on?"

"Mm." She stretched her legs out under the coffee table. "I'm analyzing studies on human behavior that might be relevant to what makes people choose to use the public library or be turned off by it. How do people respond to layout, to the kind of order librarians tend to impose, to the institutional lighting or to the way other patrons behave or dress? What subtle motivators can we use to draw people in? Why do we lose some people? One guy who's working on his 1962 Chevy borrows a manual from the library. His buddy would never think about the library as a source, even though he must have been dragged there as a school kid. Why?"

"Learning anything?"

"Oh, some of it's predictable. For example, people worry about not fitting in, to be square pegs if the holes look round to them. So a guy wanders into the library, the only other patrons are a couple of nicely dressed women with young kids, the librarian in his shirt and tie looks disdainful, and our guy with grease under his nails quietly fades back out. He felt like an idiot when he was twelve and had to use the library to research the Egyptian pharaohs, and he doesn't stick around this time long enough to discover how easy the computer is to use, that all he has to do is ask to be led right to that manual or résumé

book or *Hot Rod* magazine. If he'd come at a
different time of day, seen some other guys
that looked more like him there, his whole
experience would have been different."

"Okay. What are you going to do about it?"

Jo flashed him a cheerful grin. "I have no
idea." She slurped coffee and wiped her chin
when she spilled. "Well, I know some ways
to reach reluctant patrons. With teenagers, we
take books to youth centers, even the deten-
tion hall. We talk to women's groups. Men
are tougher. I'm not sure I know, except that
we need to be very conscious of how we as
librarians present ourselves—*and* what we
have to offer—from the get-go. We tend to
be readers. Snobs. But we don't exist just to
serve like-minded fellow citizens. I'm hoping
to find some studies that pinpoint relevant
behavioral triggers."

"You don't sound as if you believe in free
will." He considered her. "Are we really 'trig-
gered' that easily?"

Face animated, she argued, "Yeah, I think
context is more important than we want to
believe. Say I see somebody injured on the
sidewalk ahead. What if it's dark and I'm
alone? Daytime and lots of other people are
around, too? When am I likeliest to help?"

"Ah…daytime," he decided. "You'd have reason to be nervous at night."

"Ding!" she said triumphantly. "Wrong. Turns out, in the daytime I'd look around and think somebody else will do it. I don't have to. But if I'm the only hope for this guy, I'm more likely to take a chance and offer help. See? Context. The interesting part is, people don't always react the way we think they will, mostly because what we think is actually determined by what we'd *like* to believe, if that isn't too convoluted."

Ryan nodded at the book. "This could make you a cynic."

"Yeah. It could." She sipped her coffee meditatively.

The silence was comfortable, although he used it to figure out how to ask questions she might consider threatening. Finally, he just decided to go for broke.

Trying to sound casual, he asked, "After you get your master's degree, do you think you'll go back to California?"

Another sign of how far they'd come was the fact that she didn't get prickly. "You know, when I came up here, I assumed I would. Now, I'm not so sure. Libraries are better funded in other places, for one thing. The cap on tax increases in California puts such limitations on new programs and buying, it can be really frustrating. Also…" She hesitated, then shrugged. "I like it here. I even like living with Kathleen and Helen. I was thinking about it the other day. If things are still going well when I graduate, maybe I could stay on. Find a job locally. Both King County and the city of Seattle have great public libraries."

He should be glad, not mad. But he was, and he knew why. He was agonizing over whether she might ever love him enough to marry him, and she was thinking how great her present living situation was. Had she ever, even once, considered a future with him?

Unclenching his jaw, he tried to sound mild. "I have plenty of room here, too."

She went very still for what felt like half an hour but was probably only seconds. Then she drank her coffee in an obvious bid for more time, at last carefully setting down her mug.

"Is that a…proposal?"

"It would be if I thought you'd take me up on it. Really, I was just hoping you might start considering the idea."

Still not looking at him, Jo said, "You know

how I feel about commitment, marriage, children."

They sounded like two people discussing the idea of switching brands of laundry detergent: interested enough to talk about it, but with no emotional investment.

He didn't change that. "I've had the impression you might be changing your mind."

She was silent, her head bent, the curve of her neck graceful. Her hair was bundled up in a ponytail, exposing the vulnerable nape. When she finally answered, it was with a cry from the heart. "I don't know if I can."

Ryan shifted on the couch so that he sat right behind her and could reach out and massage her shoulders. Appearances had been deceptive: she was rigid beneath his hands.

"I'm doing it again, aren't I? Pushing. We've only known each other a few months, and I'm demanding you ditch your lifelong conviction."

Almost inaudibly, she whispered, "I want to."

He kneaded taut muscles and felt them becoming pliable. "What can I do to help?"

She rotated one shoulder, leaning into his hand. "You're doing it."

His grunt held amusement. "Giving you a back rub?"

Jo leaned back to look at him upside down. A tremulous smile was paired with big brown eyes welling with tears. "Being irresistible."

Momentarily, his fingers tightened. He forced himself to relax, saying lightly, "You're going to blow up my ego like a hot air balloon."

"You don't have a big enough one now. You have no idea how unusual it is to find a man as handsome as you who seems oblivious to the fact. You're smart, successful and sweet. What more could a woman want?"

"You tell me," Ryan said quietly.

She closed her eyes, and he felt her muscles tense again. "The idea just…scares me. Maybe my parents did want to be married, maybe they loved each other. But look at all the other marriages! It seems like most fail."

"Half. The other half of people who marry are happy."

Her laugh was almost sad. "You're a 'half-full' guy. I'm a 'half-empty' gal. Maybe that makes us incompatible."

He smoothed her hair back from her face, loving the spring of it, the strength and sheen and rich color. Loving just to touch *her.* "I don't feel incompatible."

"Neither do I," she admitted.

"Then?"

"Being boyfriend and girlfriend isn't the same as being husband and wife. Right now, we're the spice in each other's lives, not the oatmeal. What would it be like for our relationship to be predictable?"

Great, as far as he was concerned. He hated coming home to an empty house, hated wondering when he'd see Jo again, hated thinking of something to say to her and then having to phone instead of talk to her across the kitchen table.

"We see each other almost every day now," Ryan reminded her. "Maybe this makes me boring, but I want to be able to count on you! What's wrong with sharing the morning newspaper and the oatmeal?"

She pulled away from him, untangled her legs and stood, retreating several steps. Facing him, arms crossed protectively, Jo said tautly, "Nothing! Not the way you say it. But for most people, dullness sets in sooner or later."

He leaned back. "Is that really what scares you?"

"Yes!" Jo paced another few steps away, then swung back. "No! I mean, that's part of it. One thing I've always admired about Aunt Julia is her independence. She doesn't have to consult anybody. If she wants to spend Christmas on Cook Island, she goes. She can be spontaneous!"

He was growing to hate Aunt Julia and her globe-trotting, glamorous lifestyle, which he suspected was largely myth. "Is going to a South Pacific island by yourself really that wonderful?"

Anxiety darkening her eyes, she deftly avoided the question. "Even together! We'd quit being spontaneous! I'd have school, then work, you'd have jobs lined up, the kids would come for vacation… What if we lose all the passion and any chance for adventure?"

Adventure. Ryan mulled that.

He loved working on a banister in a turn-of-the-century house, his patience and skill stripping away the dark layers of the years to reveal the golden glow of fine wood. He loved tucking his kids in at night, pacing the sidelines at soccer games, running beside a bicycle and letting go the first time to a gasp of fear and then a crow of delight. He loved the sight of Jo Dubray sitting cross-legged at his coffee table, or munching on a sandwich in his kitchen while sitting on the counter with her heels bumping the cabinet.

That was enough adventure for him.

For the first time, he weighed the idea that maybe they *were* incompatible.

Then he considered how she held herself completely closed while she waited. He thought about the three months he'd known her and the ways they'd enjoyed each other's company.

The most adventure they'd ever had together was that French film. Or in-line skating around Green Lake—that had been scary the first time he'd trusted himself to put wheels on the bottoms of his shoes.

At his guess, the biggest adventure of Jo's life was quitting her job and moving to Seattle to go to graduate school. She'd never mentioned scuba-diving in the Caribbean or climbing in the Andes.

Adventure was another of those things Aunt Julia extolled and Jo bought into, a hazy dream like dining at the White House with a charismatic senator or walking down the red carpet in a designer dress on the arm of an Academy Award-nominated actor. They were somebody else's dreams, not hers.

He had the feeling she was waking up from them, like a star gymnast who realized she'd starved herself, suffered shattered vertebrae, given up school and friends and boyfriends all for her parents and not herself.

Or maybe he was kidding himself.

"Adventure," he said thoughtfully, "comes in a lot of forms. What do you have in mind?"

Her eyes narrowed. "You want me to list every adventurous thing I might *spontaneously*—" she became a little shrill on the one word "—choose to do over the next fifty years?"

"No," he said patiently. "What I'm suggesting is that marriage is an adventure. So is having kids. Going to graduate school. Starting a new job. Or do you have more in mind the kind of thrills you might get from sky-diving or spelunking." He frowned. "Is that how you say it?"

"You're making fun of me," she snapped.

"No, I'm not. I'm asking you how you want to live your life? Sky-diving? Touching other people's lives without fully entering them? Or do you want to take some real risks?"

Pure panic glittered in her eyes now. "You're misunderstanding every word I said!"

"How's that?"

"I'm afraid of losing spontaneity. Of not having *fun* anymore, because we get ground down by daily life."

He finally stood and went to her. When he reached out and ran his hands up and down her arms, she didn't step away, but she didn't lean into him, either.

"Daily life grinds whether you're married or not. Seems to me you can resist it best by being happy, by having someone to talk to."

Jo didn't say anything or look above his chest.

"Why can't we have fun together?"

She sneaked a glance upward. "Haven't you noticed how we already do less exciting things? I study here, you bring dinner to my house."

"I like having you here."

Her gaze dropped again. "I like being here. But…"

He understood all that the "but" implied. Commitment meant the loss of self. Parenting was joyless. The only happy person she'd had to model herself on was the carefree Aunt Julia. Jo was terrified that she'd become like her father if she took on the obligations of family.

"Forget I asked you to move in," Ryan said

recklessly. "How about if instead we plan a trip together? Let me prove we can have fun, throw off the shackles of daily life."

She looked wary but interested. "A trip?"

"Someplace neither of us have ever been. Someplace romantic."

"But...you have the kids over Christmas break," Jo said doubtfully. "And I can't miss school."

He didn't point out that she was *not* demonstrating the soul of an adventurer.

"Okay, we probably can't go to Paris." He thought. "When do you go back to school after Christmas break?"

"January seventh or eighth." She frowned. "I'm not sure. Something like that."

"All right. Melissa and Tyler fly home on the morning of the thirtieth. They start school on the second. So that gives us a week. New York City. We could take in Broadway shows, maybe ring in the new year in Times Square."

She made a "maybe" face.

Then it came to him. "No. You know where I've always wanted to visit? New Orleans. I want to see alligators outside the zoo. I want to walk through plantation houses and slave quarters—did I ever tell you I'm a Civil War buff? Imagine the French Quarter, with lacy wrought-iron balconies and narrow cobblestone streets and the haunting cry of a saxophone."

Instead of rubbing her arms, he caressed her. "Then there's Bourbon Street, where the party never ends." He made his voice a low rumble. "What do you say, pretty lady?"

Her smile tried to stay in hiding, but it crinkled the corners of her mouth and softened her eyes. "Do you mean it?" she murmured, as her face tilted up to his.

"Yeah, I mean it." He kissed her. Against her mouth, he whispered, "Are we on?"

This smile, he felt all the way to his toes.

"Mmm. I'll take you up on your challenge, handsome. You show me adventure, I'll concede we can have it together."

CHAPTER THIRTEEN

THE BOX from Jo's father arrived via UPS the same day Ryan's children were to fly in from Denver. Somebody in the house had set the parcel, perhaps twelve inches square and wrapped in brown paper, on the hall table. On her way out in response to Ryan's honk, Jo was glancing toward the Christmas tree in the living room that they had all decorated together when she saw it.

"Oh!" She stopped dead, staring at the package. Conflicting emotions flooded her, tingling in the fingers she squeezed into fists, keeping her paralyzed even when Ryan leaned on the horn again.

She wanted to take the box upstairs and open it *right now,* find out what her father had sent, what memories this gift might restore.

But, in a weird way, she was also afraid to open it. Maybe he'd sent things that would have no meaning to her, because she didn't remember her mother using them: a half-finished piece of needlework, or a cookbook.

Or what if photos didn't trigger any memories at all? What if she would never know, never remember, her mother any better than she did now?

This was her best chance—and she was scared to take it.

"Why are you just standing there?" Emma asked from the stairs. "That's Ryan's truck out there, you know." She craned her neck and peered out the narrow sidelight. "Another car's behind him and can't get by. He's starting forward. Hey! He isn't waiting for you!"

Jo tore her gaze from the package. "He's probably just going around the block."

"Why *are* you standing there?"

"I just noticed the package that must have come today, from my father."

"Oh. Yeah. It was on the doorstep. I brought it in. I'm sorry, I forgot to tell you about it." Emma crossed the entry hall and picked it up. "What's in it?"

"I...don't really know." With shocking ferocity, Jo wanted to snatch it out of her hands.

"It's kind of heavy." Mouth pursed, Emma shook it experimentally. "Like it's books or papers or something?" she said in disappointment.

"Photos and letters, maybe." Unless...was

there any chance her mother had kept a journal? One in which she wrote about the birth of her daughter, the dreams she'd held for her?

Oblivious to her turmoil, Emma asked, "Do you want me to take it upstairs and put it in your room?"

Jo stole an agonized glance outside. Ryan's truck hadn't reappeared, but it would any moment. She *couldn't* open the package now. He'd be hurt if she blew him off and didn't go to the airport with him to pick up Melissa and Tyler.

"Sure," she said, forcing a smile. "If you don't mind."

Emma shook her head. "Will you show me if your dad sent something cool?"

Jo nodded, caught a flash of red out of her peripheral vision and said, "I've got to go. Thanks, Emma. I'll see you." She grabbed a coat and fled out the front door just as he pulled up again between rows of parked cars.

"Didn't you hear me?" he asked when she got in. "I had to go around the block."

"I'm sorry." Jo fastened her seat belt. "I was on my way out the door when I saw that a package had come from my father."

He glanced at her sidelong as he maneuvered around a double-parked car. "Did you open it?"

"No, I didn't have time. Besides, I didn't want to just peek," she confessed. "You know?"

He reached out and squeezed her hand. "Yeah. Some things are meant to be savored."

Or cried over, Jo thought. She definitely wanted to be alone for this.

"Excited?" she asked, deliberately distracting him.

His grin flashed, as boyish as his son's. "You can't tell?"

"Oh, I kinda got the idea." She looked ahead at busy traffic as they neared the freeway on-ramp. "I hope they don't mind me being there."

"They liked you. Melissa asked about you the last time we talked."

"Really." Jo tried to hide her extreme skepticism about his implication that his almost-teenage daughter was dying to see her. Melissa had probably been hoping her dad would say he wasn't seeing that woman anymore.

"She wondered if you'd decided to keep that dream-catcher. Because if you did, she thought we should buy one for Emma for Christmas." His voice easily mimicked his daughter's. "Because it's, like, the *perfect* present for Emma." He resumed normal tones. "She wished she'd thought of it."

Surprised and moved, Jo said, "She did help me pick it out. Maybe it should be from the two of us."

"I think she'd like that." He was silent for a time, frowning ahead at a slowdown near the Mercer exit. "Wow," he said suddenly. "Half of me is excited that they're coming, and the rest of me is already in mourning because the visit is only for ten days and then I won't see them for almost six months. This visitation thing is awful. Sometimes I think it might be easier on all of us if I just got out of their lives."

Jo protested, "You know that isn't true."

"Isn't it?" he asked savagely, hands wrapped so tightly around the steering wheel she expected the plastic to crack. "Yeah, maybe it's good they know their father cares. But do you think they *want* to get on an airplane every couple of months and try to figure out how to accomplish a midair change of loyalties?"

"If I could have seen my mother, too," Jo said with absolute certainty, "I would have wanted to no matter what. Even if it was only for two weeks at a time."

Ryan's face changed. "Jo! I'm sorry. I'm whining, and there are plenty of people with worse problems than mine."

She bit her lip. "Just…remember. Your kids *do* want both parents."

His hand caught hers, squeezed and didn't let go. "Yeah. Okay."

They didn't say much more during the drive to Sea-Tac, south of the city and Boeing Field. Jo felt guilty. She should have listened, not belittled his misery. But she also believed with all her heart that Melissa and Tyler needed him. All she had to do was remember Tyler's unhappiness when he talked about the move and wishing he could live here in Seattle.

Melissa and Tyler's flight was on time. An attendant walked the two kids out and smiled when she saw them rush to their dad's outstretched arms.

They didn't notice Jo, standing back, until they'd started talking excitedly about Christmas and the presents they'd brought and had he put up lights yet and decorated the tree and…

"Oh." Tyler saw her. His grin didn't falter. "Hi! I didn't know you were coming."

Jo smiled. "I was here to keep your dad from pacing a rut in the carpet while he waited."

Behind her father's back, Melissa rolled her eyes, but in a friendly way. "You should have seen Tyler! He kept whining, 'When will we get there?' until I thought I'd scream!"

"Yeah, well, they're a matched pair," Jo said, while Ryan listened to Tyler. "What a pretty sweater, Melissa."

The eleven-year-old glanced down. The loosely woven, fluffy aqua sweater was paired with a tank top in the same color beneath it. "Oh. Thanks. Dad sent it for my birthday."

"Really?" Jo exaggerated her surprise. "He can pick out clothes for a girl?"

Hostility flashed briefly. "Hasn't he bought *you* anything yet?"

Jo didn't let her smile waver. "Not clothes. I haven't had a birthday since your dad and I met."

"Oh." Melissa looked down, her cheeks reddening. "Dad, um, actually always buys me cool stuff. Mom doesn't think so. She likes—I don't know—different things."

She smoothed the sweater. "Since we were coming here, I thought…"

Loyalties, switched midair. Jabbed by pity, Jo reached out and hugged Ryan's daughter, letting her go before she could stiffen or pull away.

"That was a nice thought," she said quietly, before turning to Ryan. "What say we go get the baggage?"

The kids continued to chatter while they waited for their suitcases to appear and then on the drive home about Christmas and the flight and how Mom wouldn't let them open presents from her before they left.

Tyler's excitement briefly dimmed. "Mom seemed really sad when she said goodbye. Didn't she, 'Lissa?"

His sister frowned. "I guess. Maybe because we won't be home for Christmas."

"Having your parents be divorced stinks sometimes, doesn't it?" Ryan asked. "I wish there was a way we could both have you at important times."

They nodded, subdued for a mile or two. Then Tyler burst out, "*Did* you put the lights up yet, Dad? Huh? 'Cuz I could help if you didn't."

"Oh, like *you* could help," his sister scoffed. "You couldn't reach anything."

Ryan grinned at Jo, who was laughing. Had she and Boyce bickered nonstop like this? Had *she* considered it her duty to squelch her little brother at every opportunity? Maybe sometime she'd ask him.

When she told him what was in the package from their father.

Remembering that it waited at home, she felt hot and cold. She wished she hadn't promised to have dinner at Ryan's, that she could go home, sit cross-legged on the bed in her room with the box in front of her and slowly peel back the flaps. At the very same time, she wished that she wasn't going home tonight at all, or better yet that the box of her mother's things was still a promise and not a reality waiting like a slow-ticking bomb in her room.

Why had so much had to change so fast? she wondered in sudden panic. Why couldn't she have gone along the way she was, content to hate her father? Happy with the independent life she'd chosen?

How had she come, in a dizzying four months, to pitying both her father and—of all people!—Aunt Julia?

Could she possibly be considering *marriage?* Not just marriage, but one that would make her a stepmother, even if only for a month or two a year?

Jo made herself take slow, even breaths. She wasn't married yet. *No need to freak.*

A deep rumble of laughter snatched at her, like a lifeline tossed to a woman fallen overboard. She turned her head, seeing the lines of amusement that carved Ryan's craggy face, the warmth in his gray eyes as he looked at his son, and her heart cramped.

Yes, she was thinking of marrying him. Scary as the thought was, she'd come to the point where she couldn't imagine not doing it.

However petty it made her, she just wished he didn't have children, that loving him wasn't so *complicated.*

LOCKING THE FRONT DOOR behind her and turning off the outdoor Christmas lights, Jo pretended she didn't hear someone moving quietly in the kitchen. Helen or Kathleen. She didn't want to talk to either, be offered a cup of herb tea, hear about their plans or even worries. Now that she was home, she felt as if she were being tugged upstairs by a force stronger than her fears.

Open me, the box whispered, for her ears alone.

She tiptoed to the stairs and made it half-way up before she saw movement below out of the corner of her eye. The deep auburn hair was unmistakable. It was Helen, who stopped, looked up with a face somehow distorted—and withdrew, surreptitiously, back into the kitchen.

Jo hesitated, her hand on the banister, until she understood that Helen had looked the way she did because she'd been crying. Her face had been blotchy and puffy.

Jo fought her longing to go on to her room and the magical, terrifying Pandora's box that awaited her.

Then she turned and went back downstairs, letting her footsteps fall naturally.

Helen was just turning off the lights in the kitchen. "Oh!" she said with false surprise. "Jo. You're home."

Jo hovered in the doorway. "Are you all right?"

Quiet for a moment, Helen stayed back in the darkness. "Yes." She sounded sad but calm. "I'm fine. Truly, Jo. Just…suffering one of those little blips that widows do. I'm ready to go to bed."

"You're sure?"

"Yes." Head high, Helen came toward her, not trying in the light coming from the hall to hide the ravages left by tears.

Jo backed out of the doorway. "I was just going up to bed myself."

"Did you lock?"

Jo nodded.

Helen passed her and started up the stairs, her back proudly straight. Following, Jo said, "Helen?"

Her housemate stopped at the top of the stairs without turning. "Yes?"

Before she could change her mind, Jo asked, "Do you ever regret having married Ben? Given how hard his illness was, and how sad you are now?"

Helen turned at last and looked at her, but blindly. Her face crumpled. "No." She drew a ragged breath. "No. Never. Not for a single moment." As tears wet her cheeks again, she seemed to focus on Jo with understanding and even compassion. "The joys are worth the sorrows, Jo. I promise. They are."

Jo nodded jerkily, wishing she could believe this grieving woman with her whole heart.

Helen went straight to the bathroom, then stopped in front of the door. "Do you mind?" she asked.

"No, go ahead. I'm going to…read for a while before I go to sleep anyway," Jo lied.

She closed her door and turned, for a moment not seeing the parcel. Panic and fury swept her. What had Emma done with it? She'd wake her up! She'd…

There it was, neatly centered on her desk. Jo's knees briefly buckled. How ridiculous, to get so emotional. If she'd had to wait until tomorrow, what difference would it make? She'd waited twenty years, hadn't she?

She took scissors from her desk drawer and the package to her bed, switching on the reading lamp that sat beside it. Jo hesitated, then tugged her sweater over her head. Pajamas first. She might as well be comfortable.

In a sacky T-shirt and flannel pj bottoms, feet bare, she settled in the middle of the bed. With the scissors, Jo neatly slit the tape, set down the scissors and took a deep breath. Her hands were shaking, she noticed with distant wonder, as she lifted the cardboard flaps.

On the very top lay a bundle of photos secured with a rubber band. Breath shallow, Jo picked it up and found herself looking at her mother.

A very young mother. Rhonda Dubray looked no more than nineteen or twenty. She wore shorts, a halter top and sandals. Long dark hair, parted down the middle, was pulled into a ponytail. Arms outstretched, she was balanced precariously on one foot on a driftwood log on a beach. Her laughing face looked uncannily like the one Jo saw every morning in the bathroom mirror.

In the next snapshot, she was younger yet. Jo had seen this one, in her aunt's photo albums. In it the sisters, dressed in Sunday best, leaned against each other, arms around each other's waists, heads tilted so they touched as they smiled at the camera. Rhonda was half a head taller than her slightly younger sister.

Other casual photos followed: Jo's mother playing a piano, her gaze fixed intently on the sheet music; holding an armful of cut roses, as if surprised coming in from the garden; and singing, clearly on stage at a coffee shop. In that one she was sitting, guitar balanced on her knees, the microphone close to her mouth. Her hair flowed loose and she wore some filmy white shirt with embroidery. Jo peered closely. A Mexican peasant blouse. Her mother looked like a young Joan Baez or Carly Simon.

A wedding photograph, in which Jo's absurdly young parents posed stiffly, her father in a dark suit and tie, her mother with a circlet of flowers around her head and wearing a simple white dress. The young man in the picture stared straight ahead, as if self-conscious, while the young woman's head was tilted just enough to let her look at her new husband's face.

Jo didn't start to cry until she reached the photo of her mother holding a baby, apparently in the hospital. Above the standard-issue faded blue gown, her dark hair was tangled around a face that glowed with delight and love as she gazed down at the infant in her arms.

Me, Jo realized. *That was me.*

She had an album on her shelf that she'd taken when she left home, one that held her school pictures as well as some her parents had taken of her and Boyce when they were little. A few included her mother.

But not this one. She had never seen this one.

Others followed of her mother with Jo at home, first as a baby, then as a toddler. There were lots of these, as if her father had been as eager as any new parent to freeze forever the stages of his small daughter's life. Tears wet her cheeks and kept falling as she understood that her parents had been proud. Of *her*.

Boyce came into their lives. A snapshot showed a three-year-old Jo making a horrible face at her new baby brother while her mother laughed in the background. Jo's first day of kindergarten was immortalized in a slightly different pose than the one in her album—but there she stood, small for her age, hair pigtailed so tight it must have hurt, legs skinny beneath a red dress she knew her mother had sewed.

How funny. Jo frowned in space. She'd forgotten that, but suddenly she had a vision of herself standing beside her mother, who was working on her sewing machine. Jo was watching the needle flash, up and down, up and down, as the fabric she had picked out slipped beneath it. Mom had made a pinafore, too, but Jo had refused to wear it the morning of kindergarten. Mom hadn't minded. She'd said, "You look so pretty in red, I don't blame you."

Her voice was as clear as if she were standing beside the bed right now. She sounded… affectionate, proud.

She'd walked Jo to school that first day, all the way to her classroom door. Then, when Jo froze outside, suddenly scared to go in, Mom had given her a gentle, loving push.

Other images followed, other clips Jo's memory had stored until this day. A fall she'd taken from a swing set, and the fright in her mother's eyes as she helped her up and brushed her off and took her home to bandage her scrapes. A fight with Boyce, and Mom's disappointment in her, more effective than any raised voice. A piano lesson, her sitting on the bench beside her mother, Mom gently guiding her hands. They'd owned a piano, Jo suddenly knew, an old-fashioned upright. Her fingers recalled it, the rosewood cover she lifted, the faintly yellowing ivory keys, the faded linen runner that went over the top. What had happened to it? she wondered. It disappeared from her memory along with her mother, and must have gone about the same time. Had her father sold it because it reminded him too much of his dead wife?

But she didn't linger on the piano, because she heard a song, low and haunting. Nothing she knew or could put words to, just a beautiful, lilting impression. Her mother sitting on the edge of her bed, tucking her in. Singing to her.

The box held letters, some of which she read, some of which she kept to read another day. A small book labeled *My Child* held proud notes of when Josephine Dubray had smiled and rolled over and sat up and walked. Small versions of her school kindergarten and first-grade pictures were glued inside. The entries ended there; nothing had been written for second grade, not even her teacher's name. Jo didn't remember it, either. Her mother had died in August that year.

A jewelry box held a few good necklaces and bracelets, some of which pinged at her memory and others of which weren't familiar. But with them were her mother's wedding and engagement rings, gold, the small ruby flanked with tiny diamonds a testament to their youth and optimism when Jo's parents said, "I do." Jo slipped the rings on her finger, and found they fit perfectly.

Her mother had died at thirty, only a year older than Jo was now. Her death had been

sudden, the result of carelessness. She'd been
looking over her shoulder when she stepped
into the street in front of an oncoming car.
Or so Jo had been told; she'd suffered enough
nightmares just from imagining the thud, her
mother being thrown over the hood and into
the windshield so hard her head cracked it.

So much had ended that day. The family
photos, the proud entries in *My Child,* the
piano lessons and the dresses sewn just for
her. Jo would have given anything to have had
her mother look that day before she crossed
the street.

She might have had her mother at her wedding.

Squeezing a pillow convulsively, burying
her wet face in it, Jo thought in pain and exultation, *But at least now I remember.*

THE PHONE RANG that night, well after Ryan
had said good-night to the kids. It wasn't so
late that he should have been alarmed, but
gut instinct told him the news wasn't going
to be good.

Jo, was his first, disquieted thought. Her
mood had been…odd this afternoon and
evening. Maybe because of the box of her
mother's things waiting, unopened, for her at

home. Had something her father sent upset her so much she needed to talk?

He grabbed the phone on the third ring. "Hello."

"Ryan?" his ex-wife asked, as if she didn't know his voice.

"Wendy." He should have had one of the kids call her to let her know they'd arrived safely. Of course she'd worry. "Melissa and Tyler got here fine," he told her. "They're babbling about the presents you helped them buy. Tyler is sorry I've already put up Christmas lights, because he wanted to help me."

"They're excited about Christmas." Strain thinned her voice. "Ryan…"

Something tightened inside him. He'd heard her sound this way before.

Ryan, I'm not happy. Her face lifted in sad appeal, as if he should sympathize. *You work so much, and we never go dancing or do anything romantic. You hardly touch me anymore! This is so terribly hard to say, but… Ryan, I want a divorce.*

He'd been ashamed of his surge of relief. Both emotions had been swamped in the next second by his terror of losing his children.

Now he felt some of that same fear. She was going to say something he didn't want to hear, something that threatened his relationship with Melissa and Tyler.

He imagined her breathless voice coming faster and faster once she'd gotten past the difficulty of starting.

Ronald has this wonderful new job in Tokyo. I just wanted you to know, because of course the kids won't be able to see you next summer. Maybe not for a couple of years, because it's too expensive and anyway we want to immerse them in a new culture. Oh, she would feel sorry for him, but not so much that she would tell her new husband that, no, they couldn't take his children halfway around the world.

He shifted the phone to his other hand and wiped his sweaty palm on his jeans. "What?"

"Ryan, Ronald and I have been having… problems. He didn't understand what taking on children meant."

Ryan listened blankly. How could anyone not know what having kids involved?

"You remember what it was like when we were first married. How wrapped up we were in each other."

He mumbled something she must have taken for assent, because she hurried on.

"We…we need some time *without* Melissa

and Tyler. I know this is truly dreadful, but… can they stay with you? At least for the rest of this school year?"

For a moment, he felt…nothing. Her request was so unexpected, so far from what he'd feared. Ryan waited until it sank in, shimmering beads of water blotted by a cloth.

She wanted to give up the kids. She'd chosen her new husband over them. What would this do to them?

"If they stay," he said in a cold voice, "they won't be going back to you, Wendy. This will be their last move."

A sob preceded her whisper, "I know you'll be better for them, but… This is so hard!"

Hard? He clenched his teeth to keep from a savage response. She was abandoning her children, and it was "hard." For her, of course.

"Have you told them?" he asked.

"No." Her voice was thick with tears. "I needed to talk to you first. To find out if you wanted them."

Wanted them? She must know how desperately he had missed them, how hungry he was for every letter, every email, every phone call.

Or maybe she didn't. Maybe her own emotions didn't run deep enough to allow her to understand his.

"Yeah," he said rawly. "I want them."

The sounds of muffled crying came through the line. At last she blew her nose. With a form of dignity, she said, "You've always been a better parent than I have. I do know that."

He was silent for a moment. "I pushed you to have kids. I guess I shouldn't have."

"I'm going to miss them so terribly!"

"Are you?"

"Yes! Why don't you believe me? I love Melissa and Tyler! I just..." she faltered. "I need to save my marriage."

"More than you need to be their mother."

"It's not that simple!" she cried. "Are you trying to make me feel worse?"

Me. That's all she ever thought about. If he hadn't been so young when they married, he would have noticed.

But then, he wouldn't have Tyler and Melissa.

"Do you want to tell them yourself?" he asked, knowing the answer.

"Would you?" she asked meekly. "Then I'll call. But...oh, I think it will come better from you."

Yeah. Of course it would. He'd had to tell them about the divorce, too.

How did you say, *Mommy doesn't want you anymore?*

"We'll call you tomorrow," he said harshly, and hung up before she could beg again for his understanding.

Because she wasn't going to get it. A part of him was rejoicing—he didn't have to put Melissa and Tyler back on the plane. He would tuck them in at night, chauffeur them to dance and soccer, go to parent-teacher meetings, deal with teenage sulks when they came in the next year or two. *His children were home to stay.*

But rage gripped him nonetheless, for their sake. No matter how badly he wanted them, how would they live with the knowledge that their mother didn't? Would there always be a hollow place inside them? How could she do this to them?

How would he tell them?

He turned out the lights and went upstairs, his steps heavy and slow. Light from the hall streamed in on Tyler, sound asleep, a tattered stuffed dinosaur tucked under his arm. He looked so young, no more than the five-year-old he'd been before the divorce.

Melissa slept more restlessly. She'd already thrown off her quilt and twisted the sheet around herself. Ryan gently untangled the sheet and pulled the quilt over her again, then eased out of her room as she sighed and turned over.

Tomorrow night, he guessed, they would cry themselves to sleep.

It wasn't until he looked at himself in his bathroom mirror that horror hit him.

Oh, no! New Orleans.

He was going to prove that he and Jo could have fun as a couple, that they could be romantic and spontaneous and adventurous. That week was his one chance to convince her that life with him included more than obligations and dull routines. It was his chance to woo her, to persuade her that *he* was her greatest adventure.

Kathleen would take care of Melissa and Tyler—but how could he leave them right away, even for a week, when their mother had just dumped them?

Clutching the edges of the sink to keep himself standing, Ryan let a ragged, desperate moan escape, the closest he could allow himself to a howl of despair.

How could he look his kids in the eye, say,

"See you, guys, Jo and I are off on our vacation!" and depart for a romantic, theoretically carefree getaway?

How could he not, when it meant losing the woman he loved?

And he'd claimed not to understand Wendy. Ironic, wasn't it?

The difference between him and his ex-wife was that he knew, from the roaring anguish in his chest, what sacrifice had to be made.

And his children wouldn't be the ones making it.

CHAPTER FOURTEEN

"I NEED TO TALK to you two," Ryan said.

Despite his best effort, something in his voice scared the kids. Tyler, who had been about to set his cereal bowl in the kitchen sink, turned with it still clutched in his hand. Melissa closed the refrigerator and backed against it as if facing an attacking Rottweiler.

"What?" she asked.

He nodded toward the living room. "Let's go sit down."

They sat next to each other on the couch, a rare event. Ryan lowered himself to the coffee table facing them, close enough to touch.

"It's Mom, isn't it?" Melissa said. "Is she sick or something?"

"No. She's not sick." Searching for inspiration that hadn't come during the night, Ryan looked down at his hands, splayed on his knees. "She and I did talk last night, though, after you'd gone to bed."

Melissa blanched. Tyler's face was pinched, his eyes wide. Neither said a word.

"I guess she and your stepdad have been having some problems."

His daughter gave a tiny nod. "They argue sometimes."

"The thing is," he drew a deep breath, "we decided it would be best if you two live with me."

Tyler seemed frozen, his mouth half-open, his eyes unblinking. Melissa was the one to scoot sideways, close enough to her brother so that their shoulders touched.

"She knew before she sent us, didn't she? That's why she was so sad."

"I guess she was thinking about it," Ryan admitted. "I didn't know until last night that she would consider letting you stay with me."

They said nothing.

"I hope you both know there's nothing in the world I want as much as to have you living here, with me. It's been killing me having you so far away. The trouble is, now you're going to be a long ways from your mom instead."

In a small voice, Melissa asked, "Will we visit her?"

He hadn't asked, had no idea. "I assume so," he said. "Your mom and I haven't discussed that yet. She was pretty upset. You're right. She's sad."

Tyler unfroze. "Will we go to school here and everything?"

"Yep. Your mom will have to send your stuff. The first day of school, we'll go down and enroll you here."

"Can I be in the same class with Chad?"

Ryan exhaled. "I don't know. We can ask." *Or beg, if he had to.* "Your mom is going to want to talk to you tonight. You can think of questions to ask her."

They nodded like automatons, apparently numb.

"Once you've had time to take this all in, we'll have to talk about rules here. What I expect from you, what you expect from me. We'll look into getting you signed up for whatever you want—dance, music lessons, whatever interests you."

He expected Melissa to demand instantly that she have her own bedroom. Instead, she put her arm around Tyler.

"Mom didn't want us, did she?"

He hated to lie to them, but some truths shouldn't be told.

"I think your stepfather didn't want you. Or your mom thinks, for whatever reason, that the problems she's having with him will go away if you're not there all the time. After being divorced once, she really wants to make this marriage work."

The subtext couldn't be hidden: *she wants the marriage to work more than she wants to have you with her.* Even Tyler at only eight was smart enough to understand that much.

"We'll have to buy stuff for you guys, too. More bedding, posters for the walls…uh, whatever your mother doesn't send."

Still his often pouty eleven-year-old daughter amazed and impressed him by not saying rudely, "I can't share a bedroom with *him!*"

He continued, "Melissa, if you'll be patient, I'm going to open up the rest of the attic and create another bedroom. When I'm done, you can choose which one you want, since you're the oldest."

"But…what if Mom wants us back?" Tyler asked, voice trembling. "And you've gone to all that work and everything?"

Another truth had to be told. This one might be unwelcome, but Ryan would not let them live with any more uncertainty.

"You won't be going back to live with her." He looked them in the eye, made sure they saw the steel that underlay those words. "I won't lose you again, and I won't have you two put through another move. Having to make friends again, remember what bed you're waking up in, know who you can count on. You'll probably visit your mother sometimes, but your home will be here. For good."

"Oh." Tyler looked shell-shocked, Melissa only slightly less so.

Ryan dropped to his knees and held out his arms. "Come here."

They flung themselves at him, burrowing against him, clutching him so tightly it hurt, their arms overlaying each other. He hadn't cried in a long time, but his eyes were wet right now, blurring the sight of their heads against his chest, Tyler's darker than his sister's.

They spent the day prowling the Northgate mall, partly to give themselves something to do. Tyler picked out new sheets and a comforter for his twin bed. Melissa didn't know what she wanted for hers. Tyler asked for a Mariners pennant to hang on the wall, "Since I live here now," he said firmly. "In *Seattle*."

Ryan had the guilty feeling that he was spending money as if doing so would patch emotional wounds, but he wanted to believe that instead, with a few new possessions to make the bedroom *theirs,* he was helping to root them, to convince them that this really would be home.

Melissa didn't pick out anything, Ryan noted. Of course, her room would take him several weeks if not months to carve out of unfinished attic, especially if he added a dormer, but he guessed her disinterest stemmed instead from her tighter bond with her mother. This was going to be harder on her. Tyler and Ryan had always been buddies, nothing complex to their relationship. But Melissa...she *looked* like her mother. She identified with her.

And now, at a particularly difficult age, on the brink of puberty, she'd been abandoned by her.

A man who rarely had violent tendencies, right about now Ryan would have liked to kill Wendy. Or make her sit down, look Melissa in the eyes and explain why she didn't have it in her to be the mother her daughter needed so badly.

By evening, he was exhausted. The strain of maintaining an upbeat front all day was showing. The kids got quieter and quieter while he got jollier and jollier. He couldn't seem to stop himself.

He called Wendy for them, handed Melissa

the phone and left the kitchen to give them the privacy to say anything to their mother. Out in the living room, he paced, able to hear only a low murmur of voices.

The conversation was a lot shorter than it should have been. They came into the living room with the same pinched expressions they'd had that morning, the same stiff, mechanical way of moving. "I'm sorry," he said simply, and held out his arms again.

With Melissa nestled under one arm and Tyler under the other, he kissed the tops of their heads. "Did you have a good talk with your mom?"

Sure they had, he mocked himself. *They just* loved *discussing why, after sending them off to visit Dad for Christmas, their mother had decided she didn't want them to come home again.*

Tyler shook his head. "She just kept crying and saying she was sorry."

In a small voice, Melissa asked, "Doesn't she love us at all?"

He explained the best he could. He concluded, "She does love you. A whole lot. As much as she can. But sometimes I think she isn't completely grown up herself. It's one of the things that led to our divorce. I needed her to be completely adult, a mother and wife, and she still wanted to be twenty years old and fun-loving. She *is* fun, which is one of the great things about your mother, but it can also be really frustrating."

Tyler's head bobbed against him. "She was always forgetting stuff she'd *promised* to do. Like, she was supposed to go on a school field trip to this TV studio, only she didn't show up and my teacher had to find someone else at the last minute." His humiliation and disappointment could be heard even in this flat recitation.

Melissa stiffened. "She *explained!* She *told* you she didn't forget, she just had an appointment and then traffic was really bad and she couldn't get there in time. Things happen!"

"She forgot!" Tyler yelled.

"She didn't!" Melissa's voice choked with tears. "You're trying to make her sound bad!"

"Hey! Hey!" Ryan shook them gently. "Enough! It doesn't matter whether she forgot. People *do* forget things that are important to other people, and we can forgive them. Okay?"

They went quiet and sullen. Finally Ryan got them to agree to watch a TV show they usually both enjoyed, and, leaving them sitting as far as they could get from each other in the living room, he went to the kitchen to call Jo. A cowardly part of him wanted to put off giving her the news, but he wouldn't let himself.

"Hey," she said, sounding pleased to hear from him. "Did you have a good day with the kids?"

"No. Actually, today sucked." He heard the exhaustion and anger in his voice. "Any chance you could come over? We can talk after the kids are in bed."

She agreed to come and didn't question him, for which he was intensely grateful. The doorbell rang just as he was ushering Melissa and Tyler upstairs to bed.

"Jo must be here," he said.

Their glances at each other crackled with unspoken communication, a sign that they had restored a semblance of solidarity.

"We'll go brush our teeth," Melissa said. "Won't we, Tyler?"

Her brother nodded, but his expression became anxious. "You'll come and say goodnight, won't you, Dad?"

He ruffled Tyler's hair. "Of course I will. Now, go on."

Ryan let Jo in. "Sorry to be so slow. I was just sending the kids up to get ready for bed."

She unwound her scarf. "I'm too early."

"Nope." The anguish that hadn't left him since last night twisted in his chest. "You're never here soon enough for me," he muttered, just before he kissed her.

Her lips held the chill of a night that might bring snow. They warmed quickly under his, and she sighed.

How was he going to live without her?

She was the one to ease back, her eyes searching his. "It's only been one day, and you missed me."

"You could say that." He sounded ragged.

Jo framed his face with her hands and stood on tiptoe to press a sweet kiss on his mouth, a complete contrast to the moment before.

"I missed you, too," she said softly. "Last night, after I looked at my mother's things, I wanted so much to talk to you."

In his own troubles, he'd forgotten the package from her father waiting for her at home. Ryan felt like scum.

"Talk to me now." He smiled ruefully when they both heard the voice call him from upstairs. "Well, in a minute." He nodded toward the kitchen. "Get yourself a cup of coffee if you want. I'll be back."

"Okay." She smiled. "Go. You're wanted."

Upstairs he found the kids in their own beds, Melissa already with her light turned off and her back to the door. Ryan went to her first, bending to kiss her cheek and murmur softly, "I love you, 'Lissa."

Her arms shot out for a quick, fierce hug. "I love you, too, Daddy," she whispered.

He smiled, hiding the pain he felt for her, and smoothed first the hair back from her face and then her covers over her shoulders. "I'll see you in the morning. Hey, maybe there'll be snow."

"I want it on Christmas."

"This might be the year. You never know."

Tyler still sat bolt upright, bedside lamp on. "You're not going anywhere, are you, Dad?"

"Nope." He sat on the edge of the bed. "I wouldn't leave you and Melissa alone. Your sister isn't old enough to be in charge yet."

Tyler muttered, "She already *thinks* she is."

"I heard that!" his sister snapped from the other bed.

Ryan and his son exchanged wry grins. "Okay," Ryan said, "scoot down. Time to go to sleep."

He arranged Tyler's covers, made sure his dinosaur was within reach and turned out the light before leaning down to kiss his forehead.

"I love you."

Tyler nodded. "Dad?"

"Um-hm?"

"I'm *glad* we're staying," he said with astonishing force. "I want to live here, with you. I hated Denver."

Melissa kept quiet this time. Ryan said, "I know you hadn't made friends. I'm glad you still have some here. And you know what?"

"What?" his son asked.

"I know you'll miss your mom, but *I'm* glad you're staying, too." He kissed Tyler's forehead, too. "Good night," he said softly.

From habit he left their door open about six inches and the bathroom light on so that they weren't in complete darkness.

Outside, he stood for a moment listening, but heard nothing. Tyler would have wanted him to dry his tears, but Melissa was old enough to prefer to cry alone, into her pillow. He had to respect that.

Tiredly Ryan started downstairs. Time for phase two in the rotten day.

In the kitchen, Jo turned to face him, setting down her coffee cup. "Okay. What was so awful about your day?"

No reprieve. "More than a day. The past twenty-four hours."

Creases formed in her brow. "But I'd barely left you twenty-four hours ago."

"Wendy called." Ryan pulled a stool up to the tiled counter. Fittingly, Jo stayed on the other side of it, waiting. Ryan was blunt. "She doesn't want the kids back. They're going to stay with me."

Except for a widening of the eyes, Jo didn't react. Slowly she said, "Aren't you glad?"

"Yeah!" he said explosively. "For myself. Maybe for Melissa and Tyler, long term. In the short term, they're hurting. Your mother died. Imagine if she'd left you on purpose."

Jo flinched, and he cursed his big mouth. "I'm sorry…."

"No." She shook her head. "You're right. Poor Melissa! That day at the Pike Place Market, she talked about her mother all the time. This is going to be hardest on her, isn't it?"

"I think so." Ryan rotated his head, trying to ease tension that gripped his neck and shoulders. "Tyler just told me he was glad he was staying, that he hated Denver. He might have just been trying to get in good with me because he's scared and now he depends on me, but I don't think so. He's seemed unhappy ever since they moved."

Jo nodded. "I noticed. I think after Thanksgiving he didn't want to go back."

"Yeah." Ryan released a long breath. "Here's the problem. You and I are supposed to leave for New Orleans in eight days."

Supposed to.

He saw in her eyes that she understood.

"Oh, no," she said.

"Yeah." Ryan tried to smile, felt his mouth twist. "I know Kathleen would take Melissa and Tyler, and normally that would be fine, great, but…"

Jo gave him a fierce stare. "But you can't leave them."

Confused, he said, "No. They're reeling from the news that Mom doesn't want them. I'm assuring them they're mine for good, that I won't let them be yanked around anymore. I don't see how I can say, 'Yeah, I know you're sad, and we can talk about it when I get home,' and go off on a trip. No matter how much I want to go."

"Of course you can't!" Jo exclaimed. "Ryan, did you think I wouldn't understand?"

No. What he'd thought was that she would understand all too well.

His life had just changed. He was no longer a free-and-easy bachelor. Now he was a single father, and his kids would always have to come first.

He didn't say anything. At least, not soon enough.

Her eyes narrowed. "You did. You thought I'd be mad."

"No." His voice sounded strange, not his own. "What I think is that I'm blowing it with you. I'm proving your point. Obligations do get in the way of romance and adventure. Mine are. I can't help it, Jo. I love you, but I have to put them first right now."

She came around the counter at last. "Of course you do," she said with astonishing gentleness, and, as he swiveled on the stool to face her, wrapped her arms around him.

Ryan buried his face in her hair and held her, too. She smelled wonderful, like Christmas, as if she'd been hanging fir boughs and candy canes. She murmured his name, her voice comforting.

"It's okay," she said against his neck. "It's okay."

When they finally disentangled, he knew he must look awful.

"I'll, uh, cancel our reservations."

Jo nodded and backed away, her expression suddenly...shuttered.

Now what? he wondered. Would she start making excuses when he called? And what was he supposed to do? Hire a babysitter every Friday and Saturday night, as Wendy had wanted to do when they were still married?

"We can go another time," he said, knowing they wouldn't.

She nodded again and smiled meaninglessly.

She was slipping away, sawdust through his fingers, Ryan thought with panic. He'd known she would.

"Your mother." He grabbed for any lifeline. "You were going to tell me about what your father sent."

"Oh." Jo shook her head. "Just old photos and letters and some jewelry. It was...nice. I'll tell you about it another time."

She'd chosen the same words, the same fiction: *another time.* A hazy future that somehow would never happen.

Ryan wanted to fall to his knees and beg,

"Don't leave me." He wanted to pound his fist into a wall.

He did none of those things. He sat on the stool and said, "You don't have to go."

"You look tired."

He shook his head. "Not sleepy."

"Um…Ryan?"

Made warier by her tentative tone, he said, "Yeah?"

"You'll have to take a loss when you cancel the tickets, won't you?"

Taken by surprise, he said, "You mean, will I lose money? Uh… Yeah. I guess. It doesn't matter." Right now, a few hundred bucks seemed like the most trivial thing he had to lose.

"Well, I was thinking." She knotted her fingers in front of her.

"About?"

"This is maybe a terrible idea."

Patience deflated, he asked, "*What* is a terrible idea?"

Jo flushed. "I was just thinking…what if we went anyway? Only, we took the kids. It wouldn't be the same, but we might have fun, and, well, it might be a distraction for them. You know?"

Ryan stared at her. "Take Melissa and Tyler."

"Maybe you don't want to vacation with me and them," she said hastily. "Make them think…you know. That's okay, Ryan. I understand. You could just use the reservations to take them on a trip."

Stunned, he shook his head. "You wouldn't mind taking a trip with my kids?"

"I'd rather we had the romantic week we planned," she said frankly. "But, under the circumstances, going anyway might be better than canceling.

"Melissa and I could share my room and Tyler would be with you. Maybe one night we could get a babysitter and go out? Or send them on a tour while we go to a nightclub? I've been reading about New Orleans, and I'll bet they'd love the voodoo tour of the cemetery at night."

Dazed, Ryan said, "I think that's safe to say."

"Um…" Jo backed a few more steps toward the door. "Let me know. I'd better go now. I'm sorry, Ryan." Her voice was soft, infused with compassion. "But glad, too, because I know how much you love them. You'll be a wonderful parent."

"Thank you," he said numbly. "You're leaving?"

"Shouldn't I?" Her eyes were huge and dark.

"No." Somehow he got to his feet and stumbled toward her. "Don't go, Jo. Please don't go."

She met him halfway and let herself be folded into his arms. He leaned on her as much as held her.

"Oh, Ryan." She rained tiny kisses on his cheek and neck.

"I was so afraid," he whispered hoarsely. "Jo, if you mean it, I'd love to go to New Orleans with you and the kids. It'll mean a lot to them. I love you, Jo."

"I think," her voice wavered, "that I love you, too."

They stood there a long time, held in each others' arms.

ON CHRISTMAS EVE, miraculously, snow started to fall. Tiny flakes at first, just a few scattered so far apart Jo thought she was imagining them as she knelt on the window seat and searched the dark sky. But the flakes thickened and swirled until she was sure.

"It's snowing!" she called in delight.

"It's snowing?" voices asked from all over the house. "It's really snowing?"

Soon Ginny knelt at her side, and Kathleen looked out the other window. Upstairs Emma crowed with excitement. Even Pirate crouched beside Ginny, staring out with apparent fascination, reaching out once as if to touch those odd white bits floating downward only to be frustrated by the glass.

They all went to bed at midnight, the adults—Jo, at least—as excited as the kids. Jo had never seen a white Christmas and had played in snow only a few times as a child, when her parents drove up to the Sierras. Emma had a sled, down in the basement. Would there be enough snow to use it on a grassy slope over at Cowen Park, or on a hilly street blocked at the bottom?

Screams of joy woke her at dawn. Her bedroom door burst open. "Look! Look out your window!" Emma cried.

Six inches or more had fallen during the night. Jo pressed her nose to the cold glass and gazed in awe at a cityscape transformed. The sidewalks and streets were white, untouched yet by tire tracks, and snow lay along the dark gnarled branches of the old trees and in heavy blankets on rooftops. The ugly junipers in front had become huge white sculptures, and even the cars were veiled by smooth white. The snow still fell, silent and slow.

"Ohh," she breathed.

Emma turned and grinned at her with pure, childish jubilation. "This is so cool!"

"Is there enough snow so that we can sled today?"

"If there isn't, there will be. By the time we open presents and have breakfast."

Presents. It was Christmas morning.

"Let's wake everybody," Jo said impulsively. Then she laughed. "Assuming your screaming didn't already wake them."

The rest of the household was emerging from bedrooms. Ginny was as thrilled as Emma, while the women yawned and shrugged into bathrobes. Infected by the girls' excitement, Jo felt like a kid, not one of the adults. She didn't even know why. It wasn't as if Santa had brought her anything.

She did have presents under the tree, though. Everyone did. The mound had grown through the past week and spilled across the living room floor. Now Santa's gifts for Ginny and Emma, magically delivered during the night, were heaped atop the rest.

Ginny stopped halfway across the living room, her mouth open in a circle of wonder. "A Barbie house," she whispered. "Mommy, Santa brought me a Barbie house."

Jo happened to know what that big pink plastic dollhouse had set back her mom, who could ill afford it. But she saw on Helen's face that every penny, every scrimp to make up for the cost, had been worth it.

"Let's plug in the lights," someone said, and soon the tall Noble fir sparkled with multicolored lights, and the outdoor ones strung on the eaves glowed in muted jewel tones in the falling snow.

"Are we waiting for Ryan and the kids?" Helen asked.

Kathleen shook her head. "They're going to open most of their presents at home, then come over after breakfast. We'll open the ones from them then."

Most under the tree were for the girls, of course. They ripped, tossed aside paper and bows and squealed with delight. Jo loved her precious bars of soap and intriguing little bottle of lemon-verbena shampoo homemade by Kathleen. Her brother had sent her an old leather-bound edition of *Pride and Prejudice,* one of her favorite books. She kept stroking the cover even as she opened other presents: a sweater, nubby and soft, from Helen, a mug that said, *Librarians Are Novel Lovers,* from Emma, who cackled at the cleverness, and a cute bookmark from Ginny.

For Ginny, Jo had bought a pile of her favorite children's books, and was pleased when they distracted her enough that she forgot the Barbie house.

Emma reached for her package from Jo, who shook her head. "Nope. You have to wait until your cousins get here. Melissa and I picked that out together."

"When will they get here?" Emma demanded.

"Maybe they're still sound asleep," Helen suggested.

"They can't be!" Emma exclaimed. "It's *Christmas!*"

No, they couldn't be. They arrived not half an hour later, stamping their feet and bringing in the front door a wave of cold air and a flurry of snow. Everybody babbled as they removed layers of parkas and boots and mittens. Jo got a cold kiss on the cheek and a warm grin before Ryan helped to carry their gifts into the living room.

More ripping, more cries of pleasure, followed. Ryan seemed to love the print Jo had bought him of a Shaker staircase, stark, simple and astonishingly beautiful. He gave her a necklace, two shades of gold that met at her throat in a V set with a topaz. Emma cried when she opened her dream-catcher and hugged first Jo, then Melissa.

At last everyone dispersed to get dressed for sledding.

Ryan had brought two, an old-fashioned wooden sled on metal runners and a giant plastic saucer. Bundled against the cold, they set off down the street pulling the sleds. By this time, everyone in the neighborhood had turned on outside lights, and Christmas trees shone through front windows like joyous beacons.

They found a neighborhood hill where others were already sledding. Jo went down tucked between Ryan's knees, swooshing on the tracks packed by other sleds. The cold air stung her eyes and falling snow blurred to each side as she laughed and clung to the sides and felt Ryan's arms enclosing her. At the bottom they glided to a stop, the voices above sounding tiny and far away.

"That was lovely," Jo said in complete satisfaction, leaning back for a moment against his solid body.

"Yeah." His voice was a rumble in her ear. "I think this is the perfect Christmas."

"Um-hm."

"Watch out!" someone screamed behind them, and they tumbled off the sled just as it was knocked aside by Ryan's kids, spinning on the plastic saucer and giggling helplessly.

When it came to a stop, the kids were facing Ryan and Jo.

"Isn't this *fun?*" Tyler exclaimed, his face alight.

Picking herself up and brushing off the snow, Jo said, meaning it, "I don't think I've ever had so much fun."

"You want to go down together?" Tyler asked. "*I* could steer."

"You don't want him to," his sister warned.

But Jo laughed. "I would love to go down with you. Come on." She held out a gloved hand. "Let's beat them up the hill."

Pulling the saucer, giggling, they fled under a bombardment of snowballs. On the way up, they watched as Helen and Ginny tore down, the little girl looking delighted and terrified at the same time, her mother fiendish as she wielded the ropes guiding the sled. At the top, they let Emma take the saucer next, while Kathleen assured everyone she would wait her turn.

"I'm in no hurry."

"You mean, you're chicken," Jo accused.

"Chicken, chicken, chicken!" Emma yelled all the way down the hill, until she crashed into the snow-buried curb and rolled into a drift.

"Is being chicken so bad?" Kathleen asked plaintively, before her brother arrived, handed her the rope to the sled and said evilly, "We'll watch."

Her last look at him was slit-eyed. He nonetheless cheerfully gave her a big push to get her started.

Laughing with the others as Kathleen soared down the hill, her scream trailing behind like the whistle of a train diminishing into the distance, Jo thought, *This* is *the perfect Christmas*.

She wished it could last forever. That tomorrow's dawn wouldn't bring a return to sulky teenagers and money worries and decisions about an uncertain future.

Why couldn't every day be as uncomplicated and joyous as this one?

CHAPTER FIFTEEN

THE LAST NOTES of the sax wailed, a sad refrain somehow infused with hope, fading, fading.

In the hush as the saxophonist lowered his gleaming instrument, Tyler looked up. "They're not going to quit, are they, Dad? Huh? They'll keep playing, won't they?"

Ryan smiled over his head at Jo. "I don't think they're ready to quit yet."

Around them, the crowd, mostly standing, waited patiently for music. The Preservation Hall Jazz Band, consisting of seven middle-aged men in dark suits, sat on the stage at the front of the small rustic room in a Creole Mansion on St. Peter Street. A few chairs around the outside let older folks sit, or children like Tyler stand higher to see the stage. No drinks were served here, no food. The crowd came only for the music.

Melissa was more restive, Tyler fascinated. Jo's feet were beginning to hurt after a long day spent at the aquarium and zoo. But the music was gorgeous, ranging from blues to upbeat horns weaving melodies that captured the audience. In the back, couples danced. The rest of the crowd clapped to the rhythm. The sets lasted only forty-five minutes, she knew; she could hold out that long until a late dinner.

They ate afterward at the Louisiana Pizza Kitchen, already a favorite, where the pizza didn't taste much like the rubbery fare of the chain restaurants back home, and the wraps were divine. Tyler chattered about the music and how he wanted to start a band as soon as he was allowed.

"I want to play the trumpet like that man tonight," he declared. "Did you see the way his cheeks puffed out? He blew so hard!"

Ryan told him about Dizzy Gillespie, whose cheeks had swelled and thinned like balloons because of a lifetime of blowing into a trumpet.

"That's what'll happen to you," Melissa said. "*Your* cheeks will get so huge they'll sag when there isn't any air in them!"

"I don't care!" Tyler insisted. He took a huge bite of pizza, which puffed his cheeks like a chipmunk's, then grinned cherubically at his irritating big sister.

Melissa turned pointedly to Jo. "That white gator at the zoo was so weird. Like a ghost."

"Are we going to do a swamp tour tomorrow?" Tyler asked eagerly. "So we can see alligators just swimming around? Huh, Dad?"

"You know we are!" Melissa snapped. "Why do you keep asking?"

Jo reached out and gently touched her hand. "Tired?"

The girl hesitated and nodded. "I'm glad it's not hot, like everyone says it is in the summer."

"Me, too," Jo admitted. "One hundred degrees would do me in."

Stomachs full, they ambled slowly the half-dozen blocks to their hotel on Dumaine Street. The sidewalks were empty, the alleys and doorways shadowy and dark. Overhead light spilled from open French doors onto balconies, and laughter and music burst from the doorways of restaurants as they passed. Having just read this tidbit, Jo told the kids that the streets were paved with the stones used for ballast in ships in the city's early days.

The hotel was exquisite, an 1850s mansion restored to opulent perfection. The rooms all looked out on an interior cobbled courtyard with a swimming pool gleaming deep turquoise at one end and at the other a fountain splashing day and night among lush foliage that seemed untouched by winter.

Tonight was warm enough that Jo consented to putting on her bathing suit and taking the kids down for a dip.

"I'm going to be lazy and lie here and watch the news," Ryan said. "If nobody minds."

Jo made a face at him. "You are lazy."

"Hey." He grinned. "How can you say that? We've been walking all day long! And you made me go to the zoo when I really wanted to take in that architectural salvage place."

"We promised we'd do that another day," Jo reminded him.

"Yeah, but I wanted to do it today," he whined, in perfect imitation of his children, who whacked him with pillows in response.

On the way out the door, Jo took a last peek at him, lounging on the bed. With his blond head propped on one hand, gaze intent on the television set, he was so beautiful, she wanted to shoo the kids on and turn back for a very quick kiss.

Sighing, she resisted temptation and followed Ryan's children.

The water was deliciously warm, and she

was glad she'd come when she floated on her back, looking dreamily up at the wrought-iron balconies, golden squares of windows and, above, the dark canopy of sky. Today might be chilly by New Orleans standards but compared to Seattle it felt balmy. They'd left dirty snow still lying on the ground and freezing at night on the streets. Here, gardens were still green and tropical.

Tyler dove and splashed energetically. Melissa left him to float beside Jo. Finally they shifted to the hot tub, where Jo could still keep an eye on Tyler.

Steam rose around them, making Melissa's face indistinct.

"Do you think Dad would mind if I called Mom?" she asked.

"I'm sure he wouldn't." Jo tried to make out the girl's expression. "You must miss her."

After a long pause, Melissa confessed, "Kind of. I mean, we've been so busy. But…I wish she was here. Only not really. Because you are, and she and Dad don't like each other that much, and I'm mad at her, too, but… Do you know what I mean?"

Jo nodded. "Did you know my mother died when I was seven?"

"No." Melissa sat up, shaking water off

her hair. She sounded shocked and awed. "Really?"

"She was crossing a street and was hit by a car. So it was sudden. One morning she made my lunch and sent me off to the school bus, and the next morning she wasn't there anymore. My dad wouldn't talk about her at all. I started to forget her really fast. Now I realize he got rid of lots of her things, too, because they made him sad. Her piano and guitar and clothes. At that age I felt as if she'd been wiped away, never existed. I wondered sometimes if I'd imagined her, if I'd ever had a mother."

"How awful." Melissa scooted closer, the movement sending water lapping against the sides of the hot tub. "You must have been really mad at your father."

"I was, and at my mother, too. I blamed her. Why did she have to do something so stupid?" Jo let out a shaky breath. "Just a few weeks ago, my father sent me a box of my mom's things that he'd saved, I guess on a closet shelf. Pictures and letters and jewelry. And a book of stuff she'd written down about me, like when I first walked and talked and what I said."

"What was your first word?"

"Dada." She still marveled at that. Had he been so different then, proud of his first child? Had he tossed her in the air, talked baby talk to her? "Then ball," she said.

"You must have missed her so much."

"Horribly. Especially when I got to milestones in life. You know. Girl stuff. I *hated* having to ask my father about that stuff." She remembered his expression, which she had taken for revulsion. She watched Tyler cannonball off the side of the pool.

"Maybe I could ask you things like that," Melissa said tentatively.

With an astonishing burst of pleasure, Jo smiled at Ryan's daughter. "Of course you can. But what I was trying to say is that you're lucky enough to have a mother you can ask, too. I know you must be hurt and mad at her, and I don't blame you. But…she's still your mother. Ryan—your dad—thinks she really does love you. So try to stay in touch with her, okay? Maybe your father is, oh, steadier and more reliable, but she has lots to offer you, too. And that," she concluded, "is enough of that lecture. I'm sorry! I didn't intend to start one."

As if she, who'd been afraid of having a family, was any expert!

But Melissa startled her again by reaching over and giving her a quick hug. "I liked your lecture. I'm glad Dad and you are friends. I wish—" She stopped. "Nothing. I'm just glad. That's all."

"Glad of what?" Tyler joined them by dropping into the hot tub with a splash way out of proportion to his skinny little body.

"You can't stay for more than a minute," Jo warned. "Melissa, you probably shouldn't be in here this long, either."

"What are you glad about?" he repeated.

"Nothing!" his sister said crossly, before glancing quickly at Jo. "I mean, I was just saying that I'm glad Dad and Jo are friends. That's all."

"Yeah!" he agreed enthusiastically. "This week has been really fun. And we get to miss school, too."

"We'll have to make up all the work." Melissa made a face.

"Maybe not. Since we're starting there in the middle of the year anyway."

"That's true." She looked hopeful. "Wanna go back in the pool?"

"Yeah!" he exclaimed.

Jo went, too, floating again while they played tag. She felt boneless and...happy.

How extraordinary, she thought, startled by the very awareness. She couldn't remember many times in her life when she'd been more than contented.

It was Ryan, of course. But she was having a revelation, which didn't let her stop there. Amazingly, she was *glad* they'd brought the kids. She'd had fun with them. Much of what they had seen had taken on more vivid hues for her because she'd tried to look through their eyes. As an adult, she might have strolled through the plantation house and grounds with academic interest, for example, but for the way Melissa and Tyler wanted to finger candlesticks and wainscotting and doorknobs, and peer closely and speculate aloud on what might have happened in parlors or verandahs or bedrooms. Tyler had been positively ghoulish when they walked through the simple, white-washed slave quarters at Oak Alley, but he'd been right to be so. He'd made the adults remember the horrors that had occurred here.

The fact that she actually liked Ryan's kids should have shocked her. It didn't, because, even as dense as she'd been, Jo had noticed that she liked Emma and Ginny. She was even, apparently, good with children. She knew that, because Ginny and Emma liked her. It appeared that Melissa and Tyler did, too.

She'd never minded doing preschool story hours at the library, or book talks at the elementary school to try to lure kids into summer reading. Part of the job, Jo had always told herself briskly, ignoring the pleasure she took in choosing books and finding new rhymes for the preschoolers or gory stories for the fourth-graders. She'd even known she was good at working with children. Which did not, she had told herself, mean that she wanted her own.

After all, how could she be a capable, never mind loving, parent, when her own father hadn't shown her the way? It just wasn't in her genes.

And she'd bought in, hook, line and sinker, to Aunt Julia's version of her parents' marriage. Mom had sacrificed a brilliant career for love, only to find herself changing dirty diapers. No woman could *have* career and family both. If she thought she could, she was deluding herself.

Rocking on a wave raised by splashing children, Jo thought wonderingly, *But Mom did love me. She did want me. And maybe Dad did, too.*

Did his failings automatically mean they would be Jo's, too?

Why had she never asked herself such a simple question? Her mother might have been, must have been, a wonderful parent. Ryan had once asked her how she'd come out so normal if she'd been raised so badly. Maybe, she thought now, because of her mother. By seven years old, a great deal of her basic character and sense of self had been formed. She had forgotten too much, but that didn't mean the knowledge wasn't still there, deep inside her, a secret part of her nature.

Out of nowhere, a hand grabbed her ankle and yanked downward. Rearing out of the water, Jo wrestled a slippy, wet boy into submission.

"I'm tougher than you are," she warned him, laughing. She tossed him away with a great heave. He curled into a ball and succeeded in washing a torrent of pool water over her.

"What a brat!" Melissa called, before diving on a subterranean mission to get her brother.

No, Jo thought, not a brat; just a sweet, smart boy, with insecurities normal to his circumstances, and the spirit to triumph over them.

And Melissa: she could be snotty, sure. Who could blame her? But she reminded Jo a little of herself at that age. She was so full of questions and doubts and hopes, it hurt to empathize sometimes.

Feeling light-headed, Jo drifted to the pool steps and watched them play. *I can love them,* she thought in profound amazement and relief. All these years, she'd believed herself to be emotionally stunted. Her father's fault, she had bitterly told herself.

The truth was, she had just been an emotional coward. Love opened her to loss. She had been too young and vulnerable to learn a lesson so painful. It hadn't yet been balanced by other lessons, ones about intimacy and laughter and hugs and someone to whom she could tell anything. Hurt himself, her father hadn't kept teaching her. Really, when she thought about it, she *was* astonishingly normal, considering.

Jo's chest ached, it was so filled with deep affection—no, *love*—for Ginny, Emma, Helen, even Kathleen… Melissa and Tyler, of course. And most of all, for Ryan. Afraid to love, she hadn't known she did. She could hardly believe she had been so blind. What had she done when her heart swelled with sympathy for Emma's inner anguish or Ginny's sadness? Taken an antacid and called it heartburn?

She wanted to march upstairs and throw herself into Ryan's arms. With amusement that curved her mouth, Jo thought, *Well, I wanted to do that anyway.*

Was he still thinking about marriage? Or were things different now that he had custody of his children?

Was she really brave enough to make all those promises that had once terrified her?

She was smiling again, idiotically. Oh, yes. She'd do it in a heartbeat. If he asked.

Which would not be tonight, unless he planned to go on his knees in front of the kids.

Melissa and Tyler had tired and were now drifting quietly. Jo stood, water sluicing down her body, and said, "Guys, I'm ready for pajamas and a chapter of my book. Let's go up."

They didn't argue too much. Towels wrapped around them, rubber sandals slapping the carpeted floor, the three found Ryan yawning as he turned off the TV.

"Have fun?" he asked the kids, even as his

gaze went to Jo. It sharpened, became penetrating as he saw something on her face.

"Yeah!" Tyler kicked off his sandals. "You should have come."

"The hot tub felt blissful," Jo said, trying to disguise her mood.

He dropped the remote control onto the bedside table and crossed his arms behind his head, his narrowed gaze not wavering from Jo's face. "So does lying here."

"I'm going to take a shower," Melissa announced.

"Okay," her father said, "but first, I've made some changes to tomorrow's plans."

Ready to snap his towel at his sister, Tyler turned instead. "You mean, we aren't going to the swamp?" he asked in disappointment.

"We're still going on the swamp tour. But I made a few calls while you were down in the pool, and I arranged for you two to go on a haunted history tour tomorrow night. It sounds suitably spooky. The hotel manager's eighteen-year-old daughter will go with you *and*," he added when his daughter opened her mouth to protest, "stay with you until we get in. Jo and I are going out on the town." His eyes met hers. "I made dinner reservations at

Antoine's, and we'll sample Bourbon Street afterward."

She smiled. "That sounds wonderful."

"No fair," Tyler muttered.

Ryan raised an eyebrow. "Don't you *want* to go on the voodoo tour? I can cancel…"

"No! That sounds cool. If we see a vampire," he said with relish. "It's just…it would be more fun if you came, too."

"Thank you." Ryan smiled at his son. "But I did promise Jo we'd do one romantic evening on our own. Mushy though that probably sounds to you."

Tyler shuffled his feet. "No, that's okay," he mumbled.

Ryan looked at his daughter. "Melissa?"

She rolled her eyes. "We don't need a babysitter!"

"This is a strange city. I couldn't enjoy myself if I didn't know someone was keeping an eye on you."

She huffed a little but conceded that she could survive the evening without her father and Jo. If Tyler wasn't too big a pain.

Ryan's eyes met Jo's again, and for just a moment she tried to let him see that something had changed. One charged look had to do—until tomorrow.

JO WAS IN a dreamlike state throughout the candlelit dinner at the elegant restaurant in a historic building. Her filet mignon with peppercorns melted in her mouth. Ryan, more adventuresome, tried grilled pompano, and they shared tiny, delicate puffs of potato. In a charcoal suit and tie, Ryan was incredibly handsome. Jo had bought the red silk sheath she wore tonight especially for the trip, and with her hair up and tiny diamonds in her earlobes, she felt almost beautiful. Maybe she really was, at least in Ryan's eyes. His potent gaze never left her, even when the dark-suited waiter paused to be sure they lacked nothing.

She knew even as they talked that later she wouldn't remember a word they'd said. The words weren't important. The way his eyes darkened when she smiled, that was important. So was the tone to his voice, and the slow, impossibly sweet smile that was just for her.

His hand was warm and tender on the small of her back when they left the restaurant. He made the act of tucking her black velvet wrap around her shoulders a caress, his thumbs sliding along her collarbone.

Outside the night was cool, but Jo was

flushed from the romantic byplay and the intimacy of Ryan's arm casually enfolding and guiding her. Shy with him now that she understood her own feelings, Jo found herself avoiding his gaze while helping to keep the conversation meaningless.

Bourbon Street was crowded.

They stopped briefly twice, listening to blues, raw and powerful. In neither club did they stay for long. After five or six blocks, Ryan said abruptly, "Do you want to stay?"

Jo shook her head. "I guess I'm not as adventurous as I thought I was. Do you?"

His smile was wry. "I've always admitted to being stodgy."

Jo nodded behind them. "The blonde back there didn't think so."

"Blonde?" Endearingly, he sounded surprised, as if he hadn't noticed being ogled.

"Right."

He slid his arm around her waist. "You're imagining things."

Jo laid her head against him. "I don't think so."

"What about you?" he asked, his voice a low rumble against her hair. They had turned a corner and found themselves on a dark side street. "What do *you* want?"

"I'd like a kiss," she confessed.

"Yes, ma'am," Ryan said with feeling.

Ryan turned her to face him.

"Mmm." She lifted her face naturally and parted her lips the moment his touched hers. The gaudy, noisy party behind them faded. Only they existed. He kissed her tenderly, making promises with his mouth and receiving everything she could give him in return.

On their meandering route down narrow streets, a couple of taxis passed, a few other pedestrians. Mostly this part of the French Quarter was deserted and dark but for the apartments above shops. Light streaming through wrought-iron balconies made them look like black lace. The spires of St. Louis Cathedral reared against the dark sky. A ship's horn could be heard on the broad, muddy Mississippi, only three blocks away but not visible. Restaurant doors yawned, bringing bursts of music and light and laughter. In between, unlit shop windows hinted at fascinating contents: antiques, Civil War relics, books and feather masks. Wrought-iron gates between stuccoed brick buildings allowed glimpses of dark gardens or cobblestoned carriage entrances. On one balcony, a couple seated at a tiny table looked lovingly at each other and murmured in soft voices.

Ryan and Jo stopped in dark alcoves to kiss, lingering because this time was magical, stolen. *This* was the adventure, Jo thought dreamily. She couldn't imagine how she hadn't recognized that sooner.

He lifted his head after the last kiss and said roughly, "Jo, I wish this week could have been what I promised you."

With one hand, she cupped his cheek. "In a way, it has been. Don't worry, Ryan. I've had a glorious time."

Amusement briefly infused his voice. "After this morning, I thought you might insist we take a baby alligator home as a pet."

"The kids need a pet," she said thoughtfully. "A kitten, or a puppy."

"Tyler was taken with the small gator that swam next to our boat."

"I noticed." She nuzzled his neck. "I had to hold his hand to keep him from dangling it over the side."

"Ah. Nice to know I've raised smart kids."

"You have. I like them both."

Ryan's fingers tunneled into her hair, sending pins flying. "Jo, I don't want to go back. How are we going to see each other?"

"In company."

"I'm afraid that is how it would be…" Ryan was surprised to see that Jo's expression, far from shutting down, had actually grown more open and warm.

His hands went still, and his voice almost shook. "Even after this romantic vacation, you still want to make a go of it?"

Heart swelling, she nodded.

"Jo." A tremor ran through him. "I love you."

"I know," she whispered.

"I want you to marry me," Ryan said intensely. "I want to wake up next to you every morning, come home to you after work every day. I want you to be a mother to my kids. I know all that scares you, but I need you."

Her heart must have burst, because joy and terror and love all ran like rivers through her body. Voice tremulous, she managed to tell him, "I need you, too."

Now his fingers bit into her arms. In light from a balcony behind them, his face was taut and incredulous. "What are you saying?"

"I'm saying…" Oh, no, her voice didn't want to cooperate! Jo took a deep breath and finished more strongly, "I'm saying yes. I'm saying I've figured out a lot. I can do this. If...if you really want me."

"Want you?" He gave a hoarse sound that might have been a laugh. "From the first time I saw you."

Tears dripped onto her cheeks. "Ryan..."

Ryan's big hands cradled her face, lifted it so that she couldn't miss the deep glow in his eyes. "Josephine Dubray," he said huskily, "will you be mine, to have and to hold, 'til death do us part?"

"I will," she said shakily, acknowledging to herself that she *was* afraid, but refusing to let the fear rule her life any longer.

Ryan kissed her with consummate tenderness and love. How could she have lived without this? she asked herself, as she flung her arms around his neck and kissed him back with everything in her. With her eyes closed, she seemed to be floating in emotions so powerful, they made what and who she had been seem dull and tepid and cowardly.

When the kiss ended and Ryan touched his forehead to hers, Jo said softly, "I wonder what my father would say if I asked him to give me away?"

"I think he'd be honored."

Jo nodded. Forgiveness might not be love, but it felt right. Necessary.

"I will," she repeated, and then smiled, brimming with joy she couldn't contain. "I will."

* * * * *

REQUEST YOUR FREE BOOKS!

2 FREE INSPIRATIONAL NOVELS
PLUS 2
FREE
MYSTERY GIFTS

YES! Please send me 2 FREE Love Inspired® novels and my 2 FREE mystery gifts (gifts are worth about \$10). After receiving them, if I don't wish to receive any more books, I can return the shipping statement marked "cancel." If I don't cancel, I will receive 6 brand-new novels every month and be billed just \$4.49 per book in the U.S. or \$4.99 per book in Canada. That's a saving of at least 22% off the cover price. It's quite a bargain! Shipping and handling is just 50¢ per book in the U.S. and 75¢ per book in Canada.* I understand that accepting the 2 free books and gifts places me under no obligation to buy anything. I can always return a shipment and cancel at any time. Even if I never buy another book, the two free books and gifts are mine to keep forever.   105/305 IDN FEGR

Name _____ (PLEASE PRINT) _____

Address _____ Apt. # _____

City _____ State/Prov. _____ Zip/Postal Code _____

Signature (if under 18, a parent or guardian must sign) _____

Mail to the Reader Service:
IN U.S.A.: P.O. Box 1867, Buffalo, NY 14240-1867
IN CANADA: P.O. Box 609, Fort Erie, Ontario L2A 5X3

Not valid for current subscribers to Love Inspired books.

**Are you a subscriber to Love Inspired books
and want to receive the larger-print edition?
Call 1-800-873-8635 or visit www.ReaderService.com.**

* Terms and prices subject to change without notice. Prices do not include applicable taxes. Sales tax applicable in N.Y. Canadian residents will be charged applicable taxes. Offer not valid in Quebec. This offer is limited to one order per household. All orders subject to credit approval. Credit or debit balances in a customer's account(s) may be offset by any other outstanding balance owed by or to the customer. Please allow 4 to 6 weeks for delivery. Offer available while quantities last.

Your Privacy—The Reader Service is committed to protecting your privacy. Our Privacy Policy is available online at www.ReaderService.com or upon request from the Reader Service.

We make a portion of our mailing list available to reputable third parties that offer products we believe may interest you. If you prefer that we not exchange your name with third parties, or if you wish to clarify or modify your communication preferences, please visit us at www.ReaderService.com/consumerchoice or write to us at Reader Service Preference Service, P.O. Box 9062, Buffalo, NY 14269. Include your complete name and address.

LIREG11B

REQUEST YOUR FREE BOOKS!

2 FREE RIVETING INSPIRATIONAL NOVELS
PLUS 2 FREE MYSTERY GIFTS

Love Inspired.
SUSPENSE

LISUS11B

REQUEST YOUR FREE BOOKS!

2 FREE INSPIRATIONAL NOVELS
PLUS 2
FREE
MYSTERY GIFTS

Love Inspired
HISTORICAL
INSPIRATIONAL HISTORICAL ROMANCE

YES! Please send me 2 FREE Love Inspired® Historical novels and my 2 FREE mystery gifts (gifts are worth about $10). After receiving them, if I don't wish to receive any more books, I can return the shipping statement marked "cancel". If I don't cancel, I will receive 4 brand-new novels every month and be billed just $4.49 per book in the U.S. or $4.99 per book in Canada. That's a saving of at least 22% off the cover price. It's quite a bargain! Shipping and handling is just 50¢ per book in the U.S. and 75¢ per book in Canada.* I understand that accepting the 2 free books and gifts places me under no obligation to buy anything. I can always return a shipment and cancel at any time. Even if I never buy another book, the two free books and gifts are mine to keep forever.

102/302 IDN FEHF

Name	(PLEASE PRINT)	

Address		Apt. #

City	State/Prov.	Zip/Postal Code

Signature (if under 18, a parent or guardian must sign)

Mail to the **Reader Service:**
IN U.S.A.: P.O. Box 1867, Buffalo, NY 14240-1867
IN CANADA: P.O. Box 609, Fort Erie, Ontario L2A 5X3

Not valid for current subscribers to Love Inspired Historical books.

Want to try two free books from another series?
Call 1-800-873-8635 or visit www.ReaderService.com.

* Terms and prices subject to change without notice. Prices do not include applicable taxes. Sales tax applicable in N.Y. Canadian residents will be charged applicable taxes. Offer not valid in Quebec. This offer is limited to one order per household. All orders subject to credit approval. Credit or debit balances in a customer's account(s) may be offset by any other outstanding balance owed by or to the customer. Please allow 4 to 6 weeks for delivery. Offer available while quantities last.

Your Privacy—The Reader Service is committed to protecting your privacy. Our Privacy Policy is available online at www.ReaderService.com or upon request from the Reader Service.

We make a portion of our mailing list available to reputable third parties that offer products we believe may interest you. If you prefer that we not exchange your name with third parties, or if you wish to clarify or modify your communication preferences, please visit us at www.ReaderService.com/consumerschoice or write to us at Reader Service Preference Service, P.O. Box 9062, Buffalo, NY 14269. Include your complete name and address.

LIH11B

Harlequin

Caron Todd

When Elizabeth Robb left Three Creeks, she never
expected to return. Now that she's back in town,
she hopes her arrival will escape notice. But once
Elizabeth meets Jack McKinnon, she begins to
believe there might be some good to come from
the long journey home. But Jack's got a past,
too—one he'll have to put to rest before he and
Elizabeth can find their future together.

Return To Three Creeks

Coming soon!

Harlequin®

HARLEQUIN HEARTWARMING

*A special collection of wholesome,
tender romances.*

Available wherever books are sold!